Reviews of *The Defec*

A taut thriller . . . *The*
Janac, a truly memorable anti-hero.

Christopher Moore, *The Press*

An evil storyline, with little relief and with great tension . . .
Hawke's Bay Today

This thriller has pace and immediacy.

Kate Murray, *Wairarapa Times-Age*

Throw in a love triangle, the microcosm of a boat at sea and some good sailing and you've got a fine yarn . . . Chisnell has managed to create a smart and articulate villain, always the best kind.

Kurt Hoehne, *Sailing Magazine*, USA

Never, never, never would I read a psychological thriller Just as well, then, that I didn't read the description on the back cover until after I'd finished the book, and by then was too breathless, terrified and awed to care . . .

Rebecca Hayter, *Boating New Zealand*

The Wrecking Crew

By the same author
The Defector

THE
WRECKING
CREW

MARK CHISNELL

HarperCollins*Publishers*

National Library of New Zealand Cataloguing-in-Publication Data

Chisnell, Mark, 1962-
The wrecking crew / Mark Chisnell.
ISBN 1-86950-486-0
I. Title.
NZ823.2—dc 21

First published 2004
HarperCollins*Publishers (New Zealand) Limited*
P.O. Box 1, Auckland

ISBN 1 86950 486 0

Set in Times New Roman
Typeset by Pages LP
Printed by Griffin Press, Australia, on 50 gsm Bulky News

John, Will and Glyn — not forgotten

Acknowledgements

Many people helped develop the story and read early versions, particularly Susie Aikin-Sneath and Daniela Bernardelle. Among those that provided support, inspiration and information above and beyond the normal call of friendship were Rob Andrews, Bill Ashton, Paul and Susan Boyce, Rhidian Bridge, Nina Brisius, Sian Cowen, Bruce Grant, Kevin Hall, Duncan McDonald, Jonathan McKee, Jennifer McReynolds and Sarah Nicholson.

I have to thank John Matthews, Dr Mervyn Rowlinson and the Reverend Bill McCrea for getting me aboard and showing me around merchant shipping, while I found invaluable background in Alan Branch's Elements of Shipping, Gerald Posner's Warlords of Crime and Martin Booth's The Triads. The journalism of Faith Keenan, Bertil Lintner, Nate Thayer and Michael Vatikiotis in the Far Eastern Economic Review, and research and articles by Yiu-Kong Chu, Andrew Eames, Eric Ellen, Malcolm Macalister Hall and Willard H. Myers were all helpful.

And then there's everyone at HarperCollins Australia and New Zealand — Mark Bathurst, Mel Cain, Lorain Day, Karen-Maree Griffiths, Rod Morrison, Sue Page, Lorraine Steele, Tracey Wogan and last but certainly not least, Anne Simpson — where would I be without you?

Not forgetting my family — and everyone that I have actually forgotten — thanks to you all . . .

Mark Chisnell

Each vessel that passes beyond sight of land becomes a country in itself. As with all countries, the laws are ultimately determined by power. If power falls into the hands of the mad or the bad, then there is nowhere for the helpless to run.

James Hepburn, *The Black Flag*

Chapter 1

Phillip Hamnet rattled quickly down the two flights of stairs from the bridge, his shoes skidding lightly across the steps hollowed and smoothed by countless watch changes. The master of the MV *Shawould* hit the deck at the bottom and strode along the passage to his cabin. He grabbed the handle and, with the deftness of practice, twisted and lifted. The door, with its sadly sagging hinges, still opened unwillingly. His wife, Anna, looked up at the noise and smiled as he entered. The door fell shut behind him.

'Everything all right?' she asked, watching him carefully. A white T-shirt was stuck to his wiry frame, and a sheen of sweat and grease layered his tanned forehead. He looked heroically exhausted, she reflected, the handsome face stubbled and sagging off the high cheekbones, the hazel eyes shadowed by bags. And the matted blond hair needed cutting.

Hamnet dropped into a chair by the small dinner table they had set up in his day room. 'I suppose. That damned cargo never showed up. I just got the word from the company to go anyway. We've slipped anchor and headed down the channel. It looks like there's some bad weather coming, but they want us moving, all antsy because we're late now, when it's their phantom cargo that's caused it.' He paused. 'I left Richardson up there. It's his watch, and supper's waited long enough.'

Anna nodded, and in silence served two portions of a rice dish. Hamnet stared at the electric fan, brooding. It struggled hopelessly to move the heavy air around the cabin, and the full weight of the tropics bore down on them — at its most oppressive and threatening in these moments before a storm. Anna coughed lightly. Hamnet sighed, glanced round and took the proffered plate.

'God, it's hot in here. Can I open the door?' he said, putting the plate down and rising from his seat.

'Of course. I only closed it while I was showering,' replied Anna.

Hamnet looked at his wife for the first time since entering the cabin. She was cool and composed in her light silk robe — an effect the water in the ship's tanks was just about cold enough to produce. But it wouldn't last for long. He pulled the door open and jammed a wedge under it to keep it that way, kicking it into place with unnecessary aggression.

'Hey, cheer up, it's the last trip,' chided Anna as she reached for a bottle of white wine and poured him a large glass.

'Thank God. I hate this damn boat,' said Hamnet with some feeling, returning to his seat.

'You've earned the holiday, and your new ship,' replied Anna.

Hamnet picked up the wine and took a long sip. He sighed heavily again, but the tension in his body eased visibly. He looked at Anna. 'It's coming right, isn't it?' he asked, with a hesitant smile.

Anna nodded.

'Thanks.' The smile was looser; he offered the glass. 'To us,' he toasted. The glass had little resonance. There wasn't the full, fruity hum of Waterford crystal on Waterford crystal, just the cheap chink of cheap glasses. Hamnet drained his of the not-so-chilled white regardless.

'The four of us,' replied Anna. Her chocolate-brown eyes flickered warmly, gazing through the loose fringe of her black, bobbed hair as she sipped at her iced water. Hamnet had a vague suspicion that it was bad luck to toast with anything other than alcohol, but couldn't be sure. Perhaps he should have got her to take a glass of wine. Just a sip wouldn't hurt — not now, with only five weeks to go. Four of us. Who would ever have guessed at twins? It was, he considered, a bloody terrifying thought. That's why Anna had wanted to do this trip. Last chance for a while.

Anna finished her meal first, refilled her glass from the water jug and slid across onto the sofa that lined one wall of the day cabin. Hamnet mopped up the last of the rice with a finger and moved to sit beside her, kicking off his deck shoes.

'How're you doing, Mrs Hamnet?'

'Pretty good, Mr Hamnet.' She smiled, and shifted to lie back against the cushion, the silk robe falling away from her smooth and amply distended belly.

'And all the little Hamnets?' He laid his hand gently on the soft, warm skin.

'Kinda frisky tonight.' She twitched her eyebrows up suggestively, sipped at her water and put the glass down on the side table.

Hamnet could feel the motion. 'I guess they get that from their mother.'

Her hand tugged at the buttons on his shirt, then slid up and onto his chest. 'You need a shower, darling,' she said, her pretty nose twitching.

'Maybe you should come with me,' he said, leaning forward to meet her slightly parted lips, their eyes locked together, his hand slipping down her belly, the open door forgotten.

The buzzer went on the intercom.

'Damn,' he swore. Anna frowned as he pulled back and leaned over to reach the handset.

It was the voice of the chief mate, Paul Richardson, that greeted him. 'Skipper?'

'Yeah,' Hamnet replied shortly. He couldn't keep the impatience out of his voice. This had better be good. Anna's hand ran tantalisingly slowly down his chest to his navel, and hesitated.

Richardson continued. 'Could you come up and take a look? I'm not sure about this turn.'

Hamnet glanced skywards in resignation. His eyes scanned the rusting rivet line that ran the length of the cabin. He would be so happy to get off this worthless crate and away from its mediocre crew. He covered the mouthpiece with his hand. 'Anna, I'm sorry, you know what an old woman he is. If I don't go now he'll be back on the line in another five minutes.'

Anna rolled her eyes, and sighed loudly enough for those on the bridge to hear her.

'On my way,' said Hamnet. He replaced the phone. 'Sorry, darling. I'll just go hold his hand for a while. I won't be long.' He eased himself stiffly off the couch and fumbled for his shoes. Behind him, Anna's sigh was transforming itself into a rather steady heavy breathing. He stood up and moved towards the door.

'I'll try and save you some dessert, honey,' murmured Anna.

Hamnet kicked the wedge away, stepped outside and quickly closed the door. He stood for a moment in the corridor while his eyes adjusted to the red night-lights. The engines rumbled in the depths below his feet. The moaning of steel plates and wires was louder out here. The wind and sea had continued to build. But the rain and the ship's motion cooled the air, and Hamnet could feel the sweat start to dry as he strode down the corridor and back up the steps, two at a time, to emerge onto the bridge.

'The weather's really closed in, hasn't it?' he said curtly, still thinking of Anna.

Richardson looked up from the chart table he was huddled over. His stooped figure and lined face indicated a lifetime of worry. Behind him, rain splattered suicidally against the bridge glass. Beyond, it was completely black, without even the reassuring glow of navigation lights. The company's standing orders were to run without lights whenever in close proximity to the Indonesian, Thai, Philippine or Malaysian coasts. Which for this Singapore-based tramp was most of the time. It was one of the precautions against pirates. Hamnet always added a deck watch on the stern, complete with shutters for the anchor hawsepipes, barbed wire on the guardrail and a supply of beer bottles filled with sand as missiles. The stern was always where they came from, slinging grappling hooks from fast, open boats. Creeping on board with machetes. Most of the time they could come and go without a crew even realizing. The first they knew was when the master returned to his cabin to find it ransacked and the contents of the safe gone. The thought had Hamnet reaching for the intercom just as it buzzed.

'Phil?' It was Anna's breathy voice.

'I was just about to call you.'

'Don't call me. Come on back down here, babe.' She paused, breathing heavily, rhythmically.

Hamnet could feel his face flush. 'Darling, this is a ship's intercom, not a phone-sex line.' He slapped the receiver back down. Then thought, damn, he'd forgotten to tell her to lock the door. But still, it was a filthy night — no one in their right mind would be out there in an open boat.

Richardson was talking to him. 'She just blew up from the northwest like we thought it would. Always bad, the storms when the monsoon's changing.' There was a crack and a flash of lightning, as if to emphasize his words.

Hamnet caught a glimpse of the cargo deck, lashed with rain; beyond it, whipped-up, white-capped water. There was more vibration now as the *Shawould* rolled off the occasional bigger wave. 'Hmm,' he grunted, a hand on the console to brace himself. 'So what's the problem?'

'Well.' Richardson drew out the word with his Texan drawl, but Hamnet could see from the rapid tap, tap of his hand on the chart that he was far from composed. 'We've been heading down the channel as planned, and according to the GPS we're here.' Richardson's finger finally came to rest, and Hamnet moved over to the chart table to take a look.

The Global Positioning System plot put them safely in the middle of the Bangka Channel, headed just south of east. 'So what's the problem?' Hamnet repeated.

'Well,' Richardson drawled again, 'I've been waiting to pick up the light and the radio beacon here, before I commence the turn to south-southeast round Selokan Point.'

Hamnet glanced at the chart again, at the Pelepasan Rock, whose light should have been flashing at them three times every thirty seconds, from as far as thirty-six miles away. It should have been visible from the moment they had left Muntok, on a clear night at least. He waited impatiently, his fists slightly clenched. But experience had taught him that rushing Richardson was worse. Then the Texan started to stutter. It was an inability to perform under pressure that had kept the old boy as chief mate on a boat like this.

'Now it should only be five miles away on the bow. And I still don't have a visual or a radio contact,' finished Richardson, finally.

'Not a huge surprise. The Indonesian buoyage isn't the world's most reliable.'

'Well, that's what I figured too. So I thought I would make the turn on the GPS, but that doesn't seem to agree too good with the depth right now.'

Hamnet's eyes flicked over the depth gauge: sixty feet.

16

He turned back to the chart. If they were where the GPS said they were, they should be in fifty feet of water. Not so badly wrong as to get you in a panic. But not right either. Perhaps Her Majesty's hydrographers had been a little rough and ready down here, or, more likely, had used data from someone else's survey. Hamnet checked the chart, then grunted to himself: the sources were Indonesian government charts. Another note confirmed the unreliability of the navigational aids in Selat Bangka, a third the movement of the mangrove swamp that lined the channel. He sighed. So much for the radio direction-finding beacon and the light. They were on their own.

'What about the radar?' he asked Richardson.

'Well, with all this weather I was having trouble getting a picture worth looking at.'

Hamnet contained himself with difficulty. This was the real reason Richardson had got him up here. He couldn't confirm their position with the radar. Getting clear radar vision in bad weather was an art, because the rain and sea deflected the signal back at the detector. The result was a wall of noise and clutter on the screen behind which genuinely solid objects could hide with ease. But the art of brushing aside that curtain of clutter was one you were supposed to have mastered by the time you were a chief mate in your mid-fifties.

Hamnet would deal with the radar in a moment; in the meantime, he had to believe the GPS. The US Department of Defense's ten billion dollar satellite position-fixing system was to be trusted, even if some of the residents of the Lone Star State were not. And the GPS said they would be aground shortly if they didn't turn to the southeast now.

'Start the turn to sou'-sou'east please, Richardson. And slow her down to half speed to give us a little time to figure this out properly.'

Hamnet listened to Richardson step over to the wheel and dial up the change. His eyes went to the chart; there were some low hills on Bangka Island to the east that he should be able to pick up on the radar. He checked the position on the GPS so he could measure the distance it gave from the hills. It was then he noticed the indicator light showing that the GPS unit was receiving signals from a differential radio-transmitter beacon. A differential beacon used a precisely known position on land to check the accuracy of the satellite signals. It then transmitted the necessary corrections to all GPS units in the area, corrections that each GPS automatically included in the calculation of its position.

Hamnet scanned the chart. Differential was used in places where high navigational accuracy was required or helpful — outside ports, along well-travelled coastlines. This didn't seem the kind of place for someone to set up a beacon. The only traffic through here would be the few ships headed to Jakarta via Muntok, like the *Shawould*. Anyone else would go round the outside of Bangka Island. There were some oil installations further south — they could have installed differential, perhaps that was it. Perhaps not. Could they be picking up some rogue signals bounced long distance through the atmosphere by the storm? Hamnet couldn't remember if this was possible with differential transmissions. He decided it was worth checking the GPS fix using the satellite signals alone.

'Richardson, you know how to stop this thing switching to differential automatically?' Hamnet turned to look at his first officer, whose face was creased in puzzlement.

'It's getting a differential signal?' he asked, his heavy, walruslike moustache twitching nervously.

'Yes,' snapped Hamnet, finally losing patience. 'And I would appreciate it if you would shift it to manual reception of satellite signals only, while I sort out the damn radar.'

Richardson moved forward to the GPS, the pain of a decade-and-a-half of career stasis written all over his face.

Hamnet went back to the chart and measured the distance to the hills from their GPS position. They were between nine and fifteen miles away. There was also an island in the channel; it wasn't as high as the hills but it was closer — only seven miles in front. He glanced again at the depth before he went back to the radar. It was shallowing quickly — forty-five feet. They drew forty with this cargo. The turn to the southeast should have meant the depth was increasing. Now he was worried. Damn it, what the hell was going on? He stepped over to the engine control and rang up neutral. They were coasting, and would quickly lose steerageway in the tight channel, but steerage was little use to him when he had no idea what the error in their position was or which way to turn.

The radar would help if he could pick up the island, or the first of those hills, and get a distance and a bearing. That and the depth should be enough for a position fix. The picture was full of junk as the radar signal bounced off waves and rain. He carefully tuned the display to remove the clutter, then glanced over at Richardson, who was keying the GPS from the manual.

'Bloody hell,' he muttered under his breath. But the radar screen was clearing under his deft touch, and the line of hills beginning to emerge. In front of them was a single blip — Pulau-Pulau Nangka Island. He switched the range ring on and dialled it in towards the dying glow of the radar return. The distance measurement clocked down and settled. Eleven miles. Adrenaline started to pump, and he realised how fuzzy his head had been from the wine. But it was clearing now — God knows it was clearing now. It needed only the most cursory glance at the chart to tell him what he already knew.

Hamnet had started moving when he heard Richardson's startled splutter. The depth alarm went off a half-second later. All three were too late. The *Shawould* stopped. Just like that. Nine thousand tons of decaying general-cargo carrier hit the mud bank at a little under nine knots and stopped dead. Hamnet was halfway to the wheel when it happened. He carried on at a little under nine knots, head first, and the bulkhead stayed in place to meet him. The lights went out.

Chapter 2

There was a thought, dragging him out of the darkness like a snarling Rottweiler with his arm in its teeth. What was the thought? He had to know. Phil Hamnet opened his eyes. He was instantly engulfed in the bright, white pain of light. His arm went up protectively, eyes clamped shut again. A rush of nausea, choked back.

Toby Johns, engineer, looked on anxiously as his skipper's face writhed, every muscle and sinew in the arm and balled fist clenched tight. Johns had watched Hamnet drift close to consciousness for the last couple of minutes, but now he needed him awake.

'Skipper, we have to move you. We're taking on water in the forward hold. We have a twenty-degree list. Richardson wants everyone aft, on the boat deck. There's a ship standing by — they're sending over a boat. He wants to take people off.'

There it was, the thought. It frightened him. Hamnet let himself drift back into the darkness. But the darkness was going, burning away, the fog of unconsciousness receding before the light. Phil opened his eyes again, this time slowly, carefully.

'It's OK, I've switched over to the night-light,' said Johns.

Hamnet stared into the red gloom. The room was disjointed. Diffracting in watery vision. He moved the protective hand up and gingerly touched the throbbing area on his forehead. It was bandaged, and it hurt like hell. But the thought was crowding him now. His ship, Anna — what had he done? Johns' words had been merely sounds, shifting frequencies and tones lodged in some preconceptual corner of his mind. But now they had meaning. Water, a twenty-degree list. He'd put his ship on the beach. And Anna — where was Anna?

'Skipper, we have to move. Come on.'

'Anna,' Hamnet croaked desperately as he struggled to sit up. The movement startled the pain; it charged forward, threatening to engulf and overwhelm him. But this time there was no going back into the darkness. He steadied himself and spoke again, louder this time. 'Where the hell is Anna?' The face before him was still blurred, badly lit, but recognition was arriving. 'Johns, where's my wife?'

'I'm not sure. I guess she's on the boat deck with the others.'

'And Richardson?' He had it now, the knowledge of what he had to do.

'On the bridge.'

'I'm going up there. You go to my cabin and check that my wife has left and gone to the boat deck. Make sure she's there with everyone else. When you find her, stay with her. Whatever we decide to do, I'm making you responsible for her safety.' Anna would be furious at such treatment — it wasn't as though, under normal circumstances, she couldn't look after herself — but she was eight months pregnant. Johns nodded, his face clear, happy that the skipper was back in charge.

Hamnet struggled off the bunk. His head was still pounding, his knees were shaky, but he had no time for that. 'When you find her and get her to the boat deck, call up to the bridge and let me know. Now go.'

Johns was already moving out of the cabin door. Hamnet stood for a moment, getting used to the tilted deck and his unresponsive legs. He was in the cabin they used as a rudimentary sick bay. The bridge was above him. He staggered to the door and grabbed the jamb, peering out. He saw the torn safety poster on the companionway wall. Its ripped edge spoke of carelessness. Carelessness, the bastard son of negligence. He could feel the sweat chill all over him. This would finish him — he'd never get another boat. He forced the thought away, made himself deal with the here and now, move on. There was a stairwell to the right. He let go of the door and stumbled forward. Gradually his feet and legs began to work, shuffling across the steel deck.

He could feel the violence of the storm outside, spitting down the companionway from the open starboard-side door. Feel the tremor of the waves on the plates. The seas pounding on a hull that was unable to respond — except by breaking up. He had to get to the bridge and find out what was happening. Could they salvage her? They wouldn't abandon the ship until the last possible moment. Ships were better than lifeboats. But Johns had said something about another vessel standing by — that would mean safety for Anna and nonessential crew. Then, if Richardson had contained the leak, maybe they could buoy her up and tow her off. They weren't that far from Singapore. The necessary resources would be available there. But was it worth it for this old boat? Or would the company kiss it goodbye and collect the insurance? Damn it, was he going to lose another ship? He would find out soon enough.

Arms out either side to steady himself, Hamnet lurched towards the stairwell and turned to start the short climb to the bridge. Then he saw him. If he'd had to do anything more than just fall back under the gravity supplied by the listing hull he wouldn't have made it. But his legs let him go in a spasm of reflex and he was out of sight. At the top of the stairwell was a man with a sub-machine-gun. There were no firearms on the ship — that was standard industry practice. Now there were voices too, footsteps clattering down the stairs. He pressed himself back quickly, pushing open a door. There was no time to close it. The footsteps stopped momentarily at the bottom of the stairs. He slunk deeper into the room, into the shadow, scarcely daring to breath.

'We can't take the risk,' said a voice in an American accent that hadn't seen its homeland in a while. 'The fact that they switched the GPS to receive just the satellite signals shows they suspected something. There can be no rumours on the docks in Singapore, you know that as well as I do, Mike. If we let these people go, there'll be doubt about the sinking. If the insurance company doesn't pay, we won't get paid. However much pressure I put on the little prick that owns this piece of shit, he's already bankrupt in all but name. That's why he went for this deal.'

There was a short silence. The musty smell of the room was heavy around Hamnet in the darkness. As heavy as the realisation that had struck him. A heavy blanket of grey, a leaden weight of oppression. And yet there was also wild and stupid relief. Wreckers, pirates — they had got hold of a differential GPS transmitter and sent out false position signals to lure the ship onto the beach. It hadn't been his fault. These people were conspiring with the ship's owner to collect the insurance. That's why he'd had to wait in Muntok on the owner's orders for a cargo that had never arrived. They had simply been waiting for another monsoon storm to lower visibility and mute the radar.

The sound of movement. A man appeared in the section of corridor revealed by the open door. He was dressed in battered US army fatigues and calf-high black-leather boots. Hamnet had a side view of a hard, lined face and cropped ginger hair. In the man's right hand was a big, old-fashioned, six-chamber revolver. There was a tap, tap of steel on steel as he banged the muzzle thoughtfully against the wall. When he spoke it was the same American voice as before. 'Kill the crew and lose the bodies in the hold — I don't want them found too easily. Launch the lifeboats as well — it'll give the rescuers something to think about.'

Hamnet felt the hot flush of fear and panic sweep through him. A second voice spoke — another American accent, but deeper, harsher, more recently from those shores. 'We've found a woman too. She says she's the wife of the skipper, but he isn't among the crew. She's, er,' — there was a pause; Phil could feel the sneer — 'with child.'

The tapping stopped, and with it something inside Hamnet snapped. He started to shake, his mouth open in a silent scream, nails biting into his palms as he fought to control the urge to lash out.

But the first man was already turning, moving away as he spoke. 'I'll go and get the manifest and crew list from the master's quarters. We need to know if we've missed anybody else. Keep the crew alive for now — we may need them to flush him out. Tell everybody to stay sharp while they're unloading.'

Hamnet had a brief glimpse of the second man striding past the open door — big, stubbled, greying blond hair, dressed in black. Then footsteps were clattering down the stairs as the two intruders headed for his cabin and the working deck. He fought to control an upsurge of anger, then the panic and fear again. Forcing himself to move slowly, quietly, he inched his way towards the door. He peered out into the corridor. It was deserted. Just the heaving of the ocean and the groaning of the ship. The noise was loud enough to hide the sound of anyone moving cautiously. That was both good and bad. He stepped out of the room, gently closing the door behind him — nervous, out in the open, in the light.

He had to get help. The radio was on the deck above, at the back of the bridge. He could go up the stairs to his left, but he would be completely exposed. There was a crash behind him and he spun round, pulse hammering. The open starboard door swung back and smashed against the wall again, propelled by another violent gust of wind. It beckoned him outside, where there was a ladder to the wing deck on the side of the bridge. That had to be safer, but not on the windward side. He moved quickly along the corridor to port, stepping through and down, into the darkness of the shadow thrown by the interior light. The rain swirled through the air, rising and falling in waves, whipping over his head and away. But it was quieter here on the leeward side, protected from the wind by the bulk of the ship's superstructure. He waited for his eyes to adjust to the darkness.

He was looking downwind, which, unless the wind had shifted, was southeast. The leg of the channel they had been trying to turn into had run southeast too. He was sure they had hit the mainland shore by turning the corner too early. With the bow hard aground, the wind and waves had swung the stern, pulling the vessel broadside on to the weather. There was a heavy list to leeward, the ship being pounded that way by the storm. Break-up or capsize was a real possibility.

To his right, the companionway ran up to the wing-deck ladder and the glow of the night-light on the bridge. Below him there were much brighter white lights, and now he saw motion too. One of the cranes had sprung into life, hauling out crates from the hold. To his left the companionway was unlit, disappearing as it dropped down another ladder to the deck that held the officer's accommodation.

Hamnet moved forward carefully, keeping below the rail, in the shadow cast by the lights on the cargo deck. He reached the ladder and started to climb, bubbles of rust rough under his grip.

The view down onto the cargo deck below him opened up as he gained height. A barge or lighter had pulled alongside to leeward and was being made fast. The covers had been removed from over the centre hold, and men appeared to be unloading the crates of machinery from number three 'tween decks. The rain blew across the scene in sheets, illuminated by the deck lights. There were fourteen pirates that he could see, all armed, mostly locals, plus a couple of whites, who appeared to be controlling the operation. It took him a while to spot what he really should have seen first. Directly below the main cargo crane stood his crew. Huddled together under the guard of brandished weapons, they stood in a variety of attitudes: despair, defiance, resignation. All were soaked to the skin, rain running in rivers off their clothing. Hamnet pressed himself against the ladder in the shadow and counted — all eleven were there. And so was Anna, the flimsy robe glued to her body, feet bare, hair plastered to her face. Hamnet pressed the side of his head back against a rung and stared into the rain-soaked night.

The Tannoy crackled into life three metres above him, cutting through his anguish. The sound came through the storm sporadically, gusts of wind whipping away half-words. 'Hamnet. Understand me. Give yourself up, or your crew will die. In three minutes' time I kill your first officer. Then the rest, one by one, three minutes each. Don't make me do it. Give yourself up now, Hamnet, and you'll all be safe.'

Hamnet slumped on the ladder. A familiar sense of dread was rising in him. What good could he do by giving himself up when they planned to kill everyone anyway? What could he do in three minutes? Or six, or nine? How many would have to die for him to save the rest? If he could save the rest. Seconds slipped by. He was frozen in pain — the pain of memories he thought he'd beaten. But he had to move; if he wasn't to surrender he had to do something. He glanced up the remainder of the ladder. The door to the bridge was closed against the storm, and he could see it was safe to pull himself up onto the wing deck. He eased himself over the metal rim, keeping low, close to the wall, inching forward. Surely there would be someone on the bridge — they wouldn't have left that unmanned — and when he opened the door, the blast of weather from outside would instantly give him away.

The Tannoy crackled again. A hiss of static, then the voice.

'One minute, Hamnet.'

He still had a clear view of his crew bunched together on the cargo deck. The rain and wind swirled amongst them. One of the pirates pushed into the group and pulled out Richardson, so that he was standing in front of them, body hunched. He had lost a shoe. A fussy, tidy man, whose shirt-tail now flapped in the wind. His hands hung loosely by his side. The pirate raised his gun to the chief mate's head.

'Thirty seconds. Show yourself, Hamnet, and no one will be hurt.'

Hamnet buried his face in his hands. There was nothing he could do. He didn't hear the shot, any sound dispersed by the wind, deadened by the rain. He stared at the water running down his hands. There was a thin, painful wail from the cargo deck, a high-pitched keening. He couldn't stop himself from looking. Richardson was prostrate on the deck in front of the others. A pool of blood was washing away as quickly as it formed, running in diluted rivers across the deck. Anna was on her hands and knees, vomiting, held by Johns, the man he had sent to look after her. Sent to his death.

Chapter 3

Inside Phil Hamnet a terrible rage was slowly building. And as the rage grew, it swept away fear and caution. He stood and opened the door to the bridge. The red night-lights were still on inside, and the glare from the cargo deck threw most of the room into dangerous shadow. His ears gave him the clue he needed — a hiss of static from the radio room, on the starboard side. He strode quickly across the bridge, and was halfway to the door when he heard the words, 'That you, boss?'

He accelerated into a run, and got to the door to see a man half out of the swivel chair, reaching for a machine pistol propped against the wall. The man had a hand on the barrel when Hamnet lashed a foot into his groin. The force of the blow both doubled him up and flung him back against the table. His scream of pain was choked off as Hamnet buried the side of a fist in his throat. The blow snapped the pirate's head back and smashed it against the steel case of the radio. His bones appeared to melt as he slid into a heap on the floor.

Hamnet wasted no time. He picked up the microphone of the long-range single-sideband radio, hit the emergency-frequency button and snapped down for transmit. 'Mayday. Mayday. This is the MV *Shawould*. We are aground on the south shore of the Bangka Channel and under attack from a pirate crew. Do you read me?'

He forced himself to wait. Glanced down at the figure on the floor — another Caucasian, more army fatigues. The pinched face had relaxed into a serene expression, in contrast to the signs of violence — blood matting the dark hair and spreading around his feet. It occurred to Hamnet that he had killed the man. The adrenaline rush of hate and rage that had driven him onto the bridge was starting to recede, and he realised he was shaking violently. He pushed down on the transmit button again. 'Mayday. Mayday. This is the M.V. *Shawould*. We are aground on the south side of the Bangka Channel and under attack by a pirate crew. Does anyone hear me?' He released the transmit button. There was another silence, as the message propagated through the rain and into the night.

'Come on, come on,' muttered Hamnet under his breath, casting an eye anxiously through the door and onto the bridge.

Then, through the crackle of static, came a response. '*Shawould*, *Shawould*. This is the oil installation AP Vargo. We receive your Mayday. Please give details.'

A jolt of relief cracked through Hamnet's body, but before he could press the transmit key again, the frequency dissolved into static.

The answer came before he'd had time to formulate the question. The short-range VHF radio strapped on the dead man's belt told him what was happening. 'Boss, there's someone on the SSB. You should get up there.'

'Shit.' He'd been a fool not to think of it. They were monitoring the emergency channels from the pirate boat and were now transmitting a jamming signal.

'It's happening,' snapped the VHF again — the recognisable voice of the American leader.

Hamnet looked in despair at the whining SSB. He could try another frequency, but no, that would be hopeless — the operator on the oil platform wouldn't dare leave the emergency channel while waiting for his response. And he was all out of time. He just had to hope they had understood enough of his message to send help. He had to get off the bridge. He picked up the short-barrelled machine pistol and moved to a starboard-side window. With the unloading happening to leeward, the pirate contingent was focused on the port side of the ship. There was no one coming up the starboard ladder, no one on that wing deck. He slipped outside and shut the door. Wind and rain whipped at his clothing. Down on the cargo deck he could see things were proceeding as before — the cranes still working, his crew gathered in the same place. Richardson's body remained where it had fallen. Hamnet slung the machine pistol across his back. They were going to get one hell of a surprise the next time they tried to shoot one of his crew.

He moved to the aft end of the wing deck, as far out of sight as he could get, and stepped up onto the railing. From the top of the bridge he would have a commanding view of the whole cargo deck. With his feet on the rail, one hand steadying himself on a pillar, he felt cautiously for a grip on the lip of the bridge roof. It was a dangerously exposed position — the wing deck was built out to the full beam of the ship. Apart from the risk of being spotted, the ocean churned violently fifteen metres below him as it threw itself against the hull. A fall wouldn't kill him outright, but he would be pinned helplessly against the steel wall by the waves. Helpless in every sense. Unable to save himself — or Anna. Churned around in the washer until he drowned, while they killed his wife and crew.

His legs started to shake at the thought. He crouched, trying to take some weight off them, to return the muscles to conscious motor control; fighting for the composure to start the climb. He could find little purchase on the wet paintwork, and the wind and rain were lunging at his body, trying to tear it away. His hands felt along the roof edge; somewhere there had to be something to get a hold on. He moved carefully forwards, feet slipping on the railing, increasingly exposed to any casual glances to windward by the pirate crew. And anyone arriving on the bridge. There was a crash as the leading wave of a big set pounded into the hull. The railing hummed with the impact; spray licked up the side of the ship and doused him. He held on, white knuckled, blinking hard to clear stinging salt water from his eyes, as the next three waves did the same.

In the momentary lull that followed, his right hand finally located a support-wire fixing for the radio mast. He took a firm grip with both hands, kicked his feet clear and heaved. He got one elbow onto the edge but that was all. The wire felt like a cheese cutter, and the pain sliced into his palms. There was nothing to provide his feet with any support — they kicked uselessly in the air. Already his arms were feeling the strain, the pain spilling out from his hands, creeping up his forearms, tightening insidiously as it sought to break his hold.

Hamnet dug as deep as he could go, dredged the pits for that extra strength that came with desperation. He knew it was there — he'd been down there before. With a howl of pain and fear and anguish that was whipped away by the wind, he flung his body sideways. It was just enough — his right foot hooked over the roof edge. Immediately he could take the strain off his hands, slip the wire into the cradle of his elbow. He levered hard with his leg, shoe leather skidding on water-streaked steelwork. A final heave, and he threw himself onto the roof — and lay staring up at the bruised clouds, rain hammering his face and body, gasping for breath.

At the crash of a door below he rolled onto all fours. Someone had got to the bridge. Hamnet scuttled softly across to an air vent to listen. There were footsteps and loud curses from inside. One of the Americans — the one he'd seen first, he reckoned — had found the radioman. A quick command on the VHF to the support boat cleared the SSB of the blocking transmission. The oil platform immediately came crackling over the air. Hamnet had difficulty making out what was said next, but figured the American was trying to persuade the rig that its help wasn't required. The crash of a weapon as it slammed lead into the radio indicated he had failed. Hamnet was motionless, rooted in place. The American's voice grew louder as it moved from the radio room to beneath the air vent. 'The oil installation has birds and armed security. We don't have much time — they've already left. Get the barge away from here, fast, up the river and into the mangroves. Kill the crew, like I said, but not the wife — she's coming with us. Get her in the inflatable with the boys.' A pause, then: 'He's dead — forget him. Get on with it.'

Hamnet heard footsteps retreat to the stairs. He hesitated, still crouching by the air vent, grasping for a plan, some notion of how best to respond to the situation. The rain drummed down on the steel roof all around him, the wind sweeping it past him in rivers.

A sudden commotion on the cargo deck made him look up. The crane had stopped, diesel engines were revving hard. Then the Tannoy again. 'Hamnet, hear me. We're leaving now. With your wife. One single word reaches the authorities about how you ran your boat aground, and she dies.'

The words jolted him into action. He slithered quickly to the front of the bridge, keeping back from the edge, just in the shadow thrown by the light from the cargo deck. He fumbled the weapon off his back. The unlit barge was moving away to leeward, soon to be swallowed up by the rain. The high, whining revs of a pair of outboard engines reached him as a rigid inflatable boat pulled alongside in its place. The remaining pirates were gathering by the leeward rail, preparing to disembark. His crew were still by the crane, but now the guard was urging them forward, towards the edge of the hold. Hamnet could see what was coming. He

33

had to take the guard out first to give them any sort of chance.

He lined up the sight. His experience of firearms being limited to fairgrounds and air pistols, he knew his chances of hitting anything were slim, but maybe some of his men would be able to get clear in the confusion. He breathed out, tried to settle his pounding heart. It wasn't happening. Giving up the attempt, he tugged the trigger. Nothing. 'Shit! Shit! Safety catch, the fucking safety catch. Where the hell is it?' He fumbled with the unfamiliar weapon, found a switch by the trigger guard and snapped it down — two clicks.

As Hamnet took aim again, the gaunt figure of the American commander approached the prisoners, grabbed the guard's machine pistol and pushed Anna to one side, towards the pirates by the rail. It would be harder now — he couldn't turn his weapon on the main group for fear of hitting Anna.

But the American was already bringing up the machine pistol, and Hamnet stopped thinking and squeezed his trigger blindly. Unknowingly, he had set the Heckler and Koch MP5 on automatic. The barrage surprised him, and he didn't see where the burst went, but those on deck saw where it came from and their reaction was immediate. He heard the first rounds clang into the front of the bridge below him and slammed his head down. A hail of lead pelted the steelwork around him, a continuous clatter of death delivered at eight hundred kilometres an hour. Hamnet's cheek pressed hard into the warm deck, rain puddling into his nostrils as he willed the racket to stop. For minutes it seemed to rage — then, suddenly, silence.

Cautiously, anxiously, he lifted his head. There was no one, nothing. No crew, no pirates. The sudden roar of outboard motors told him where the gang had gone, and he caught a brief glimpse of the rigid inflatable as it pulled out from the cover of the ship and disappeared into the murk. Nothing moved below him. He wondered briefly if any of his crew had survived, but his head told him that the pirates would have made sure there was no chance of that. And Anna had been swept off in the inflatable.

Then, through the ringing in his ears, came another noise — the distant but unmistakable throb of helicopter rotor blades. The sound grew louder, approaching from the port side. With the cargo-deck lights ablaze, it wouldn't take them long to find him.

Hamnet stood, dropping his weapon to the deck. He wiped the rain from his face, tried to think clearly. A foundered ship, a lost crew. How the hell was he going to explain all that without telling them about the GPS? And there would be an enquiry. He could remember the last time. Press, questions, tribunals. No where to hide from it all. And no one you could trust — he remembered that most of all. He knew then that he would have to find Anna himself. The beat of the helicopter blades was heavy on his ears. He only had seconds. The inflatable had pulled out to the east. He had to do it now. He stared at the leeward edge of the ship. How deep was it? She drew forty feet. There would be plenty of water. So he ran. Hamnet sprinted across the deck and launched himself into the air.

Hurtling downwards he whirled his arms to keep himself upright, pulling them in to protect his head the instant before he hit the water. The impact pounded the breath out of him in a blast of bubbles, and he plunged forever before remembering to spread his arms and legs to slow his descent. Then he started fighting, trying to pull himself back to the surface, as he realised how deep he was and how little air he seemed to have in his lungs. He could feel the turbulence all around him, and when he opened his eyes there was only white froth. His legs were kicking hard, his arms pulled in to his sides. But he had to breath. Automatic reflex kicked in and he sucked in a lungful of seawater even as he broke the surface. As the water went down it tore at the delicate tissue. He coughed and retched violently, unable to suck in the air he needed but expelling the seawater in one explosive heave. He thrashed at the surface, trying to draw breath, and oxygen slowly filtered into his racked lungs.

He bobbed in the waves, a dozen metres to leeward of the looming hull of his former command, still choking and coughing. He could hear the helicopter but not see it. It was circling somewhere in the rain and cloud above, testing the situation to see if it would draw fire. Hamnet rolled over and started to swim. The first forty metres, in the flat water that extended in the lee of the ship, were relatively easy. But as he swam beyond the illumination of the ship's lights, he entered a maelstrom. The forty-knot winds had tortured the surface of the sea into a heaving morass. But Hamnet had spent his childhood on Sydney's Cronulla Beach. A lifetime's passion for surfing had made him supremely comfortable in the ocean. It was only panic or exhaustion that would kill him, and he wasn't about to panic.

A sudden explosion of light dazzled him. He rolled onto his back to look at the scene behind. He could just make out the chopper, hovering above a parachute flare. Below, all was bathed in an eerie glow. The stricken ship was now some four hundred metres away, cloud tumbling over the superstructure. Wind, current and his painfully slow swimming had allowed him to cover some ground. The helicopter crew would never see his head bobbing in such confused seas from that distance. He swivelled himself through a full circle to check his surroundings, fighting to keep his head clear as he popped up on waves, trying to see any sign of a shoreline. There was nothing. He looked back at the ship, and realised how fast he was being carried directly down-wind. The current must be taking him out into the channel. He needed to swim across it, parallel to the ship, to stand any chance of reaching land. He struck out again, now across the waves rather than with them.

The light from the flare was dying slowly. He could hear the chopper descending close to the stricken vessel, the sound carrying on the wind. The crew had finally satisfied themselves that there was no danger from gunmen. But Hamnet was in no mood for further spectating. Energy was draining from him fast. The ocean rolled over and under him, in walls of green water or churning foam, determined to frustrate his progress. He ducked under the big waves, searching for the calm beneath the surface on his own terms, fighting the ocean's effort to pull him under when he wasn't ready.

Slowly, the sea started to change. The waves became steeper, pitching up, dropping and hurling him sideways so it was almost impossible to swim. But he knew what that meant. The bottom was shallowing beneath him. It might be possible to body-surf the breaking waves.

He changed his angle again, swimming down each wave as he felt it rise under him. It was a struggle to swim fast enough, but finally he caught one. He twisted hard to pull himself across the face, and suddenly he was rushing into clear water. The wave carried him a useful distance — forty, fifty, sixty effortless metres — before the white water sucked in his legs and slowly, inevitably, washed past him, leaving him floundering. Once again every metre was a battle.

He caught a second wave. Another. And one more. But exhaustion was biting hard and he could no longer summon the energy. The waves simply broke over him, tumbling him forwards, a whirligig of limbs. There was no point in fight-ing it. He let each foaming monster suck him in and throw

37

him around until it was ready to spit him out. Or not. Maybe he would hit the beach first. Maybe he would die. There was little he could do in his weakened state except hope. And breathe when opportunity allowed.

As he dropped off the lip of one wave into a full somer-sault, crashing down unseeing, he felt something hard. Sand or mud scraped across his face, and energy returned. Floun-dering, uncoordinated energy, but energy all the same. He was bounced along the mud, and then hurled into the arms of a mangrove bush, which he grasped with the very last of his strength. Pulling, crawling, struggling out of the ocean's reach as the wave receded, he was utterly drained, but alive.

Chapter 4

The rigid inflatable boat had pace on — too much pace. But the pirate captain paid no heed as it threw itself off the back of a wave and into the air. The twin engines howled as the propellers flew clear of the water. Anna braced herself. The RIB came down stern first with a smack, the engine note dropping to a stuttering moan. Water flushed from under the impacting hull, and the boat rolled wildly from gunwale to gunwale, spray rails throwing huge fantails into the rain. Anna had one hand wrapped round the lifeline; with the other she struggled desperately to steady her children's passage. She jammed herself harder into the aft port corner, on the floor beside a petrol tank, her legs braced against the rear seats in front of her.

Three times so far the RIB had become airborne as it tore up the ocean away from the *Shawould*. The American was good. He wove across the wave pattern with a tight professionalism, using all two hundred horsepower available to him and some intelligent steering to avoid the breaking faces. But when forced to tackle the white water, he displayed a recklessness that verged on the psychotic. He hurled the boat off the waves with total disregard for the consequences. And all the passengers could do, captors and captive alike, was hang on. White-knuckled, grim-faced. Only the grace of whatever godless being was watching over these men had stopped their vessel from flipping.

Anna shut her eyes, ignoring the stinging salt that filled them. The driver had the hammer down still, tracking the smooth water on the back of a wave, heading up towards the breaking lip. Again the RIB was quicker than the peel of the wave, and the driver was faced with the drop. But this time he put the wheel down hard. The boat responded immediately, the stern slewing round so fast that it skipped and skidded, scattering chunks of wave into the air as the driver turned into the clean water of the unformed face behind. Anna clung on desperately, teeth clenched against the shuddering slide. But the turn had been too hard. The protesting outboards had had enough. They wailed at the cavitation, coughed on re-entry, and stopped.

The silence was instantaneous and ominous. As one, the passengers looked behind them. A gentle rolling slope was going vertical. The RIB had stalled in a trough before a massive breaking wave, which lurched up and towered over it. The boat started to slip down the wave face, slowly rolling sideways. A sinister, hissing roar filled the air, drowning the splutter of the engines as they turned over, once, and the cries of panic from the stricken passengers. The driver tried again — still nothing. Anna wasn't screaming — that was worse than pointless. She pulled herself onto the floor and lay sideways, breathing deep and hard, filling her lungs with air, ready for the inevitable roll.

Then the engines choked into life. The driver reacted with intuitive brilliance. Too heavy on the throttle and the still struggling motors would have cut out again. But he didn't need that much power. The lip of the wave was toppling into the boat as he applied the revs. For a moment it seemed he was too late — water cascaded and sluiced around the crew, and the RIB lurched and staggered, pitching both sideways and forwards. Then, as the props found something to bite on, they pushed the boat with just enough speed to catch the wave. It was all that was needed. The boat accelerated down the face of its own accord, the driver applying power for steerage and control, until the engine note steadied and he hit the throttle hard. The RIB lunged through the curtain of spray to safety.

It was the last hurdle. That final monster wave had been pitched up by the shallows on the bar at the entrance to a river. The wave height dropped quickly as the boat slid into a power turn round a spit and headed towards the shelter of the windward shore. The engines cut as the water finally flattened out, and Anna eased herself off the floor into a sitting position. Branches rattled and tossed above them in the wind, and rain hissed through the leaves, bouncing off the hard rubber sides of the inflatable and splattering her as she tucked her knees against her belly. She pulled the sodden silk robe tight around her. Even as her muscles relaxed after bracing for the ride, she tensed in expectation of new dangers. Why had they stopped? Surrounded by the pirate crew, Anna felt naked to the core of her terrified soul. She could feel movement inside her too, could sense that her fear had been communicated to the tiny human beings growing there. She was no stranger to pain or fear or deprivation, but tonight she had seen things she had never imagined she would see. Things she would never forget.

Richardson's tall, frail body as he had stepped forward to his death. The bewilderment on his face — on all their faces — as Phil had failed to appear. The growing terror as the minutes had ticked away. The accusing looks cast at her by the others. And then the sudden explosion of violence. None of them had tried to run. She closed her eyes again as she recalled the scene, but the images only returned all the more vividly. They had just stood there, dithering away the last chance they had for life. A wide burst of continuous fire had brought all of them down, followed by a carefully aimed bullet for each twitching body — until the only motion among the litter of corpses had been the splash of rain, clothing tugged by the wind and the steady flow of blood. Then the dead had been casually kicked into the hold. And all the

41

time the din of automatic gunfire as they had tried to kill her lover. A tear trailed down her cheek.

But questions tumbled through her mind. What had happened on that ship? Why hadn't Phil come forward? What did he know? Where was he now? Had he survived the shooting gallery that his rescue attempt had become? Her thoughts whirled onwards, diving to ever-darker depths as she sat silently waiting.

She didn't see the helicopter land on the *Shawould*, but its descent over the parachute flare was the signal for the American to put the boat into gear again and pull out from under the security of the mangroves. His crew remained silent. Surviving the roller-coaster journey they'd just endured would normally have left them giggling like schoolchildren. But the American was angry. In a land where people lived on a dollar-and-a-half a day, life was cheap, yet his capacity for violence still frightened them. They knew to be quiet, to let the anger burn slowly rather than provoke it into explosive combustion.

The driver gradually increased power until the RIB was churning a phosphorescent wake through the dark water. Engine noise and wash bounced off the silent mangroves, which steadily closed around the narrowing river. The moonless night, thick with swirling rain, allowed no visibility beyond the shadowy outline of encroaching foliage. The men on the boat were silent, faceless shapes.

The inflatable motored past the barge. No one spoke on either vessel. The journey continued through tightening turns in the river. Then, ahead, the suspicion of a light was reflected in the falling rain. Soon, a handful of individual glows were distinguishable, strengthening as successive layers of mangrove were peeled away at the rounding of each bend. Finally, stilted houses could be made out, fires and gas lamps bright through doorways and fissured walls. The RIB slowed and turned towards a group of dark figures squatting on the porch of one single-storey wooden building.

The American manoeuvred alongside, and as a couple of the crew stepped ashore with mooring lines, he turned to Anna. She was staring at her left hand in the firelight, knuckles stark and white, blood oozing between her fingers. Only now did she see that she had torn the skin while holding on during the journey to the river mouth. The American indicated she should be taken inside, then jumped out ahead of her. She allowed herself to be pulled up and off the boat. She stumbled on the uneven planking, her arms held firmly and protectively across her stomach. She was frightened for herself now. Frightened for her babies. The horrors of the ship, of the massacre, receded as she focused on her own immediate future.

Inside the building a woman squatted over a fire, the lid of a steaming cooking pot rattling quietly. Anna was led to a mat in one corner. She sat watching as someone lit a couple of gas lamps and yellow light flooded the room. By the door the American was staring out into the rain. This was the first time Anna had got a good look at him. Her eyes ran over his sodden tunic, taking in streaks of dirt, a heavy revolver in a shoulder holster under one arm. A gaunt, stubbled chin. Water trickled through cropped ginger hair, across a face lined and freckled by the sun. He blinked occasionally to clear drops from the lashes that hung over relentless grey eyes, but otherwise he was motionless. And everyone else waited.

Finally, the man turned to his second in command, who had brought her in — a barrel of a man, heavy and awkward. 'So, Mike,' he said, 'what do you think? Did he stay on the boat?'

Mike Bureya remained silent, staring intently at Anna. He knew the question was rhetorical — the boss would answer it himself soon enough.

The American commander sucked at his teeth, thinking. That Hamnet had survived the hail of gunfire he had no doubt. It was unfortunate there hadn't been more time, either to hunt him down and finish him off for sure, or to force the issue with his wife, which, considering how he had let the thin officer die, might have taken a while. So the question now was as he had voiced it: had Hamnet stayed on his ship and waited for the bird from the oil rig? If he had, would he report their differential transmissions? And if he hadn't, could he survive in the water long enough to get ashore? And what would he do then? Certainly he would take the threat to his wife seriously. Surely that was enough to keep him quiet — wasn't it? Too many imponderables — he didn't like it. The name meant something too. Hamnet: where the hell had he heard that before? She would know. He turned to Anna: 'Coffee?'

Anna nodded tightly, and he waved a hand at the woman by the fire. She ladled liquid from the steaming pot into a cup and carried it over. Anna took it carefully with her good hand, searching for eye contact with the woman, for some kind of reassurance. None was given.

The American commander spoke again. 'My name is Janac. As you will have gathered, I am responsible for tonight's events. My apologies for the rather dramatic turn your evening has taken. It is of course your misfortune to have been in the wrong place at the wrong time.'

Anna was staring at the black liquid in the cup but listening to every word.

'I must assume that your husband is still alive. I need to keep him quiet, and while he remains so, you get to stay alive. As you know him rather better than I do, you can make your own judgement as to your chances.' Janac watched her carefully. Even in these circumstances she was, he judged, very beautiful. Latin blood, perhaps — dark hair, soft brown eyes and a caramel complexion to match. A lucky man, Phillip Hamnet. At least until tonight. 'Phillip Hamnet,' he continued. 'I've heard of him. Tell me why.'

Slowly Anna looked up from the cup at Janac. The line of his mouth was zipper straight. His grey eyes seemed to pin her to the spot.

'Tell me.'

'Tell you what?' she replied, creases at the corners of her eyes now.

'Tell me why I've heard the name Phillip Hamnet.'

Anna blinked slowly. Would this be a betrayal?

Even her short hesitation was too much for Janac. It had been a long night — he didn't need this. He sighed and stepped towards her, pulling his heavy revolver from its holster and flipping it round so that he was holding it by the barrel, all in one smooth motion. The butt clattered the cup away. Anna stifled a scream as hot coffee splashed across her bare legs. With his other hand, Janac pushed her hard, forcing her off balance. She fell backwards. He dropped on top of her, a knee across her thighs, his hand round her throat. He held the gun above her stomach. Anna's arms reached across her belly protectively. Her brown eyes were wide, locked on Janac's face in the sudden stillness. The wind moaned, and the rain clattered on the corrugated-iron roof above them.

'Of course,' he said, 'what kind of damage I do depends on how hard I hit you.'

He choked off her scream with a little more pressure from the hand on her windpipe. 'It's real simple,' said Janac. 'Just tell me what I need to know.' He raised the gun a couple of inches higher.

Anna's lips were working, but only a gurgle emerged. Until Janac eased the pressure on her throat, and then the words came in a hoarse rush. 'The Lifeboat Man, he's the Lifeboat Man.'

Janac smirked as he let her go and stood up. She rolled onto her side, curling into the foetal position. Now he knew what Hamnet had done. He turned to Bureya. 'He won't have waited for the helicopter. He's out there somewhere. We'll start a search at first light. Use the fishing boats so we don't attract any unnecessary attention from whoever's on the wreck. Sweep south from the river mouth — if he hasn't drowned he'll be down tide and wind.' He glanced at the heavy stainless Rolex watch on his wrist. 'We have a lot to do. The barge should be here in a couple of hours. Get the people fed before then. I want it unloaded tonight so everyone is out looking in the morning. I'm going to Palembang first thing. I want a full inventory of what we've got off the *Shawould* by then, as I'll be seeing the owner tomorrow. But hold the stuff here — we'll decide exactly how we get it out when we know how badly the shit is going to hit the fan over this. It's not going to be as simple as I planned, what with a dead crew and Hamnet loose.' Janac shook his head. 'And I need that money.'

Bureya nodded silently. Janac turned and walked slowly back to the door, where he stared out into the dark and rain again, his anger gone as quickly as it had flared. He snapped out the cylinder of his revolver and spun the chamber thoughtfully before reholstering the gun. He glanced over at Anna, still curled up defensively.

Anna's mind was ablaze with conflicting emotions. The fear she felt at the possibility of losing her babies was altogether different from the fear she had felt before. And she hated it because of the anger that swelled beneath it. Anger that she had snivelled in the face of this man instead of spitting in it. Anger at the babies for making her so helpless — she hated them for that. And she hated herself for feeling so.

There were heavy footsteps on the wooden floor as Bureya moved to the fire to help himself to coffee. He took a sip and joined Janac at the door. Janac glanced at him, then spoke softly into the rain. 'I'll be away for a couple of days, to find out how this thing is being reported, to see if Hamnet turns up on the outside. I want you to look after things here, Mike.' He nodded at Anna. 'If Hamnet doesn't turn up, or keeps his mouth shut, we'll need to get her out of here. I'll sort that out while I'm away. In the meantime, keep her safe — I don't want anyone touching her. Get her some clothes and feed her properly. But if you find Hamnet, don't wait for me. Kill them both.'

Chapter 5

The rain and wind had stopped as abruptly as they had started. Hamnet had stirred constantly through a cramping, endless night, lying with his head propped in the crook of a mangrove branch to stop it slipping into the water when he dozed off. On one of the countless occasions when wakefulness had broken the shallow veneer of sleep, the elements had become still and quiet. On another he had been aware of light — a weak orange glow — off to the east. But by then he had been too tired to react, and sleep had finally sucked him down from the surface and into its swampy grasp. Just when it was time to move.

In the end it was a fleeting thought of Anna that jerked the impossible weight from his eyelids, as sharply as if he'd woken to the thunder of a rumble strip under the wheels of a car. His collision with the bulkhead when the ship had run aground had left him with a stupefying headache. He gently brushed his fingertips over the bruise — the bandage was long gone. The skin didn't seem to be broken, and there was no blood. He struggled to sit up, and the pain rolled out through his body. He sat still and looked around. The sky above him was clear, but glowering cumulus topped the low hills of the island, and haze hung above the steaming mangroves. The water of the channel shimmered blackly. To his left he could see his ship, resting peacefully with a forty-degree list. There was no sign of life. No indication of the bloody mayhem that had taken place in the night. But he had to forget that — the ship was no longer his problem. His only concern was to find Anna. At the moment he had nothing — no money, no papers, no food or water. And there was only one man he knew he could trust, who would help, who would know where to look. He had to find him first.

Hamnet scoured his memory for details of the chart to work out which way he should proceed. He knew there was a port city called Palembang about eighty kilometres inland, and a major river that led there from the Bangka Channel somewhere to the north, but he could remember nothing of what lay in between. He glanced behind him at the mangroves. It would take him hours to do just a couple of kilometres through them, and they could extend for ten or twenty. It made more sense to stick to the coast — he would have a better chance of finding people, a fishing village perhaps, somewhere he could get water and food. But he had to be careful. Most of the pirates had been locals, and doubtless the word had gone around that he was wanted. He needed to put some distance between himself and the ship before he could come out into the open. He would head north, towards the traffic that he knew plied the river up to Palembang.

He pulled himself unsteadily out of the shallow water, and a further wave of pain rippled out. He moved off, skirting the mangroves, stumbling over the uneven mudflat. As the sun rose, the air grew hot and steamy. The light glared down, reflecting off the water, dazzling in its intensity. Hamnet's mind drifted, unprompted, back to the events of the night.

It was a variation on the old 'rust-bucket' fraud: hiring a crew to illegally sell a valuable cargo before scuttling the ship in deep water and collecting the insurance as well. The scam with the GPS should have achieved the same end with less risk. No weak links. No chance of anyone getting drunk on the pay-off and blowing the story all over the docks.

He had worked it out, but not fast enough. He should have been sharper, and it was his crew who had paid the price. And Anna — what of her and the babies? Their future could still be in his hands, but only in return for silence, allowing the pirate crew free reign. Yet what if they continued to murder indiscriminately aboard the ships they attacked?

Time passed, measured in steps forward. His head throbbed to the uneven rhythm of his progress. Two steps, a slip, a splash, a foot jammed under a root. The struggle to get free. The untiring resistance of the water to his progress. The constant desire to slake his thirst. His vision, blurred and uneven, pulling in and out of focus unbidden. And overlying everything, the heavy silence of moisture-laden air.

Until a steady tick-tick-tick broke that silence. It was growing rapidly louder. Hamnet stopped, recognising the even beat of an outboard motor. The sound seemed to be coming from his left, apparently from deep in the mangroves. He crouched down in waist-deep water until only his head was visible. Just in time — a slim wooden dinghy burst out of the foliage about a hundred metres away. The starboard gunwale dipped as the boat made a right-hand turn and headed towards him. On board were three men, all staring intently at the passing shoreline. Hamnet caught a glimpse of a rifle propped up in the bow. There was no time for anything else. He hauled in a breath, slid below the surface, found a submerged mangrove branch near the bottom and hung on.

The seconds ticked by. Hamnet knew from experience that he could manage just under a couple of minutes underwater. That was a long time at the speed the boat was going. At ten knots, it would cover some six hundred metres. He'd be safe. He started to count. One thousand, two thousand, three thousand . . . He scanned the water surface above him. He could see no sign of a wash — perhaps he would feel it as it rolled over him. One minute. And one thousand, two thousand, three . . . No vibrations, no ripples — the water remained still. He had to start coming up while he had enough air in his lungs to be in control, not charge for the surface at breaking point, sucking back frothy seawater. Thirty thousand. He was close to his limit. Keeping his legs locked in position, he eased his grip on the branch and slowly sat up.

The water streaming down his face made vision difficult, but he didn't need to look far — the dinghy was ten metres away. An adrenaline surge burned what was left of the oxygen in his lungs. His eyes bulged, fixed on the three men. They were so close he could have spat on them. But they were all looking the other way. As his mouth came clear he grabbed a breath and slid back to the bottom. Every inch of his skin tingled with the anticipation of a bullet.

He must stay down until they left or he drowned — but he knew he couldn't hold himself under until he passed out. He was considering using his belt to strap himself to the branch when the water ten metres away exploded into a white froth. They had restarted the engine. The wake was already carving away from him, through the murk. He had only to hang on a few more seconds.

He forced himself to count to ten, then eased his way airwards. The top of his head broke the surface, eyes peering cautiously while mouth and nose remained submerged. He was safe. The boat was fifty metres away, the occupants' attention firmly directed ahead of them. He lifted his nose and mouth clear of the water and sucked in deep breaths of air with the relish of a smoker taking the first drag of the day. Slowly his body re-established some sort of equilibrium. Oxygen flooded into his blood stream, and the adrenaline receded, although a nagging tension persisted. He remained motionless until the dinghy had moved out of sight round a curve in the shore. Then he dragged himself, still half-submerged, deep into the mangroves.

He fought his way towards the river from which the boat had emerged until he was just back from the edge, facing a hundred-metre-wide expanse of brown water. To his left the river disappeared round a bend. To his right, the southern shore on which he stood became a spit, extending into the Bangka Channel. At the end of the spit was his foundered ship, still silent and lifeless. Hamnet swore heavily under his breath — they had so nearly missed it. But more interesting at that moment was the opposite shore. Fringed with forest, it curved away sharply to the west, offering a view up the channel. No more godforsaken mangroves. He would be able to move fast and in good cover. How quickly could he swim a hundred metres? A couple of minutes? It would be a long time in the open, but the risk was worth it.

Hamnet stood and listened. The boat engine had gone. He pulled off his shoes, tied them together by the laces and hung them round his neck, then pushed through the remaining screen of mangroves. He slipped into the deeper water, electing a steady breaststroke — that way he could still hear. He soon realised there was a lot of water running out of the river from the previous night's rain, and the current was carrying him towards the channel. He adjusted his direction to compensate, using two trees to keep his bearings. He kept listening, kept swimming, kept hoping he'd stay lucky.

The silence remained unbroken, and finally he felt his feet kick the bottom. Staying belly down, he slithered through the mud towards the forest cover before collapsing in the safety of the trees.

He watched the ship for fifteen minutes while he recovered a little energy. It remained quiet. He moved on, keeping a hundred metres back from the shoreline, paralleling the channel west. Although still marshy in places, the ground was much easier going than the mangrove swamp, and the trees provided shade from the intolerable blast of the sun.

He made his way cautiously at first, tensed in anticipation of another search party, choosing good cover over easy walking. But as the hours slipped by, exhaustion and thirst made caution a luxury he couldn't afford. Weakened, hurting, priorities shifting, Hamnet knew he must find water — or nothing else would matter. But there was none — and slowly, inexorably, dehydration tightened its grip. The light began to soften, the shadows lengthened. He stumbled on unseen undergrowth, lurched into a tree, hanging on even as the earth dragged him down.

Every muscle was burning with lactic acid build-up. His head pounded, his throat was on fire, his tongue was cracked and swollen, his lips, burnt by the sun, were split and bleeding. He felt himself falling as his eyes closed, sliding down the tree, toppling onto his side. Something told him that losing consciousness was a step towards death. But there was nothing left to draw on. Nothing left to resist with. It was all gone. He sank onto the soft bed of the forest floor, and there, in the distance, he could hear Anna calling him.

Chapter 6

It was the crash of thunder that brought Hamnet back —
that and the rain. He didn't know where he was, or why he
was there. He knew only that his thirst was a harsh, domi-
nating pain that permeated every cell in his body — and
that now there was water all around. He rolled over, press-
ing his face into the soft mud beneath him, lips and tongue
kissing the wet earth — wonderful, miraculous moisture.

He knelt shakily, pulled off his soaking shirt and wrung
it out into his mouth. He then tossed it over a nearby branch
and scrabbled around in the darkness looking for pools of
clean water in hollows of bark and root. He wrung out his
shirt again, then lay back, mouth open, to let the downpour
pummel him. Finally, instinct forced him onto his feet. The
darkness was complete, but the familiar hiss of rain on still
water led him to the channel, where he found a narrow sandy
foreshore. He turned left, and once again began tramping
west. He stopped regularly to drink, but was unable to save
any of the water that was now so plentiful.

He thought he was imagining the light, that it was a trick
played by tired eyes and an overanxious mind. But there
was another — and a third and a fourth. He walked for another half hour before the beach swung to the left, and now
it became clear that the lights were out in the channel. A
couple were flashing — navigation beacons indicating the
entrance to the main river. For the first time in twenty-four
hours, Hamnet's spirits lifted a fraction. But then the beach
turned a further ninety degrees to the left, forcing him to
walk away from the glimmer of hope. A little further on the
foreshore itself started to disappear. The ground became

marshy once more, and mangroves closed in around him.

The most logical explanation was that he had reached a branch off the main river and was now headed upstream into the hinterland. It meant another swim. He went through the same routine as before, slipping over the slime and into the water, into his tired and awkward breaststroke. But he was soon kicking the soft bottom of the narrow stream, and stumbled to all fours in the shallows. Struggling to his feet, hesitating only to put his shoes back on, he moved off at a crawling pace. Only when he finally saw lights to the north did he stop. They appeared through the trees, both near and far. With the first blush of dawn easing over the eastern horizon, he took shelter in the undergrowth and slept.

It was his constant companions — heat, hunger and thirst — that woke him. The view from his hide-out was much as he had expected. Directly north he could see the port of Muntok, where the *Shawould* had been anchored two days earlier. He watched a ferry pull out from the harbour, headed for Palembang. Nothing else moved. Muntok would be closer than Palembang — only fifteen or twenty kilometres away. If he could just get hold of a dinghy to cross the channel . . . Wooden buildings on stilts, with attendant fishing boats, dotted the bay. These must have been the source of the closer lights he had seen in the night. The boats were there for the taking if he could manage the swim.

The channel was placid in the sunshine, showing little sign of tide or current. But thirst was still nagging, and although lack of food was slower to inflict its damage, the steady decline in energy reserves was real enough. He knew he had little strength left. If he got in trouble out there, he would have nothing extra to call on.

Such were the thoughts that spun around in his head all afternoon. He dozed, shifted his position, tried to rest, his hunger and thirst growing. Eventually he gave up on sleep and spent an hour cutting and tearing the legs off his trousers with the help of a stone. He would leave his shirt behind — the less resistance while swimming the better.

The fishermen came and went, but of the three buildings closest to him, one had a boat beside it as the sun went down. He guessed it to be between two and three kilometres distant. There was little point in waiting any longer. It would be easier to start while there was still some daylight. He wormed down the beach, crawled into the cool water, and settled once more into a steady breaststroke that allowed him to watch and listen.

Clouds were gathering behind the low hills of Bangka, but for now the water was rippled by only the lightest of breezes, and glowed with the deepening orange of the western sky. Hamnet paced himself carefully. His parched throat cried out for him to wash back the liquid that streamed across his face with every stroke, and he had to work hard to fight the temptation. The sun's rays finally disappeared, to be replaced by a weak moonlight. Occasionally he heard a distant engine, and once felt a wash ripple past him. He kept a careful eye on his target. It remained unlit, which he hoped meant the occupants were sleeping. He took his bearings off a distinctive group of four lights on the far shore. He judged there was no tide carrying him off course, but it was difficult to estimate distance, and harder still when the clouds finally shut out the moon. The water around him was dark and oily.

He stopped, ears straining to listen. He let himself sink low in the water, kicking gently with his feet to hold position without splashing. There was only silence ahead of him, broken by a faraway clap of thunder. The air was heavy with anticipation of another storm.

A sudden noise sent him reeling with its proximity. Then a lamp threw the shack into stark relief. Light escaped through every crack in the walls and glittered across the water, shining off his face. The building was only ten metres away, to his right. Beneath it was deep shadow. He sucked back a huge breath and dived as quietly as he could.

Hamnet swam hard for the darkness with the minimum of motion, without expelling any of the air in his lungs. Stealthily he entered the shadow and glided to the surface. He breathed out as quietly as possible. The floor of the hut was two metres or more above. Had they heard him? A creak, a sigh. Then a stream of liquid splashed and bubbled centimetres from his face. Someone was urinating off the porch. Hamnet barely stifled a curse and the reflex to recoil.

He backed carefully away from the froth and turned. He needed to locate the boat while there was still light. It lay on the far side of the hut. More creaks, a few words in a language he didn't recognise. A phut as the lamp was extinguished, then silence and darkness.

This was the most dangerous moment. He forced himself to wait, for his eyes to adjust, for those above him to return to sleep. Gradually he tuned back into the environment. The wind was building, the odd rumble of thunder no longer so distant. Sudden flashes of lightning lit up Bangka Island, and in those instants he could see the boat more clearly. But the rain that would cover the noise of his movements so effectively refused to come. He swam over to the boat and pushed gently against it. It was brought up short by lines at both bow and stern. He draped his shoes over the gunwale before moving to the bow and groping for the rope. It was tied up high on the building, well above his reach. He cursed himself for not carrying a knife.

More frustrating still was that the freeboard of the boat stopped him reaching inside to release the rope at that end. Either he would have to climb one of the stilts and untie the line from the shack, or he would have to pull himself into the boat. Neither was an attractive proposition, but climbing aboard silently from the water would be impossible. He decided to tackle the stilts. Where the hell was that rain? The thunder had stopped and the wind had settled to a gentle ten knots. Ripples slapped against the hull. That would have to be cover enough.

He swam to the closest stilt. He was just able to grab a strut, and from there he reached for the lip of the porch. As he pulled himself up, water began to cascade off his shorts. He quickly lowered himself back. No sign of detection from above — yet — but the shorts would have to go. He emptied his lungs and sank quietly. It was the only way to get the shorts off without thrashing around on the surface. He wrung them out as gently as he could, then hung them over the side of the dinghy with his shoes.

He went back to the stilt and tried again. He cleared the water silently, but felt more exposed than ever. He pulled himself up so his head was level with the bottom edge of the porch and slowly peered over. He couldn't make out anything. Stepping on it would be too risky, judging by the creaking and groaning that had accompanied the owner's movements. Instead, he moved arm over arm along the edge of the porch, lifting his feet slightly so they didn't drag in the water, until he felt the bow line brush against his body. Muscle burn was starting to bite in his forearms. He transferred his right hand to the rope and pulled. It didn't budge. And it was clear from the angle that it was tied up well out of reach unless he could climb onto the porch itself. Despair began to flood into him, as fast as the strength was pouring out of his arms. He ground his teeth with frustration. He had come so far — it was ridiculous that this part should be so hard.

Then, with a flash of inspiration, he realised he was holding the solution. He pulled the line in the opposite direction and the bow of the boat turned obediently towards him; then, by lifting his body, he got the dinghy to slide directly underneath him. He shifted his weight to the rope and gently let himself down onto the thwart, before working his way to the end of the line to untie it. One down, one to go.

He stared at the bottom of the boat for a long while before accepting he could see nothing. It was too risky to try working his way down to the stern — there would be fishing gear, ropes, uneven boards and God knows what else to trip over. He grabbed the bow line, pulled himself up and out of the boat, and lowered himself back into the water.

It had been the perfect technique. All he had to do was repeat the manoeuvre at the stern. He swam there, found the nearest stilt and edged himself up it until he held the lip of the porch in his hands again. Arm over arm he moved towards the stern line, which he then tugged to bring the boat towards him. This time, without the restraint of the bow line, the dinghy kept coming — and bumped into one of the stilts. It didn't make much of a noise, but there was a rustle, a murmur, from above. He froze, suspended from the porch, feet touching the water, looking down into the shadow of the open stern.

He pulled up his feet and felt for the edge of the boat with them. Another creak. He hung motionless again, arms throbbing — he had to get his weight off them. His searching feet found the outboard motor. There was no casing on it. Would it start if he had to make a run for it? The chances of getting it going quickly enough were slim. But if he just paddled away from the shack any half-competent swimmer would catch him. He pushed such thoughts aside — he could still get away unnoticed. Slowly, he lowered his weight towards the stern. A little more slapping of water as he rocked the boat in the search for somewhere flat to put his feet down. No convenient thwart this time. He reached over for the stern line, gripping it to transfer his weight and drop himself into the boat.

He knew it was a mistake even before he had fully shifted his weight. But it was too late — he couldn't find his hold on the porch again. The stern line was badly fastened. It slipped once, just a little — enough to freeze his heart. Then it went completely. He crashed to the deck of the boat with a cry of pain, coming down heavily on an ankle. There was an immediate response from inside the hut — a shout, sounds of movement. Hamnet staggered to his feet, reached out for the porch and shoved as hard as he could. The boat slid quickly away. He fumbled for the outboard starter. There was the fizz of a gas light from inside the hut, and suddenly everything was illuminated. He glanced behind him, saw a body throw itself off the porch with a yell, the splash as it hit the water. The oars were stored just inside the gunwale. He grabbed for one as a hand reached over the edge.

He brought the oar down hard, and there was a scream of pain. He tried to get the boat into motion with a couple of strokes, but its owner wasn't ready to give up his livelihood that easily. He threw himself on the blade to stop Hamnet using it. Hamnet pushed the oar at the assailant and let go. The man went under. Hamnet flipped the second oar up off the gunwale and brought the blade swinging round. As the man resurfaced, spluttering, the oar crashed down on his skull. Hamnet didn't stop to watch or wonder. He lodged the oar in a groove at the stern and with a few quick strokes sculled the boat away, out of the light. A last bellow from behind, more splashing.

He barely noticed. He unshipped the oar and reached for the outboard starter. First pull, it spluttered — no petrol. He felt for the pump on the hose — three quick squeezes. Then he remembered the airlock inside the petrol can and felt for the lid. He flipped it off and squeezed again. This

60

time petrol rushed down the rubber tubing. He grabbed the starter rope and pulled a second time. Nearly. One more go. The engine fired into life. He reached for the throttle and wrenched it open. The surging revs drowned out all sound behind him. The propeller bit, the boat leapt forward and Hamnet sat down heavily, grabbing for the tiller. He got the thing under control and looked behind him. His wake was carving a foaming trail away from the pool of light. There was at least one person in the water, while others were standing on the porch holding out sticks to grab on to. Hamnet turned his back. He was gone.

Chapter 7

Anna was sitting on the porch, legs dangling over the water, lightly warmed by the early-morning sunshine. The sounds of the village as it woke were sharp in the cool air. Homely sounds, but not comforting. A single fly buzzed irritatingly around her right eye. She flicked at it half-heartedly.

Two days of keeping vigil over the imprisoning sea of mangroves. Two days during which nothing had happened, nothing had changed. She had spoken to no one. All her efforts to communicate with her captors had been rebuffed. Although she had been well fed and no one had touched her since the incident with Janac, the isolation was intense. This was something she had formerly been good at handling, but the information vacuum left her reading everything into nothing. She couldn't stop imagining what was about to happen. And what had happened, on the *Shawould*, to Phil.

There was the creak of a footstep on the bamboo floor, and she reacted instantly. A glance told her it was Janac approaching the pots over the fire. She turned away again, hiding her reaction. This was the man. The nothingness of the last two days had corresponded exactly with his absence. What did his return mean? She could feel her pulse quickening as she listened intently to the familiar sound of a plate being filled. The fly was back, the hum loud in her left ear. She flicked at it again, then winced at the use of the still painful blistered hand.

'It's eighty kilometres to the nearest town.' His voice was coming towards her. 'And every step of the way is through that.' It was above her now, very close. She remembered his hands on her, that yellow-toothed grimace, and shuddered involuntarily — then was instantly angry for doing so. She forced herself to keep staring out across the river. Janac took note, turned to sit on the bench that backed the porch, and took a couple of mouthfuls, sucking air over the hot food.

'So, what did you think when your beloved husband refused to show himself and let his crew die?' he asked through the sticky rice.

Anna's lips tightened. She eased round to face him and leant back against the balustrade. 'That he had his reasons,' she replied, quickly casting her eyes over him. Smart but casual dress — jeans and a cotton button-down. The stubble had gone, along with the revolver. She felt dirty in the T-shirt and shorts she'd been given.

Janac swallowed before he replied this time. 'Like saving his own neck?' His tongue worked on something stuck between his teeth.

'Like saving everyone.'

Janac spat whatever it was that had come loose into the water. 'Well, he didn't do much of a job, did he? Eleven dead, wasn't it? So do you think he's going to save you now?'

'Yes.' She pulled her knees up and wrapped her arms around them, careful with the sore hand.

Janac emptied the plate, chewing the last mouthful as he set it down beside him. He leaned back, hands behind his head. 'A buck-naked white man stole a boat last night from one of the villages up near the mouth of the Upang River. Whoever it was, he killed the owner — clobbered the sad bastard with a paddle. He drowned.'

Lightning snapshots of Anna's reaction flickered across her face. Was it Phil? He was alive! Thank God! Had he killed someone?

63

'The trail of blood and destruction that accompanies Phil Hamnet seems endless. How many's that? Eleven on the boat, twelve including my man, one last night — and four before, wasn't it?'

Anna looked away, closed her eyes, her face draining. Nothing would ever be the same. Whatever happened, to either or both of them, it would be different after this. Last time had been bad. This was worse.

Janac pulled a packet of Lucky Strike out of the top pocket of his shirt and a Zippo lighter from the packet. A cigarette flared, he exhaled noisily. Anna looked round and he offered one to her. Smoke drifted over her on the listless air. She shook her head.

'So tell me,' he resumed after another slow drag, 'were you married to him then?'

'When?'

'Fortunately for you, this morning I have a little more time — but not much. You will tell me what I want to know.' He pulled his feet in under the bench and sat up straight. His grey eyes bored straight through her. She could feel the sweat in her palms, and tightened her arms round her knees, her babies. 'How about we start with how you met?' he continued.

She took a deep breath and let it out slowly.

'It was eight years ago. I was doing a single-handed round-the-world race in a sixty-foot yacht.' She saw Janac's eyebrows go up, and the tiniest smile twitched her lips before she continued in a clipped monotone.

She had hit something in the Southern Ocean — a container, or a whale perhaps. It had taken the rudder off and shifted the stock so that the bearing had leaked badly. Then a storm came in, and she pumped almost nonstop for five days. The boat was rolled twice, lost its mast, and was going down when help arrived in the shape of a container ship.

The skipper positioned his vessel across the waves, with Anna's boat in the lee. Then Phil Hamnet descended a rope ladder, swam across and found her below. She was so exhausted she had strapped herself to a bunk to prevent herself slipping under the rising water. She was barely conscious, but Hamnet got her into a sling, and in a ten-metre swell, subzero temperatures and forty knots of breeze, his crew hauled them both to safety.

Her rescuer was there when she woke two days later, miraculously transported from a living hell to a world of crisp linen sheets and regular mealtimes. They had been together ever since.

As Anna finished the story, Janac stood quickly, ground the cigarette butt under his boot and moved away to examine the contents of another pot over the fire. He ladled some coffee into a mug and lifted another enquiringly towards Anna. She shook her head. He noted again the fetching bob of dark hair, the sad brown eyes. His jaw tightened the tiniest fraction. Yes, a pretty and spirited woman. 'This was before he lost his own ship?' he asked. 'Where were you when that went down?' He strolled back towards her.

Anna watched him. 'I was sailing at a regatta. In Hawaii.' She had got off the plane from the States at midnight and found an answer-phone message at home saying Phil's boat wasn't reporting. It had been the second-longest night of her life, thanks to the idiot who had left the message but no number to call back.

'And when they found him?' Janac prompted her, sitting back on the bench and putting the coffee on the floor beside him.

'I was at home.'

'And what happened?'

Anna closed her eyes momentarily. 'The ship had gone down in a hurricane, late in the season. It was Phil's second command — an old grain carrier, eight crew. The cover failed on a forward hold. They made it into the lifeboat, got blown around for two days before the storm backed off. By then all of the food and most of the water had been lost or spoilt.'

'And when he got back, did you talk about what had happened?'

Anna shook her head. 'Not really.'

'I find that hard to believe.' The coffee was still on the floor, untouched.

'Maybe a little — after the stories came out in the media.'

'Ah yes, the media. I checked some old news reports — and you're not telling me anything I don't already know. In fact, according to the enquiry, one of the crew didn't make it onto the lifeboat. Leaving seven men, who — after the storm subsided and the trade winds pushed back in — were a good seven days away from drifting anywhere near a shipping lane.

'We can imagine that some of them were already in a bad way — dehydrated, weak with seasickness. The lifeboat's awash in puke and piss and shit. Shared out evenly, the water that remains won't keep them all alive for seven days — not even close. But it might keep two or three of them going long enough to be rescued. A moral dilemma: some should die so others might live. So far so good. But what I really want to know is: what did Hamnet do next?'

Janac waited, motionless, but for a moment only. His indulgence stretched little further than his own speeches. 'Please.' The word had rarely been used with less sincerity. 'Don't make this unpleasant for yourself.'

Anna looked away under the withering gaze, unconsciously resting her good hand on her belly. During the previous two days she'd had plenty of time to think about the information Janac might demand. The price of her life was apparently Phil's silence, but what was the cost of that

66

silence? Ships? Cargoes? More lives? She knew better than anyone how Phil might balance such things and make a decision. But if she told Janac about that, what impact might it have on Phil's chances of saving her? It seemed better to say less rather than more — but, as she had already discovered, saying nothing was not an option.

'Phil told me —' She hesitated. 'Phil told me that they all talked about it. They decided to draw lots. Four would leave the lifeboat, the other three would share the remaining water equally. As the ship's master, Phil was ultimately responsible, but he always said that they discussed it.' She looked back. 'That was it. He wouldn't tell me any more. They were picked up after eight days. Three of them survived and Phil was one of them. But you know that.'

Janac reached for the coffee mug and sipped. 'Indeed. And then the media picked it up.' The searching eyes flicked back onto her face, but his voice was a little softer, his tone neutral. He didn't think he was going to have to beat this out of her. 'The speculation was that there had been a fight, that someone had been killed with a flare gun. And we can imagine that those who picked the short straw might have decided not to go quietly. They would have had nothing to lose by trying to take the water by force.'

Anna's eyes were locked on his, which were no longer menacing but almost mesmerising. She twitched at the fly again, but this time the movement was an automatic reflex — she barely noticed it. 'He never talked about that. He only said that they all supported the original decision.'

'I think not. The media thought your husband was a murderer, and I agree.'

'No,' she bit back. 'All that talk of criminal charges, but nothing happened. Phil kept his licence and went back to sea.'

Janac smiled, stood up and walked to the rail, flicking

the remains of his coffee into the water. 'And then I came along.' he said. He remained staring out at the mangroves. 'What Hamnet does next is of some importance to both of us. We can assume he's clear of the area, and if he's found some trousers he'll already be close to a phone. Will he keep his mouth shut to keep you alive? Or will he report what's happened to stop me doing it again? He must balance the lives of men he doesn't know, and ships that are insured, against the woman he married. And his children.

'The distinction is important: saving those we know against saving those we don't. People will go to vast effort and expense to rescue two or three men trapped on a mountain, or in a crippled yacht, when logically they could save many more lives by investing the money in a clean water supply for an African village. But those villagers rarely have names or faces, or distraught wives and mothers giving tearful interviews in a familiar language. It's an empathy with those at risk that seems to change it for people. It seems to remove rationality from the moral equation and leave it driven by emotion.'

A shrug, a mirthless smile. 'So, normally, I would have to say we're in with a good chance — and it would be a shame if my expensive equipment became useless on its first outing. Unfortunately, your husband may be rather more rational in these matters than the average. Lives were in the balance in the lifeboat and he decided on a coherent plan to save the greatest number. Even when it meant the deaths of people he knew. Deaths he would be responsible for as the ship's skipper.'

Janac turned, walked slowly back to the fire and dropped the mug beside it. 'Quite how far he was prepared to go to defend and enforce that decision — those deaths — is still a question without an answer. An important one.' He turned, and the stare was cold, appraising.

Anna had remained motionless throughout this speech, and now she gazed back at Janac impassively. It seemed, she thought, that even with the information he had he was no closer to understanding what Phil might do.

Janac nodded at her pregnant form. 'How long?'

'Little less than a month,' she answered automatically.

Janac nodded. 'We're moving out of here. You're going north, somewhere more permanent, with rather less primitive facilities. The boat will be here in an hour. It's a long trip — be ready.' He swung on his heel, and left.

Chapter 8

Hamnet pulled hard on the rope, heaving on the turns so the fibres bound tight. He wiggled the tiller and the whole boat shook — it was firmly lashed in place. He fired the engine up with a quick whip of the starter, and then stepped out into the warm water, fine mud squishing between his toes. He pushed the bow offshore, then leaned over and clunked the outboard into gear. He watched critically as the dinghy accelerated, eyeing the white wake as it cut through the dark water. It was straight enough. He sloshed out of the sea and collapsed onto the wet mud.

His shorts and shoes, a plastic bottle and some scraps of dried fish lay beside him. He'd half filled the bottle by wringing rainwater into it, although he wasn't sure about its previous contents. He pulled on the shorts and shoes before sniffing the bottle — nothing, just water. He drank slowly. It tasted fine. He scratched and wriggled — he'd been bitten alive while asleep.

The whine from the outboard was already faint. Hamnet watched the boat recede, veering a little to the right now. With luck the tides of the Selat Bangka would sweep it miles clear before it was found.

He had run the boat aground as the storm had broken around him, stumbled ashore with the painter and collapsed gratefully in the mud. Now he must move inland fast. He nibbled tentatively at a piece of dried fish, then, suddenly and painfully hungry, swallowed it whole. Another mouthful of water washed it down.

The land was open, dotted with palm trees and scrubby bushes. The morning smelt wet and fresh and he was filled with a new hope. This was the beginning of the search. He needed clothes, then a phone. He had landed the boat between Muntok and a much smaller group of four lights just to the east. He set off to look for a road linking the two settlements, and soon a thin strip of badly potted dirt road glistened palely through the trees in the orange light. Keeping to the scrub, he turned right towards what he hoped would be a village.

Hamnet hadn't gone more than a couple of kilometres before he heard voices. He edged cautiously towards the road, eyes scanning the remaining cover. He saw the roadside stall first — a sad-looking wooden affair, with Coke and Marlboro signs hanging unevenly from rusty nails. Then, lounging on the wooden steps, a young Western couple: colourful T-shirts, tie-dyed trousers, idle talk and laughter. They weren't speaking English, but he didn't recognise the language. Parked off the road beside the stall was a lightly loaded Honda trail bike, half-empty panniers draped over the seat. To one side was an open backpack, in which he could see an assortment of clothes. Hamnet smiled — a shirt and some new shorts or trousers were all he needed to rejoin the world.

He skirted carefully through the scrub. The back door of the stall was open, screened by plastic strips that stirred sluggishly in the light morning breeze. He couldn't see inside. He had ten metres of open ground to cross. He swept his eyes over the dirt for anything that he might kick or scuff noisily. The ground was drying fast, but there was nothing that would crack underfoot. He listened to the rhythm of the voices, waiting until the tempo of the conversation picked up a little. Then he stepped out, strode quickly to the pack, pulled on the drawstring to close it and picked it up.

There was laughter from the front of the stall — so close.

And then silence. Hamnet hesitated, waiting for the conversation to resume. The sound of movement. He started to back away quickly, ready to drop the bag and run. Another laugh — the young woman, light and happy. A second later and he was back under cover. He turned and retreated a couple of hundred metres before swinging left, loping along at an easy jog for another five minutes and stopping next to a large palm tree. There was no sign of pursuit.

He swung the bag onto the ground and slumped beside it. He leaned against the tree, wiped the sweat from his eyes and stared at the pack. He shook his head and pulled the top open with a reluctant hand. There was a wash kit, a guidebook and a map, a bottle of water, which he emptied in seconds, a couple of big, loose men's shirts and some jeans. There was also a handful of dollars and rupiahs wrapped in a bikini — emergency money. This was an emergency, he thought, but guilt prickled — more so when he found some letters stuffed into the leaves of a paperback. An Amsterdam address established that the couple were Dutch. At least he couldn't read the writing. He shoved everything back in, pulled the drawstring, rolled the pack onto his back and headed east once more.

The shaded stream, with its clear water and stony bottom, was exactly what he was looking for. He investigated the wash kit, daubing after-sun onto his burned and blistering skin and treating the cuts and bites that had spread like a rash across his body with antiseptic lotion. He found a mirror and blade and scraped at his chin. It was an improvement, but his eyes told the truth. One of the shirts was a good fit, the jeans a little loose. He rolled up the legs and found a scarf to use as a belt. He swapped his trashed shoes for a pair of espadrilles. He thumbed through the guidebook but learned little: there were some decent beaches on the other side of the island, and a map told him the village up ahead was called Belolaut. He pocketed the cash, put the remaining clothes and toiletries back into the bag along with the books, letters and his own cast-offs, and stashed it in a hollow under a dead tree.

He moved closer to the road again but continued to parallel it, keeping to the scrub. Before long he could see the village. He skirted round onto the beach and approached from the shore. A naked child watched him from the shade of a stand of fishing floats. The village was just a scattering of run-down wooden houses set around a muddy beach, on which lay a handful of fishing boats. There was a simple bar — a one-room shack with a few tables tucked under a canopy of palm leaves. The barman was fixing a fishing net when Hamnet found him round the back of the building. Hamnet held his hand up to his face, finger and thumb extended in imitation of a phone. The man ran his eyes over him, then nodded. He went inside and reappeared with an ancient payphone, which he placed on the nearest table. The instructions were in Dutch.

Hamnet looked at the instrument doubtfully. It obviously wasn't going to take any of the money he had. The barman rubbed his fingers together to indicate he wanted payment up front.

'Singapore?' said Hamnet.

The man shook his head. 'Palembang, Jakarta.'

Hamnet looked back at the machine. There was one chance. He pulled out the stolen cash. The man picked out five hundred-rupiah notes, then, apparently satisfied, returned to his net. Hamnet punched in the Indonesian access number for his phone card. If that didn't work he would have to go into Muntok. The 'ping bong' and fluted American tones of the computerised voice were a powerful flashback to a past life. They had been the prelude to countless transcontinental phone conversations with Anna. He held until he got a real operator, then asked for directory enquiries. Two minutes later he had the number he wanted. Another minute while the operator connected him — silence broken only by the occasional clunk and crackle. Hamnet glanced around him and wiped the sweat from his forehead. Finally the phone began to ring.

'Dubre,' a voice answered.

Hamnet leaned on the rough wooden table, closed his eyes involuntarily. It was the bouncy confidence he needed to hear. Dubre had been the loss investigator for the sinking of the grain carrier. He had been the one fixed point in the whirlwind of the aftermath. They had become friends.

'Hello? Dubre.'

Hamnet tried unsuccessfully to speak. He coughed and tried again. 'Dubre, it's Phil Hamnet.'

'My God, Phillip, are you all right? You're all over the TV and newspapers. What the devil happened?'

'First off, this conversation goes no further than the two of us. Promise me that, or I ring off right now and I'm gone for ever.'

A momentary hesitation, then, 'Alrighty.'

'You read any reports on the *Shawould*?'

'Yes. As I say, it's everywhere.'

'What do they say?'

'Confused — boat on the beach, crew dead, you and Anna missing . . .' He hesitated. 'Is Anna OK?'

'She's alive.'

Dubre waited for Hamnet to say more. When he didn't, Dubre continued: 'There's some speculation in the English papers about your role in this.'

'I bet,' replied Hamnet grimly. 'What's the gossip on the insurance?'

'The tattle I get from the floor is that they think it was an accident and you got looted by some locals. They're

74

expecting your body to turn up any day.'

'They going to pay?'

'I expect so. The murders confuse it, but robbery and looting — well, it's common enough in this area.'

'I heard you're freelance now — you have some kind of incentive deal with the underwriters. That true?'

'It's true.'

'Then I know something that could make you a lot of money, Dubre. Things are not what they seem out there.'

'And?'

'First you've got to help me.'

Dubre's reply was a noncommittal grunt.

'What I know has got half of Indonesia looking for me. I need you to get me out of here. That's just the start — there's more. But I'll tell you what I need when I'm safe. Can you help?'

The silence was a long one this time. Hamnet glanced nervously around him. Nothing moved under the hot sun. Then Dubre's distant voice was in his ear again. 'It's a big step in the dark.'

'You'll have to take me on trust, Dubre. Believe me, what I know will make you a lot of money.'

'It's what I have to do to get it that worries me.'

'I've got no one else to turn to, Dubre. You going to leave me out in the cold?'

'Tell me what the devil's going on.'

'I can't. Not yet. I'm sorry.'

Hamnet heard a sigh.

'Alrighty, I'll do what I can.'

Hamnet felt the tension in his body relax, just a fraction. 'I'm on Bangka, just outside Muntok, with no papers and no money. Any ideas?'

'Let me think. Can you give us another tinkle in five?'

'No problem.' Hamnet hung up.

Five minutes — Hamnet glanced at where his watch had been. He counted to three hundred, fidgeting. Then waited a little longer, which was as much as he could manage, and dialled again. Dubre answered instantly.

'Here's the deal. I can get hold of a seaplane for tonight. I use it a lot to get to investigation sites, so it won't attract any attention. I'll fly in and pick you up. Should be simple enough. Name the spot.'

'There's a village called Belolaut, to the east of Muntok. Make it the first bay west of Belolaut. I'll be at the western end. Say ten o'clock tonight?'

'Alrighty.' Phil could hear Dubre scribbling. There was a pause, then, 'I'll be there, Phillip. I'll try and figure out where to take you in the meantime. See you then, chap. Love to Anna.' And he was gone. Hamnet replaced the heavy receiver. Love to Anna.

He thanked the barman and bought a bottle of water and some sad-looking fruit. Then he followed the shoreline from the village out to the west. He found the first bay, a small sandy beach with rocky headlands at either end. It was just under fifteen minutes' walk. He returned to the stream. The bag he had stashed was crawling with ants. He left it where it was. He drank some of the bottled water and ate the fruit slowly, trying to eke it out. But the stream water he had drunk earlier cramped his stomach, and he threw everything back up.

The day dragged wearily. The sky was clear and the land steamed under the unrestrained sun. The bottled water was gone by midafternoon, and with the heat, thirst and hunger came clouded judgement.

At nightfall he returned to the empty village bar, ordered a dinner of fish and rice, and drank water and Coke till his stomach was bloated. The food came and his body absorbed the nutrition like a sponge. The barman sat at a nearby table

76

and smoked. Hamnet had only to look up to get another drink. The soporific hiss of the gas lamp and the sleepy atmosphere seemed to ease the strain out of him.

There was no clock in the bar, and he was thinking about paying and leaving when he saw a small group of people approach. But it wasn't until they stepped into the pale-yellow circle of light that he saw a uniform. And a young couple — the pair he'd last seen laughing outside the roadside stall that morning.

The young man pointed — he had recognised his clothes. Hamnet's chair crashed to the ground as panic jolted him out of it. He had gone several paces before the first yell, heading straight for the water. On foot he had no hope on the road, but the beach and the rocky headland would even the odds. He swept right along the sand, footsteps behind him pounding in pursuit. It was dark, but not impossibly so under the weak moon. The food in his stomach threatened to come back up. Blood and adrenaline swirled through him in a heady mixture of fear. The soft, calf-stretching sand gave way to heel-jarring rock. A torch beam flickered on the headland in front of him. Then, behind, the crack of a gun shot. He neither heard nor saw where the bullet went, but he didn't have to. He was being shot at, and that was more than he needed to know.

He sprinted up a slab of rock and jumped recklessly into the darkness beyond as another round whirred over his head and slammed into a cliff face. Somehow he landed flat and level, stumbling only slightly, and pitched himself forward into the unknown. He leapt from rock to rock, relying on faith, driven by fear, skirting the base of the cliff, heading for the next bay and his rendezvous. With no idea when Dubre was going to arrive. Heavy footsteps grated on the rock behind him. The torch beam flashed wildly across the cliff face, then disappeared. More shouts. A cry of pain as someone went down. The pace of pursuit was slowing. They were going to a lot of trouble for a backpack — unless these people knew who he was. Could the pirates' search have got this far?

He rounded a corner of the cliff and saw moonlight reflecting off the water ahead. Then he heard the faint drone of an engine. It was coming in low from over the sea, without lights. In the nick of bloody time, he breathed, stepping off the rock and stumbling again across the sand. The strength-sapping softness underfoot took a heavy toll as he struggled round to the western end of the bay. The seaplane landed, with plumes of white spray from the floats, only a hundred metres to his left. He shouted and waved, attracting more gunfire. None of it went anywhere near him, but he could see lights off to his right — three torch beams moving restlessly through the scrub at the back of the beach. More shouts. He cut closer to the water, onto slightly harder sand, his breath rasping as his dinner burned the back of his throat. Behind him, he could hear footsteps kicking up spray, another shot, almost continuous shouting. This was clearly not about a pair of jeans and a T-shirt.

The seaplane had ended its landing run some forty metres out. As he glanced across, Hamnet saw the door open.

'The rocks!' he yelled, waving frantically at the next headland along. A forty-metre swim would be much too long in the water. But if Dubre could get the plane close to the headland, he would have only a few metres to cross. More gunfire cracked behind him, and this time he saw where the bullet hit the sand with a soft thwack.

Dubre had got the idea. The plane was turning, motoring towards the rocks only fifty metres ahead. Hamnet glanced over his shoulder for the first time. His suicidal speed round the previous headland had given him a hundred metres on the first group of pursuers. The second group, on the right, had just reached the beach and were slightly further away. Their flanking operation had failed. Dubre had the plane turned and headed offshore, motoring parallel to the headland. Hamnet was twenty metres away when he saw a shot hit the water just to the left of the plane. Dubre's bulk filled the starboard door — he hadn't heard the shot over the noise of the engine. But as Hamnet drew level they both saw the next round slam into the starboard wing. Hamnet heard Dubre's shout of alarm even as he dived, plunging into the cool water. His momentum carried him almost the whole way. Two strokes and he had hold of a strut. With a massive effort he heaved himself out of the water and onto the starboard float.

'Where's Anna?' yelled Dubre.

'Go, go, just go!' screamed back Hamnet.

Dubre pulled his head back from the door and hit the gas hard. The seaplane skated over the water. There was more shouting and shooting from the beach but Hamnet didn't notice. He tried to struggle to his feet and into the cabin. The plane wobbled under the movement. Dubre turned and waved a clenched fist — the signal to hold on. He was moving out of range of the guns. Hamnet looked behind. There were three or four lights, all pointing at the plane, but none was strong enough to reach it. He felt the power slacken and the seaplane slow down. More steadily this time, he climbed to his feet and into the tiny cockpit beside Dubre's heavy form. The plane slid across the water and lifted into the air before Dubre turned to Hamnet with a look of thunder.

'What the devil's going on?' he demanded.

But Hamnet had slumped against the window. He shook his head, wheezing back air. Dubre would have to wait.

Chapter 9

Hamnet stared out of the cockpit window in silence. Dubre had shaken him awake a few minutes earlier, wordlessly pointing out the sprinkling of lights off their starboard side. The black carpet below them was airbrushed with an ellipse of orange on the eastern horizon and splashed with a paint stroke of moonlight to the west. Hamnet was still incapable of anything more than a grunt of acknowledgement, and Dubre seemed to understand. The hours of sleep had left his mind freewheeling. He struggled to re-engage it, gazing unfocused into the future. A quick stock check of his body brought up a long list of deficits, but the sleep and the security of the tiny cockpit had relieved the worst of them. Bizarrely, he realised the thing he was most anxious to fix was the disgusting taste and texture inside his mouth. If only that were his biggest problem.

Dubre broke into his reverie. 'I filed a flight plan for this place. If anyone wonders why I'm late, I'll tell them I had to put down a couple of times to let an overheating engine cool down. But I can't be seen to arrive with you aboard, so I'm going to land her just this side of the headland, before the village. You slip out and swim ashore. There's a plastic bag by your feet with a change of clothes. I have another bag of stuff that I'll give you later. Get cleaned up as best you can and meet me in a bar called the Smiling Buddha in a couple of hours. It's by the beach. The place is tiny so you can't miss it.'

Hamnet nodded and started to strip off. 'Where are we?' he grunted as he fumbled for the plastic bag.

'An island called Phi Phi off the west coast of Thailand,

just north of the Malay border. No one asks any questions. Here we go. You ready, chap?'

The engine blipped a couple of times as Dubre levelled out over the water and adjusted the angle of the glide path. The hush of anticipation was broken as the floats kissed the smooth surface, trailing an even curtain of spray. Dubre leaned over and unlatched the door. 'Go!' he hissed. Bag in hand, Hamnet hesitated, watching the bubble and froth. Then he plunged into the warm water. By the time he surfaced Dubre had gunned the engine and the plane was moving quickly away. Hamnet bobbed in the wash trying to orientate himself. The nearest land was a black mass of rock less than a hundred metres away. It sloped gently out of the water at an inviting angle. He kicked out, lying on his back, the bag clasped to his chest.

Dubre had prepared well. The bag contained saltwater soap, a toothbrush and paste, a towel, a pair of sandals, a pair of baggy chinos and a faded T-shirt which declared itself to be a lousy present from Singapore. The rock was the perfect bathroom. Hamnet scrubbed and wallowed while the sun launched itself over the hills behind him. It revealed spectacular rock formations, climbing in a series of steps from the sea onto two headlands that enclosed a tiny bay. A towering, chirping wall of palm trees backed a beach of pure white sand. Hamnet dressed and stuffed the toiletries and stolen garments in the plastic bag — an early-morning bather returning for a hearty breakfast.

He walked along the beach until a pathway opened in the foliage. Progress was easy through a tunnel of dappled greens and yellows. Too perfect, too stunning. It fitted badly with his mood. The path rose gently over the back of the furthest headland and descended to a beach on the other side. Dubre's plane was anchored at the far end. Wooden houses with roofs of leaf thatch were scattered among the palm trees. Fishing boats reclined indolently along the fore-shore, and nets were staked out in front of the buildings. Smoke drifted gently down to the water through the lazy air of early morning. Little else moved.

Hamnet kept to the beach and found the Smiling Buddha after a further couple of minutes' walk. It was more a canopy than a building, with an open kitchen at the back. The smell of cooking food awakened a ravenous hunger. A young Japanese couple sitting near the water didn't bother to acknowledge his arrival. The woman giggled loudly as he sat down in a creaking wooden chair at a back table. The menu offered little but fish and rice. He ordered it fried, with a pot of black coffee, from a slip of a boy with eyes like pools of oil. Even allowing for his more than healthy appetite, he judged the meal about as good as fried rice and fish could be. He was halfway through a second pot of coffee when Dubre appeared in the doorway.

Hamnet watched him approach, smoothing the nonexistent hair on his pate. It was a familiar gesture, and not for the first time Hamnet wondered what colour Dubre's remaining grey hair had once been to match his startling green eyes. He kicked the chair opposite him out from the table and said, 'Thanks. I guess I haven't said that yet.'

'Anything for you, old chap. Though I have to admit to being a trifle disconcerted by the fact that someone was shooting at us.' He hesitated, staring at Hamnet appraisingly. 'You look like shit.' He dropped the canvas knapsack he was carrying by the table. 'You should find everything you need in there. I packed a first aid kit, and there are more clothes and some money.' He lowered his pot-bellied bulk into the chair. 'So I think it's your turn, old chap. What the devil is going on? Where's Anna? And who the hell was shooting at us?' Then he added, 'In any order you like.'

Hamnet twitched his nose, rubbed his cheek. 'The local

police on Bangka were the ones taking pot shots. I stole some kid's clothes and he spotted me in a restaurant.'

'And they shot at you for a pair of jeans? Indonesia has a human rights problem, but I think that's pushing it a bit even for them.'

'Maybe they connected me to the *Shawould*. What I know is going to cost someone a great deal of money. Well worth killing me for.'

Dubre picked up the battered menu as he said, 'Talking of killing, some white chap topped a fisherman the night before last. Stole his boat from a stilt house at the mouth of the Upang. You know anything about that, Phillip?' he finished, eyebrows raised enquiringly as though he had asked how Hamnet had found the fried fish.

It stopped Hamnet dead. He could feel Dubre's eyes on him. He could feel his throat dry. And he could almost feel the kick in his forearms again as the paddle came down on the man's head. He knew he'd hit him hard. He'd just blocked it out. Struggling for an innocent reaction, he sat up, pushed his empty plate away and leant forward on the table. 'Christ, no,' he said hoarsely. 'What happened?'

Dubre's eyes stayed on him. 'The chap knocked him out and he drowned. I checked out the latest on the *Shawould* yesterday after you called. The police I spoke to down there mentioned it in passing — having a busy week, they said. But they don't think it's connected.'

'Hard to see why it should be,' said Hamnet.

'I can't help you if you were involved in that, Phillip. Whatever's going on, this is different from last time. You're not out there on your own, man against the sea and all that. This time you're in someone's country. There are rules.'

Hamnet could feel his face flush. 'I didn't hit anyone,' he said, hating himself for the lie.

'Then how did you get to Bangka?'

83

Something deep in his memory rescued him. The pirate leader had ordered the ditching of the life rafts and gear. 'I was in a life jacket. Got swept around in the squall. When it flattened out in the morning, I was close to the Bangka shore.'

'You were lucky,' said Dubre. The green eyes hesitated on Hamnet's face for a second longer before flickering away to the menu.

'Very.' Hamnet nodded, his pulse easing. 'What did they tell you about the *Shawould*?' He took the chance to change the subject.

'Went aground in bad weather, boarded by unknown parties. Somebody got off a Mayday, but by the time the helicopter from an oil rig got there it was too late. Eleven crew dead, the master and his wife posted as missing. They won't close the file until the bodies turn up. But I don't think it will hold up the insurance payment.' Dubre was watching him carefully again. 'So where's Anna?'

'They took her. To keep me silent. If we can find her and get her back, I can tell you what I know. I can save the insurers every single penny of the payout on the ship and cargo.' Dubre's smooth brow wrinkled as his eyebrows rose.

The boy waiter appeared at Dubre's shoulder. Dubre spoke quickly to him in Thai and he slid away. 'And what makes you think I can get her back?' he asked Hamnet.

'You know people — the right people. You've got contacts throughout South-east Asia at all levels of law enforcement. You're well thought of, and you know as much about piracy as anyone. If you don't know these people, no one will. And besides, there's no one else I can trust.' Uncomfortable words, spoken so shortly after his lie. 'If it becomes public that I'm alive, it'll be a circus just like last time. And if I'm out in the open, I'll be a target. Simplest way for the bastards to solve their problem is to kill Anna

84

and me. No, we have to find her ourselves — the two of us.'

Dubre tapped heavily on the table with a big gold ring on the little finger of his left hand. 'Let's assume I decide to help you. What can you tell me? Where do we start?'

'She's with a group of pirates led by two Americans. I got a look at both of them and one name — Bureya. He was the number two. There can't be many whites involved in piracy; it's normally locals. But these guys were organised — rigid inflatable boats, a goddam lighter and crane to take the cargo off. It was a serious piece of work — organised, with money behind it. Someone must know something about these people. They didn't come out of nowhere.'

'Americans though. No Chinese?'

Hamnet hesitated as Dubre's breakfast, a fresh pot of coffee, arrived. 'You're thinking of the Triads?'

'Triads if you want a simple label. The Chinese are the only real criminal power in this part of the world. If you want organised crime, that's the place to look.'

'I didn't see any Chinese. Just the Yanks and some locals.'

'So what did they look like?'

Hamnet described everything he could remember about the two Americans while Dubre listened in silence, scribbling the occasional note in a small book. When he had finished, Dubre snapped the book shut and fixed him with a steady gaze. 'I'll have to go back to Singapore to check this out, chap,' said Dubre.

'Sure. What do you want me to do?'

'It's not such a good idea for me to come back here again so soon. Why don't we meet in Bangkok? I can get some false papers for you while I'm in Singapore — you shouldn't need them for the journey. Take one of those cheap buses with the backpackers — you won't have any problems.

Have you ever been to Bangkok?'

Hamnet shook his head.

'Alrighty. There are plenty of cheap hotels around Khoa San Road. They won't ask any questions and you won't need papers. We'll meet at Wat Benjamabophit — it's near the Chitlatda Palace. I'll see you in front of the filthy great gold Buddha — you can't miss it — in exactly a week.'

'We don't have a week.' Hamnet leaned forward.

Dubre hesitated. 'I don't know how long this is going to take.'

'Three days.'

'No can do, old chap. I've got a lot of other work to clear. Five days.'

'Three. It's Anna's life, for God's sake.'

'Four. I can't do it in less than that without people wondering where the devil I'm off to in such a flying hurry and why. Take your pick.'

'OK, four days,' said Hamnet. 'At eight thirty a.m.'

'Any problems call me at home like you did before. But don't leave a message if I'm not there.' Dubre swallowed the last of his coffee and stood up. 'Maybe I'll know more when we meet again. I can't make any promises here, Phillip, even about being of any more help. But I'll check out this guy — we owe you that much after last time.'

Hamnet shook his head. 'No "we", Dubre, just you and me — OK? I don't trust those other bastards.'

Dubre nodded. 'I remember.' He pulled a slim camera out of the top pocket of his shirt. 'I need a photo for your papers. Smile, for God's sake — it may never happen.'

'It already has,' replied Hamnet, stretching his lips in a rictus.

The camera flashed. 'I guess that'll have to do. I'll fly out this afternoon. Have to make it look like it was worth coming. But you might as well get out of here straight away.

There's a midday boat to the mainland.'

Hamnet nodded. 'I'll be on it. Good luck.'

'You too, chap.'

Hamnet watched him go. Dubre had accepted there were questions about what had happened on the lifeboat that simply shouldn't be asked. For that reason Hamnet had never had to lie to him. It had been the foundation of the bond between them — until now. Dubre had ambushed him with the question about the fisherman. And he had lied. Dubre had been right — it was different from last time. That bond had been broken. But did Dubre know?

And Hamnet had killed a man with his own hands. An innocent man. He buried the thought deep. If there were a price to pay — moral, legal or emotional — it would have to wait.

Chapter 10

Janac leant over and tapped the mouse with a thin finger. The swirling colours of the screen-saver disappeared and the chart display redrew itself. 'I would prefer it if you turned that thing off, Jordi. It's beginning to annoy me,' he said.

The man seated in front of Janac turned to the computer and fiddled for ten seconds. Then he glanced over his shoulder at the figure standing behind him. 'Apologies,' he muttered, before returning to the box that been holding his attention.

'Is it all right?' asked Janac.

'It seems so. The power output is down a fraction, but it's still adequate. Would you like me to start the sequence?' Oversized ears either side of a thin face twitched a little as Jordi spoke.

'One mile of divergence to the west, input over thirty minutes,' replied Janac.

'Affirmative.'

'Let's do it.'

Jordi pushed a button on the black box, which was the signal generator for the differential GPS transmitter, then snapped a couple of switches on the radar unit beside it. He glanced at the SSB and VHF radios to his right to confirm they were set to the emergency channels. Then his fingers clattered quickly over the keyboard, pausing only briefly to make a couple of adjustments with the mouse. He stopped and leaned back in his chair, a chewed fingernail hovering before the laptop screen. 'In red is the ship's actual position; in green is where his GPS is telling him he is.' The fingernail came up to his mouth while his gaze stayed on the screen.

'OK.' Janac's eyes narrowed as they focused momen-
tarily on the back of Jordi's head. Then he turned to where
Bureya was propping up the cabin wall behind him. 'The
RIB ready?'

Bureya leaned forward slightly to acknowledge. 'Yes,
boss.' His arms remained folded across his barrel chest. His
face was dripping only slightly less than the walls of the
enclosed, fuggy bridge of the barge. Condensation streamed
off the window beside him. Outside there was only the grey
swirl of a dawn fog.

'Weapons check?'

'Complete.'

Janac pulled the pack of Lucky Strike from the breast
pocket of his tunic and snapped the Zippo. After the first
deep drag, he looked back at Bureya. 'You did a good job
getting the girl up to Lee's place. There are some broads
there to deal with her.' He paused for another pull. 'The
kids might be useful.'

Bureya nodded slowly, heavy eyelids half closed.
'Thanks, boss.'

Janac turned back to the screen. The minutes passed as
the red and green lines slowly diverged, cigarette smoke
adding to the suffocating atmosphere. The green line headed
for the Selat Limende channel, while the red line made
straight for the Kelemar shoal.

With the target half a mile from the reef Janac turned to
Bureya. 'Saddle 'em up.'

The big man pushed himself upright and picked up the
automatic weapon beside him. He moved through the bridge
door silently. Janac pulled out the heavy Smith and Wesson
from his shoulder holster and dropped out the cylinder. A
quick spin confirmed what he already knew. He reholstered
the weapon.

'Any moment now,' whispered Jordi. The red line crept

89

off the white of navigable water and onto the green of the shoal. It stopped. Anticipation lay as heavily on the bridge as the fetid air. Finally the SSB crackled, once, twice; then came the urgent tones of accented English.

'Mayday! Mayday!'

'Nice job, Jordi,' said Janac. 'You know the script and the codes. Keep me informed.' He tapped the tiny VHF radio hooked to his webbing belt as Jordi picked up the microphone. He stepped through the door and disappeared forward into the fog.

Jordi breathed out loudly, wiped the back of his hand across his mouth and glanced across at the barge captain. They exchanged the briefest of looks and the tension palpably eased. Jordi pressed the transmit button. 'Station calling Mayday, this is the freighter MV *Hope*. What is your position and your situation?'

Janac tossed the bow line down and swung himself into the RIB in a single motion. The twin outboards burped and puttered. Janac took the wheel, clunked the motors into gear and swung the boat slowly away from the side of the barge. He snapped the VHF off his belt. 'How we doing, *Hope*?'

'They're taking on water quite badly. They're expecting you and want to get some men off.'

'Roger.' The stricken ship was only a mile ahead, and the two hundred horsepower of the RIB's big engines covered the distance across the flat, silent sea in just under two minutes. Lights loomed out of the fog and Janac cut the power. The boat fell off its bow wave and rolled awkwardly as he spun it sideways. Janac turned to the five men stationed in the stern. 'Tosh, you and the boys under the tarp.'

Tosh responded with a bob of a grey ponytail and a quiet 'Aye' in a soft Scots brogue. He threw the butt of a crumpled roll-up over the side before the five men flattened themselves onto the deck and Bureya threw a tarpaulin over them. Two remaining Indonesian crewmen in the bow tucked Heckler and Koch MP5 machine pistols under their loose jackets, Bureya following suit.

'You know,' said Janac, dropping his shoulder holster to the deck as Bureya returned to his side, 'it'd be a lot more fun doing this with cutlasses in our teeth and the skull and crossbones flying.' He almost smiled as he hit the throttle and the boat eased forward.

He slowed again as the RIB drew alongside the steel hull of the stricken ship. It was clear something was badly wrong. The stern was jammed high in the air, exposing half the rudder, and the hull sheered away at a thirty-degree angle. Faces peered from above as a rope ladder tumbled down to the inflatable. Janac held steady beneath it with minor adjustments to the throttle and waved his point-man — one of the Indonesians — upwards. Bureya followed, surprisingly agile for someone of his size.

There was a shout and a crash just as the American arrived at the top and stuck his head over the rail. Bureya saw his man go down to a blow from a pickaxe handle. Another crewman was wrestling the automatic from his lifeless hands. Bureya ducked and swore loudly as a bottle whistled over his head. He glanced down at Janac and yelled, 'Trouble!' as he pulled his weapon out from under his jacket. But he was hampered by his hold on the ladder and the ship's crew were quicker. The wooden shaft struck his cheekbone as he pushed away from the ship in a frantic effort to avoid the blow.

Janac was reaching for the revolver at his feet. He didn't see Bureya bounce and roll wordlessly down the side of the hull, missing the bow of the RIB by centimetres as he smacked into the ocean. But he knew it wasn't Bureya with the machine pistol as he looked back up. He fired twice, and the soft-nosed, heavy calibre shells exploding against the superstructure kept the gunner's head down. But they didn't stop the man pointing the pistol over the rail and opening up blindly. Janac had no choice — he hit the throttle and spun the wheel. The boat launched forward. Over the howl of the engines and the chatter of machine-gun fire, Janac didn't hear the stifled scream of the still groggy Bureya. But he knew what the bump and churn of the prop meant as he accelerated. He glanced behind even as bullets peppered the fibreglass and rubber around him. The wash turned to blood red in the grey fog as Bureya's body bobbed briefly into view. Janac slammed his hand onto the console in a white-hot lash of fury before his professional instincts cut in. He snatched the VHF from his belt. 'X-ray Zebra, *Hope*, X-ray Zebra,' he snapped into it.

Aboard the barge, Jordi started jamming the emergency channels and scanning the others for transmissions from the crippled vessel.

The RIB was quickly hidden by the fog. The machine-gunner aboard the freighter stopped his barrage. Behind Janac there was an excited buzz from the five men emerging from beneath the tarpaulin. Two of the boat's inflatable sections had been ripped open and flapped uselessly as they trailed in the water. Seating and deck had been shattered in several places, including less than half a metre behind Janac, who glanced around to assess the damage. A couple of holes were taking water, but as long as the boat kept moving it would be flushed out of the stern. He spun the boat hard on its rail and silenced the crew with a raised hand. 'Tosh — you and Edi put down suppressing fire.' He indicated the other two. 'Grappling hooks, then use the frags.' As the men prepared the ropes and grenades, the surviving bowman moved back beside his boss. Janac slid his shoulder holster on, and the engines whined as the hammer went down and the boat sped back to re-engage.

Janac powered past the stern of the freighter at twenty knots. Bloody foam indicated where the previous action had taken place, but the rope ladder had gone and there was no sign of Bureya's body. And no heads along the rail. But someone could see them, for the machine gun chattered out again, kicking up a trail of splashes on their port side. The Heckler and Koch's in the stern immediately opened up and the inbound fire stopped. Janac spun the wheel to bring the inflatable along the other side of the hull. The grappling irons clattered as they found purchase and the ropes pulled taut as the climbers' hooked up jumars and stepped into the loops. Nothing moved above. With the boarding party on its way up, Janac took the RIB back out to give the supporting fire a better angle — from just on the limit of visibility.

An eerie silence descended — sharply broken when a figure appeared heading towards the assault ropes. Tosh was first to react, with a single measured burst, and the figure disappeared from sight. The two boarders were making heavy weather of the overhanging hull. Janac cursed their lack of fitness and technique. With Bureya gone, Tosh, Soey and Edi were the only ones he could rely on. The climbers paused a metre or so from the top. A grenade arced over the rail and went off three seconds later with a flash and a fog-muffled 'wumf'. The two men followed, and Janac had the boat back under the ropes as the machine guns opened up above him.

Tosh, Edi and Soey were on their way as Janac waved the remaining man to the wheel. As he started to climb, the gunfire stopped. He slid over the rail, the Smith and Wesson in his hands. He appraised the situation with a glance. His five men held covering positions that commanded the aft deck. He could see little beyond fifty metres, and an uneasy silence fell once more. The fog seemed to soak up sound as well as visibility.

Janac indicated as he spoke. 'Tosh, take your buddy and go to port. Edi, you and your man hold starboard. Kill anything that moves, but don't start to clear inside until we've got the bridge. Soey, with me.'

The two other pairs moved off cautiously as Janac led Soey towards the starboard companionway to the upper decks. He walked with a soft but solid step, upright, the barrel of the Smith and Wesson cradled business end forward in the crook of his forearm, following his eyes. The bridge-deck lights glowed above him. The pair passed two steel doors, both locked. There was a crash and the extended clatter of automatic fire from below. Finally, the radio on Janac's belt buzzed with Tosh's voice: 'We got three.'

A ladder led up to the wings of the bridge, looming overhead. No movement, no sign of resistance, but Janac didn't like it: the bridge and the radio room were the places to make a stand. He backed up, checking the white steel wall that rose sheer two storeys above him, retreating to the far end of the walkway. Here, a service ladder ran upwards. He indicated to Soey, who slung his shotgun onto his back and started to climb. The pair paused as they drew level with the wing deck, but there was no sign of life. Once on the roof of the bridge they eased forward, Janac checking cautiously over the edge until they were above the side windows. He took the two grenades proffered by Soey.

'On three,' he said.

A quiet count and the two men dropped lightly onto the wing deck below them. Soey's feet had hardly touched when the shotgun tore out the window. Janac lobbed the grenades through the hole and both men flattened themselves against the wall as the explosion ripped through the bridge.

Janac snapped open the door and led inside with revolver and torch raised. Nothing moved in the gloom. The beam danced over the wreckage of paper, plastic and glass. Still nothing. Then he heard a plaintive cry from the back of the bridge. He flicked the beam up and found the radio room, with two figures prone on the floor, both stunned by the blast, one bleeding from the eardrums.

Janac strode towards the shattered pair. He raised his revolver at the closer of the two officers. The blood from the man's ears was spreading a stain across his white shirt. He stared blankly up the barrel's darkness with no apparent comprehension. Janac put a bullet through his forehead, and the top of his skull was whipped back into the second man. The mess of brains in his lap appeared to shake the survivor out of his stunned state. Fear flooded his face as the blood drained from it. The revolver crashed out again, and he, too, parted company with the top of his head. With the sound still ringing round the bridge, Janac lifted the radio.

'Bridge is secure, begin clearing. No prisoners. Repeat, no prisoners.'

The radio confirmed the order and Janac clipped it back on his belt. He glared at the chaos around him. 'Fuck!' he swore. 'So, Phillip Hamnet, what are you going to make of this little fiasco?'

Chapter 11

Hamnet woke up sweating. He had gone to sleep sweating, too. He opened his eyes. Less than half a metre from his face a ceiling fan circled in leisurely fashion through air so heavy and moist you could wring it out. He watched it for a while, slowly absorbing place and circumstance into a mind befuddled by lack of sleep. Bangkok. The trip had been simple enough, but the time had passed so desperately slowly. Every minute on the boat, on the bus, in the fraught heat of this nightmare city, spent while Anna's fate remained unknown.

But today he was to meet Dubre. He sat up quickly. 'Ahh!' He had forgotten about the fan. He fell back on the bed, and it was all he could do to hold back the tears. The desire to pull the sheet over his head to make it all go away was almost overwhelming. But today was a day that had to be faced — somehow. He rolled out of the bunk and dropped heavily to the floor, then peered through red-rimmed eyes at the room around him. A dozen bunk beds, in four three-tiered arrangements, all painted a hard, metallic grey. Inert forms in five of them. The wreckage of several budget world tours was scattered about: backpacks, T-shirts, damp towels dangling. The hostel was a pit, but Dubre had been right. In the cosmopolitan crush of budget travellers, no one noticed a solitary, melancholy Englishman.

Hamnet dressed slowly in the cheap shorts and T-shirt Dubre had provided, then walked down the corridor and through the single room that was lobby, restaurant and bar all in one. Tanned, pierced and pony-tailed youths sprawled and chatted over coffee. Hamnet glanced at his cheap new watch and kept walking. He had plenty of time but no stomach for breakfast. Outside, a side street was crowded with the bustle of a market. The smell — that humid putrescence of which all Bangkok seemed to be possessed to some degree — grew steadily as he approached. Already his shirt was clinging to his sweating body and dirt sticking to the cotton. But Hamnet didn't notice any of it.

The temple was clearly visible in its chastely landscaped gardens as he entered through the steel gate. A red-tiled roof rose in three steeply pitched, overlapping layers above polished marble walls rising sheer out of granite paving. Hamnet slipped past the statues of guarding lions, pausing only to shed his shoes as local custom dictated. He looked over the early-morning sprinkling of tourists. There was no sign of Dubre. He glanced at the watch again: eight twenty. He was early. He stepped to one side and sat down with his back to the end wall.

He didn't have to wait long. Dubre rolled in, his normally cherubic face clouded, sweat patches darkening both armpits of his white shirt, grey trousers hanging loose and misshapen. He held a square manila envelope in each hand. He saw Hamnet immediately, walked over quickly and said, 'We'll talk outside.'

Hamnet followed Dubre out into the gardens. His mouth was dry, and there was a tingling in his spine, a tightness across his chest. Dubre led him past canal-like ornamental ponds to a bridge, rust red across green and turgid water. Dubre stopped on the far side and slumped onto a concrete seat by a little jetty. Hamnet sat beside him, desperate to know, fearful to ask. Dubre handed him one of the envelopes. Hamnet looked at him, terrified of what it might contain.

'Photos,' Dubre said. 'Take a gander.'

Hamnet felt his stomach flip as he slipped open the envelope and pulled out four 24-by-15-centimetre glossy colour prints. He drew in a sharp breath. The first was of a body on a slab. Large areas of flesh and organ in the abdominal region had been slashed; likewise the muscle tissue on both calves and thighs. One arm had been almost severed at the elbow. But the face was still there, curiously undamaged. And still recognisable.

'Bureya.' said Hamnet. He looked up at Dubre, surprised.

'Michael Toliver Bureya,' said Dubre. 'US citizen and formerly with Special Forces, Vietnam. Known companion of one Paul Robert Janac. Who fits your description of the second American aboard the *Shawould*.' His tone was strained, formal. 'Mr Bureya was found yesterday morning in the Limende Strait, near a general cargo ship that had grounded on the Kelemar shoal some hours earlier. His injuries are consistent with being run over by a powerboat. Which is not in itself a problem. Mr Bureya was, by all accounts, a particularly nasty piece of work. The trouble is that all twelve of the crew are every bit as dead as he is.' There was a long and painful pause. 'What the bloody hell is going on, Phillip?' Dubre leant towards Hamnet, fists clenched.

Hamnet felt his head grow light. He wasn't sure if he was going to faint or throw up. Twelve more dead: A breeze ruffled the trees, playing their shadows across the paving, bringing a moment's mild relief from the heat. Chilling the sweat. Chilling his soul. What had he done?

'Talk to me, Phillip. Can you help me stop this? What do you know?' demanded Dubre, fists working on his knees.

Hamnet looked at him hopelessly, struggling for words when there were none.

'What do you know?' insisted Dubre.

'Anna . . .?'

'This Janac character's psychotic. I'm truly sorry — Anna won't make it through this.' Dubre flipped over another photo. 'But there are others you might be able to save.

Men like these.' Hamnet caught a glimpse of a row of bodies lined up on a dock before burying his face in his hands and screwing his eyes shut. The rumble of distant traffic and the bright birdsong overhead barely pierced the heavy silence between the two men.

Sunlight crept between Hamnet's fingers, lit the red blood that pumped through his eyelids. The world was still there. A world in which thirteen men had been lost for Anna's life. The blood of all of them was on his hands.

'Do you know where she is?' Hamnet ground out through clenched teeth and clasped hands.

'Maybe.'

'Where?' Hamnet dropped his hands and looked at Dubre.

'Burma.' Dubre wiped the sweat from his palms onto his trousers.

'In Burma? Anna's up there now?'

'It's a best guess. Near the northern Thai border. Janac's been on the run since he was chased off an island in the Gulf of Thailand a few months ago. The Drug Enforcement Agency have a couple of sightings from the border region which they believe to be Janac. He has strong links with an old drug warlord and it's possible he's gone to ground with him. Piracy and murder obligations permitting.' There was a bitter edge to the sarcasm. 'He runs a heroin ring in Australia and does his buying at this time of year up in the Golden Triangle, along with every other drug-dealing scum in the Pacific Rim. So it's a good bet he'll be there at some stage soon. Whether he's based in Burma and took Anna there, or if he has her stashed away somewhere else, I don't know for sure. It's a best guess,' Dubre repeated. He swept his hand agitatedly through the imaginary hair. 'If she's still alive . . .'

'But it's the place to look,' said Hamnet, sitting up.

Dubre shook his head slowly. 'Even if she's there, there's nothing you can do. These opium warlords command armies ten, twenty thousand strong for pete's sake. Nothing short of a full-scale invasion by the Thai military will get her out. And if they won't engage those people for the US government's antidrug money, they sure as hell aren't going to do it for some Farang woman.'

'I want to go there.' Hamnet's voice had a new firmness. He gazed levelly at Dubre. 'Give me a week. If we haven't found her by then, I'll tell you everything. We can stop this happening again.'

'Then tell me now.'

'I'm sorry, I can't.'

'You can't save her, Phillip.'

'Take me there. Give me just a little more time. Then I'll tell you.'

'I can't do that. Two ships and twenty-three lives already — I can't risk any more.'

'You don't understand, Dubre. I'm not going to tell you anything until you get me as close to Anna as you can.'

Dubre caught the intensity of Hamnet's gaze full on. He had seen that defiant look before. He was losing this argument. He looked away, his hand stroking the top of his head again. 'We don't have a week. This boat was hit six days after the *Shawould*.'

'I gave you four days. You do that for me.'

'Phillip, for pity's sake, there are untold lives at stake here,' retorted Dubre with a sudden flash of anger and frustration. 'He will kill Anna — if he hasn't already. There's nothing you or anyone else can do to save her. Help me save others. Tell me what's happening.' Dubre thumped his fist onto his knee.

'Christ! You think I'm happy about this?' Hamnet slapped the pictures in disgust. 'But I can't just give her up, walk away. I can't. How do I live the rest of my life after that? She's pregnant with my children. Four days, that's all I want. To try and reach her. He can't set up another boat in that time, believe me. Get me close and I'll tell you everything.' And as he spoke, Hamnet prayed silently to an unknown god he barely believed in: please let it be so. Give me four days before he strikes again.

Dubre stared off into space, his anger draining. It had been his last shot. Across the water a young girl posed prettily for her picture by the lions at the temple entrance. There was the distant crack of thunder. The moisture-laden air was heavy with the menace of violence in the coming storm.

'I'll take you up there,' said Dubre. 'I know a chap in the DEA in Chiang Mai. He owes me a favour. He'll tell you it straight from the horse's mouth.' He sighed in resignation. 'After that you'll come to your senses. Get used to the idea that you're not going to see her again, Phillip. I'm sorry.'

Chapter 12

Hamnet returned to the hostel, where the same upturned but uninterested faces greeted him as he walked into the lobby. There was no reflection in those innocent expressions of the hollowness — the gut-wrenching emptiness — that he felt. In the dormitory, just regular breathing and periodic fits of unconscious movement. He sat, trying to adjust to the new, even darker world that now surrounded him.

Eventually he pulled open the second of the two manila envelopes Dubre had been carrying. Inside was a forged British passport, in the red of the European Union and bearing the name Michael Toliver. He had arranged to meet Dubre at nine o'clock the following morning at a hotel in Chiang Mai. He used the freedom the new passport gave him and stepped from the traveller ghetto into the embrace of another, first-class, Thailand. He glided all the way to the hotel Dubre had named. There was still another long night of sweat-soaked sheets that even the Suriwongse's impressive air conditioning and a sleeping tablet couldn't alleviate. But by the time Hamnet faced himself in the mirror the following morning, he had found new strength in a decision made. He dressed as smartly as he could in yet more borrowed clothes — a pair of 501s and a grey, collared T-shirt. Then he sat on the bed and waited. The man he was to meet was his last real hope of saving Anna; the only alternative was both desperate and final.

At five past nine the phone rang. Hamnet stared at it for a moment before answering.

Dubre was curt. 'I'm downstairs.'

Hamnet was with him in less than a minute. On seeing

him, Dubre turned and strode through the wood-panelled lobby without a greeting. They were in a taxi before he spoke.

'We're going straight to the DEA's compound to meet one of their chaps. He'll tell you everything you need to know.'

'And what does he know about me?' asked Hamnet as the taxi clattered off.

'I've told him that you're a friend of mine, a journalist called Michael Toliver. This guy Janac murdered half the crew of a yacht six or seven years ago. It was big news at the time — he made them play some kind of crazy game to see who would live and who would die. You remember it?'

Hamnet shook his head. 'No.'

'Well, I told the DEA chap you're doing a follow-up story and want to get some background on Janac. I think that way you'll learn all you need to know. Naisborough is something of an expert. But if you want more from him, you'll have to figure out what you're prepared to tell him.'

Hamnet nodded slowly, staring out at the life spilling towards them from the pavement, crowding ever closer as the streets became poorer. Brick gave way to tin, three storeys to one. Finally, they rounded a corner, to be faced by sheer concrete walls and massive steel gates. The taxi pulled up, Dubre paid and they climbed out.

Dubre spoke a few words to a guard and showed some ID. After a thorough search the gates opened and they stepped from the dust and poverty of northern Thailand into the manicured and surreal calm of Middle America. The gentle thump of tennis balls and the swish of sprinklers was all that disturbed the air. Crisp, white-painted, two-storey houses nestled amidst perfect lawns and swimming pools. They were led to a three-storey office block and up a flight of stairs. Their footsteps echoed down the wooden hall. Finally they stopped outside a heavy door. A swift knock and they were ushered into a large office. Its occupant was already halfway across the floor, hand extended.

'John Naisborough,' he said in a clipped voice, after nodding a greeting to Dubre. The grip was painful as Hamnet proffered his own hand. From the close-cropped salt-and-pepper hair to the polished black calf-length boots, Naisborough was the all-American serviceman. Only the dragon tattoo on a muscular forearm spoke of an irregular past. Hamnet judged him to be in his late forties and in frighteningly good shape. Naisborough moved to sit down, indicating two chairs opposite him on the other side of an enormous desk. Hamnet's gaze flicked quickly round the room as he sat. An assault rifle was propped against the back wall, the American flag kissing the barrel as it hung from its standard.

'I understand from Dubre that you're a journalist,' said Naisborough in a voice that didn't go far towards disguising his distaste.

Hamnet glanced quickly at Dubre before saying, 'That's right. I'm interested in a man by the name of Paul Robert Janac.'

Naisborough sat back and the big leather chair creaked. He folded his hands in his lap. 'Janac, yes, I served with him in Vietnam, Mr Toliver, before he went off to work for the CIA. We were on long-range recon patrols together. It was an unpleasant business. Lurps didn't take many prisoners but that suited Janac just fine.'

He paused. The silence was broken only by the hum of the air conditioning and a slight scuff as Dubre shifted his bulk in his seat. Hamnet stared fixedly at the wall behind Naisborough until he continued.

'I understand you're writing a story about the incident

in the boat off Papua New Guinea. So you'll already know that Janac has a sadistic streak. But it's not cruelty for its own sake — he's motivated by what he sees as some kind of enquiry into the human mind. That was the case in the boat incident — the series of games, pivoting on a decision between self-interest and collective good. And all targeted on a man whose life had turned from good to bad on just such a decision. It was typical of Janac, as much for the fact that his own code of honour ruled that he let the survivors go as for the cruelty of the final game of Russian roulette.'

It was Hamnet's turn to shift uncomfortably. 'Dubre thought you might have up-to-date information on his activities and whereabouts,' he said.

'Yes,' drawled Naisborough. 'But this is unattributable. I'm only doing it because I owe Mr Dubre a big favour. Understood?'

'Understood.'

'Then it'll be easier if I give you a little background first. This is a war zone up here.' His hand indicated a wall map bright with coloured markings and tiny flagged pins. 'Right now we have a very fluid situation. There are many causes, but the result is a bunch of competition in the opium business. And the only common factor in the whole stinking business is the Chinese. The Golden Triangle armies, the supply routes and the distribution networks are all controlled by elements of the Chinese diaspora. Now this is not a criminal organisation like the Mafia or the Colombian cartels, with an extensive hierarchy and vertical control like a multinational corporation. It's more of a huge group of small freelance operations that come together for particular deals, forming and re-forming depending on the capital, manpower and logistical requirements of each task.'

Naisborough leaned forward, warming to his theme, elbows on the desk. The dragon rippled. 'It's a very modern business model — flexible, responsive — but it only works when the different parties have a strong relationship of trust. You do a deal and you stick to it. If you take money off someone, you deliver what's agreed. Guanxi is what they call it — networks of obligation and responsibility, favours and requests. Now, obviously, Janac is not Chinese. And his lack of respect for this Chinese way of doing things is what has landed him in his current situation.

'But I'm getting ahead of myself.' He paused for a moment's thought before continuing. 'Janac was originally sent to Laos by the CIA in the '70s to help organise insurgency armies. The Kuomintang in particular — the Chinese nationalist army defeated by Mao — was maintained and assisted by the CIA as a barrier against communist expansion. But instead of retaking China they used CIA weapons to build a massive opium export business.

'So Janac hooked up with an old KMT general and made some good friends — people who control opium fields, refineries and supply routes. And when the moment was right, he set up as an independent operator. He built his market in Australia using some Aussie buddies he'd met in Nam. It got Janac started, and whilst we helped break up parts of the network occasionally, he was Australia's biggest importer for some time.

'Contacts in Sydney tell me that the situation has now changed. He's getting hit on the streets by the new Chinese traffickers — people who went there ahead of the Hong Kong handover. And a year ago, someone — we think a Hong Kong-based Triad — started to squeeze him in Thailand as well. His protection collapsed, and he cleared out of his stronghold on Ko Samui, an island in the Gulf of Thailand, just before our boys down south got to him. He was off the scene for six months before he popped up here.

'This has been coming to Janac for a long time. As I

106

said, he doesn't respect the Chinese way of doing business, and you can't run heroin out here unless you deal with the Chinese. Janac believes that self-interest is the only driver in any kind of relationship — as you'll know if you've talked to the survivors of the boat incident. So he just doesn't get Guanxi. He has no concept of a trust relationship. You give him an inch and he'll screw you over. I'm sure the boat victims wouldn't fail to see the irony in the fact that it's this very attitude that has wrecked Janac's drug business.

'But the Chinese are practical people, and they put up with it while they needed him. Once his dealers started getting hit and he lost market share, though, his position here was weakened too. Someone decided to get even and he's been running ever since they closed him down on Ko Samui. A lot of stock and cash went down the river then, and what I hear now is that his dealers are not getting supplied. But there's one man who will still deal with him up here: the KMT general he's known for twenty-five years. I'm sure Janac is seeing old General Lee, trying to buy enough China White to put himself back in business. How the hell he's going to pay for it we're not so sure.'

Hamnet had listened to every word of this long speech in silence. He knew — in his gut, in his blood — that Anna was here, that she was still alive, with Janac, with General Lee. He would not let her die alone. He had kept himself alive on the *Shawould* to try and save her. If that could not be achieved, his life was forfeit — payment for all those who had died as a result of his quest. And he'd known it since that morning. He knew what he had to do, but he needed this man's help.

'Mr Naisborough, I appreciate what you've told us,' he started. 'But we've come here under slightly false pretences.'

Naisborough swung a heavy glance at Dubre.

'I must ask you not to repeat anything that I am about to

107

tell you,' continued Hamnet.

Naisborough opened his hands and shrugged. 'That depends. Will the information help me do my job?'

'No. It doesn't concern drugs.'

'OK. But I can't make a complete commitment. It still depends on what you have to say.'

Hamnet rubbed his cheek. He needed this man. He would have to take the chance. 'My wife, Anna, was taken hostage by Janac just over a week ago. We now believe he's taken her to General Lee's.'

'What makes you think she's still alive?' asked Naisborough.

'He said he'd let her live in exchange for my silence on a matter that concerns Dubre.'

'Ah, I see. Well, knowing Janac, if you remain silent, she'll live. If you don't, she'll die.'

'Too many others will die if Michael doesn't reveal what he knows,' said Dubre.

Naisborough took a long slow breath. 'Then if Janac's got her up there, she's as good as dead.'

'That's it?' said Hamnet.' You're saying you won't help me?'

Naisborough shook his head. 'This is a very big game, Mr Toliver. I represent the most powerful state in the world in its most operational frontline drugs-enforcement office. And I am powerless to do anything about these people in Burma. General Lee's base is thirty kilometres north of the border. It's easy to find him. But I can't cross that border, whatever you may hear in the bars around Chiang Mai. The State Department would have a shit fit if they thought I was even having dreams about going up there to do a black-bag job. And the truth is, even if I could get permission, I'd need a US marine division and air support to get in and out of there without serious loss of life. This KMT general commands an army of about fifteen thousand regulars. We're not talking dope-happy amateurs here, we're talking a real army — uniforms, ranks, discipline and training. And some excellent hardware. The best a bunch of money can buy. I'm sorry, but even assuming that your wife is up there, you have an army as well as Janac to deal with.' Naisborough leaned forward. 'There is nothing I can do for you, Mr Toliver. Believe me when I say I am sorry for your loss. Please go home and mourn your wife.'

Hamnet's reply was quick. 'I will see her, Mr Naisborough. She will not die alone. Whatever the personal cost might be, I will go in there and find her. If you will show me where to look.'

Naisborough frowned slightly, running a finger across a tidy eyebrow. 'I don't think you understand, sir. There is no question of what the cost "might" be. You'll die, along with anyone I send with you.'

'Then perhaps you can provide me with a map, or directions to this general's camp?'

A ripple of impatience passed through Naisborough's taut figure. 'Have you not understood a single word I've said, son?'

'I've understood every word. I intend to join my wife. I will try and exchange myself for her. And I'll die with her if that is the cost of trying.'

Naisborough looked at Hamnet a few moments longer. He had seen a lot of living and a lot of dying. And he knew when men were serious. He turned to Dubre.

Dubre looked at Hamnet. 'You know, I . . .'

'Save it.' Hamnet returned his gaze. 'I've had plenty of time to think about it, Dubre. This is what I have to do.'

Chapter 13

Hamnet snapped the clip shut on the borrowed DEA backpack. A couple of hours had passed since they had left Naisborough. The American had eventually agreed to provide him with a guide as far as the border and instructions as to how to proceed from there, but only after Hamnet had threatened to ask for help among the Chiang Mai trekking companies. The DEA's man was due to pick him up in a couple of minutes' time. Hamnet sighed deeply and turned to Dubre, who was leaning against the wall by the door.

'Is there nothing I can say that will stop you, Phillip?' asked Dubre with a resignation that reflected every second of the previous two hours of trying.

'Nothing.' Hamnet managed the briefest of smiles for his friend. 'On the ship I had the chance to give myself up, supposedly in exchange for the lives of the crew. I didn't — because I already knew he intended to kill everyone regardless. But Anna doesn't know that.' Hamnet hesitated, frowned at the floor. 'I can't let her die believing I deserted her.' He looked back up at Dubre, his face clearing a little. 'And if I can possibly save her, I will.'

Dubre nodded, shifting his weight from one foot to the other. He opened his mouth to speak, then closed it. He tried again: 'I know this isn't . . . I mean, I don't want to appear heartless, but how do you intend to tell me about the *Shawould* if you don't . . .'

'If I don't come back?' Hamnet finished for him, gazing levelly at Dubre's quickly averted green eyes. He stepped over to the coffee table and picked up one of the hotel's envelopes. It was sealed but not addressed. Hamnet tapped it against his fingers a couple of times before turning back to Dubre. 'It's all in here. Everything you need to know to stop it happening again. I have three days left. If Anna or I aren't back or haven't been in touch by then, you can open it.' He held it out. 'Agreed?'

Dubre looked at him. 'Of course,' he said, and reached for the envelope. 'Midday, in three days' time.'

Hamnet watched his precious secret all the way into Dubre's pocket. Then he picked up the backpack. 'We might as well wait in the lobby. I have to check out anyway.'

Dubre nodded, held the door open and followed Hamnet downstairs. Dubre's steel-heeled shoes clicked loudly on the floor as they walked across to the reception desk. There was no one else around. As Hamnet paid his bill, Dubre stood and stared out into the street. When Hamnet had finished, he had to cough to regain Dubre's attention, so deep in thought was the other man. Dubre turned, his face heavy. Hamnet was holding out some cash — the remainder of Dubre's loans.

'There's some other stuff in that envelope, including a letter to my parents and one to Anna's,' Hamnet said. 'They'll return the rest of the cash I owe you from my estate. Your time, of course, will be paid for by the fee from the *Shawould*'s insurers.'

Dubre — still deep in reverie — started to take the wad of notes, then stopped himself. He held up both hands. 'You keep it, you might need it.' He hesitated. 'When you get back.'

Hamnet looked at him, then at the money. And could think of nothing to say. The hotel door opened on the burning silence with a heavy breath of heat and dust. They both turned. A stocky Thai, dressed in black work trousers and a faded fatigue shirt, eyed them quickly before introducing himself with a limp handshake as Moh. Sensing the tension

111

between the two men, he turned wordlessly on his heel and led the way out of the front door. Hamnet watched him climb into a battered Jeep, then turned back.

'Thanks for your help, Dubre. I wouldn't have got this far without you.'

Dubre just shook his head, tight lipped, eyes cast downward. 'Good luck,' he managed finally. 'I hope you find her.'

Hamnet nodded, once, slapped Dubre lightly on the shoulder, swung on his heel and left.

The Thai guide turned the Jeep north and headed out of Chiang Mai. The city quickly fell away behind them and the countryside opened out into scrubby land and fields. They stayed on a metalled road for a little more than three hours before pulling off onto a track. The gradient steepened, the track twisting and turning. The pounding, pothole-plagued ride continued uphill for twenty jarring minutes before the ground flattened out. Then the track disappeared completely as the jungle thinned onto the top of a ridge, which they followed for another twenty minutes. Moh stopped just as the gradient started to dip.

'Walking,' he said, and climbed out.

They pulled their packs out of the back of the jeep and Moh led off at a brisk pace. He threaded his way downward, and through the screen of trees Hamnet caught the occasional glimpse of the jungle spread below them. Even in the shade it was stiflingly hot, and Hamnet was soon lathered in sweat. They traced a gradual decline across the contours, until they reached the bottom of a valley. A shallow stream, a couple of metres across, lay before them. Moh pointed to the other side. 'Burma,' he said.

Hamnet nodded. Moh rolled the pack off his back, pulled out a book-sized brown-paper package, carefully taped, and handed it over. Hamnet started to unwrap it. He heard Moh resling his pack as he pulled off the tape. Inside was a single sheet of paper — a photocopied section of a map — and a weighty object wrapped in linen. He glanced up enquiringly — but Moh was gone. No sound, no movement amongst the trees. Hamnet opened his mouth to shout — and thought better of it. Moh's instructions had obviously been to leave him here, and yelling about it wasn't going to change that.

He settled down to examine the map. The black-and-white photocopy wasn't particularly clear, but a red circle and dot marked a point on what was presumably the stream beside him. An arrow pointed upstream towards a second circle and dot, next to which was written the word 'Janac'. The stream extended continuously, by way of a couple of tributaries, as far as his destination. It seemed a simple enough piece of route-finding.

He tucked the map in his pocket and turned his attention to the linen package. He pulled away the cloth and sat staring at a semiautomatic pistol. He took a deep breath. Was this going to help? The last thing he needed was to get himself shot before he had had a chance to talk to Janac. The blued finish of the weapon had been ground down on the slide, presumably to lose the serial number. Naisborough was a careful man. Hamnet rewrapped the gun and stuffed it in his pack, deep in the sleeping bag.

It was almost four-thirty, no more than a couple of hours before sunset. He pushed the pace hard. It was a thirty-kilometre hike and the clock was ticking. He wanted to approach the camp after dark, which left him twenty-four hours. A path slowly developed beside the stream. This made for easier walking, but heightened the chances of meeting someone coming the other way. Hamnet moved about fifty metres up the side of the valley and continued threading his way through the scrub, until gathering darkness had him stumbling on

113

unseen roots and rocks. He picked a flat spot with the last of the light and stopped. He ate a quick meal of bread and tinned fish, then turned in. And this time he slept.

It was the slightest of human sounds that woke him. What had he heard? He stared into the half-light of dawn. The crack and grunt was repeated. Distant but definite. It wasn't a sound that someone was trying to muffle. He rolled over and out of the sleeping bag in an instant. Then stopped and listened again. It was getting closer — several layers of noise, lots of people, maybe animals. All moving down the stream towards him. He rolled the gun back into the sleeping bag, packed quickly and moved off along the valley side until he found a covered vantage point from which to view the path.

The noise was loud now, a steady clattering of hardware and the murmur of low conversation coming along the valley floor. Out of the gloom loomed a figure, a soldier with a rifle across his back. He walked openly down the footpath, followed by a second soldier and a third. Then came the first of the mules, laden with panniers. He had stumbled on an opium shipment. He counted forty animals, each with at least four soldiers in attendance, every one of whom looked alert and professional. Ammunition, water bottles and grenades were clipped to their webbing belts, rifles and mortars slung over their shoulders. Naisborough hadn't been lying.

Hamnet sat motionless for a quarter of an hour after the last of the train had gone by, the jungle assuming its former silence. Then he set off, contouring along the valley side above the stream. The foliage grew thickly, making it difficult to navigate. Several times he made his way back down to the path to check his directions and get water, and he almost missed the second of the two tributaries.

It was midafternoon before the map told him he was close. The stream had petered out to mud as the valley sides had flattened and the downward gradient he had been following had levelled out. The trees began to thin, cut back deliberately. According to the map there was a plateau ahead, three-quarters ringed by a ridge of hills that dropped almost sheer onto its tabletop expanse. The camp was on the plateau. But Hamnet didn't need the map. In fact he could have walked in blindfolded. His ears told him everything he needed to know. He heard the first sounds from a couple of kilometres away — the clatter of engines and hardware, shouted orders borne to him on the thin mountain air. He stopped. It was five o'clock. He was as close as was safe in daylight; further reconnaissance would have to wait until nightfall.

It was an eternity before the stars emerged in the darkening dome above him, and two hours after sunset when he finally set off. He contoured to his left, and the ground beneath him steadily steepened as he skirted round the plateau and onto the slope of the hills that backed it. The vegetation thinned until he was completely exposed on what had become almost a rock face. Judging he had gone too far, he backed up into some cover, then he turned upwards and started to climb. He picked his way as silently as he could. It wasn't easy — the moon provided enough light for him to be seen, but not enough to see where he was stepping. And however carefully he placed his feet, the occasional rock would break loose and tumble noisily downhill in the still night. At each sound he would stop and listen, breath steady but pulse charging. And each time all he could hear was the distant hum of generators, the soft babble of voices and the occasional clatter of a vehicle.

Ahead of him was a powerful glow, which threw his side of the hill into shadow. But he was unprepared for what he saw when he crawled to the top of the rise and looked down the other side. Thirty metres below him, a huge parade ground dominated the centre of the plateau, from which all vegetation had been removed. Set around it along three sides were parallel rows of buildings, all backed up against the slope that dropped away beneath him and to his left and right. The fourth side, which faced the valley he had walked up, was fortified with barbed wire and gun emplacements. A track led through the defences towards the jungle, across as much as a kilometre of open space. Every couple of minutes a truck would set off along this, and just as often another would return. Hamnet could see people everywhere — walking, running, in groups, alone. Many were eating in huge open-sided dining shelters. The chatter and buzz of army life radiated out to him on the warm air. The sheer scale of the enterprise took his breath away. But it didn't have a fraction of the impact achieved by the sensation of warm steel on the back of his neck.

Hamnet froze. There was a moment's silence before the click of a torch, the dazzle of a light in his eyes. Then voices, gabbling excitedly in a language he didn't recognise, and hands on his arms, wrenching them behind his back. His pack was pulled away, then there was a sharp stab of pain as a loop of rope tightened around his wrists. He was hauled to his feet and pushed forwards, up and over the lip of the hill. The slope was steep, and his weight ran away from him as he struggled to keep his legs beneath his upper body. Slipping and sliding on the rubble underfoot, he kicked up a cloud of dust which swirled into the harsh light of the camp's arc lamps, announcing his arrival as effectively as the yelling behind him. Figures he had been watching only moments earlier now stopped and turned to observe his noisy approach.

'Janac!' he shouted, and kept shouting, 'I want to see Janac!' Hands pushed him forward down a steadily growing gauntlet of uniformed figures. The faces were silent, impassive.

He kept going, prodded and goaded — past the dining shelters, across the parade ground and between rows of brick huts. They approached a shadowy compound, enclosed on all sides by barbed wire and accessed by a narrow gate. Inside were several bamboo trapdoors, all opened to reveal a hole in the earth. Hamnet was pushed towards the nearest. He twisted and turned, walking backwards now, trying to tell them again. 'Janac! Janac!' he bellowed, louder and louder. The faces remained blank — uncomprehending or uncaring or both. Then he missed a step, felt the ground slide away beneath him, and realised he was losing his balance. He lurched in a reflex bid to regain control, only to find himself staring down a black hole as it rushed up to meet him.

Chapter 14

Falling has its own fear. A fear driven by the knowledge that what has happened has happened. That while body and soul might yet be intact, in an unstoppable instant they will be dashed against something hard and unyielding. The fear is barbed when the fall is blind. All this in a moment, then he hit the ground, an ankle turning awkwardly. At the sharp stab of pain Hamnet rolled sideways and fell hard into the wall of the pit. He was unlucky to take the impact in the same spot as when the *Shawould* had run aground. Unconsciousness rolled over him, a foggy cloud of pain, as the still healing wound thumped angrily at this new contusion. Until, a threshold passed, his mind shut down.

When he came to, Hamnet was painless, floating. Where and why slowly began to return — sensation also. He dragged his aching body across the pit and wedged himself against the side. Staring upwards, he blinked and screwed up his eyes to try and restore his vision.

When he could finally focus, he saw that the top of the pit was five metres away. The slats of the trapdoor were silhouetted against the glow of the camp lights. The walls were only two-and-a-half metres apart. The sides were supported and panelled with slabs of rough dark wood. But the floor was earth.

He remembered his watch, and twisted round to take a look. He was surprised to find it still on his wrist. It was four in the morning. It would be daylight soon. Dubre would release the information in thirty-two hours. He had to make them understand that he must see Janac. He tried out his voice gingerly: 'Janac.' Then he drew a breath and yelled,

'Hey!' Silence. He tried again. And again, with mounting frustration: 'Come on, you bastards. I'm awake. Come and get me. Janac, I want to see Janac.'

Hamnet pushed himself to his feet against the side panelling and took a short step across the pit, wincing as his weight came onto his twisted ankle. He limped to the other side and yelled for Janac again. But the world above ignored him. And kept on ignoring him. He struggled back and forth, calling repeatedly. Each time the same words, always for Janac. He limped and yelled through sunrise, and on into the building heat. When his voice started to crack, he yelled every two turns across the pit, then every three. His throat closed, his head pounded and his ankle swelled. The laps slowed and then stopped as he fought dehydration and exhaustion. His voice died to a hoarse whisper, a whimper — and for Anna, not Janac. He slid down against the rough boards and curled into the foetal position on the dirt. He was out within seconds.

When he woke the ground under him was damp and cold. He knew instantly where he was. The sunlight had gone. He checked his watch in the bluish artificial light that crept through the slits in the trapdoor. It was ten in the evening. Six hours had slipped away like water through sand. He struggled to his feet, pain jabbing at him from cramped and stiff corners of his body. 'Janac!' he tried to scream, but there was only rasping. His throat was parched and painful. He'd had nothing to drink for over twenty-four hours. 'Sons of bitches,' he moaned to himself. 'Come and get me. Please come and get me.' But there was only silence. Not even the sounds of the camp reached him down here. Loneliness swept over him like flood water. He was so close, but so helpless.

The sun woke him with its light and heat. Hamnet couldn't believe he had slept. Couldn't believe he had been left there. If the bastards wanted to torture him to death, why couldn't they do it personally so he could beg for Anna's life?

His watch told him there was little time left. He could never have imagined, even in his worse nightmares, that he would set Anna's execution date. He could picture Dubre, anxious to slit open the envelope, hovering by the phone. The news would be flashed out as a Navtex warning and the whole world would know in moments. And she would die wondering why he hadn't come. Wondering where he was, where he had been on the *Shawould*. Why he hadn't been there for her. She filled his mind with her touch, her smell, her voice, her laughter. His throat tightened and choked. The tears came now, as the sun burned its arc and took away the time. He wanted more than anything — more than it was possible to believe anybody could want anything — to see her. The tears rolled unbidden and unstoppable.

It was a change in the light that told him something was happening. Dappled sunlight had been replaced by a bald glare, as if from a spotlight. He looked up and saw the trapdoor had been raised and a couple of faces were peering down at him. Expressionless, shadowed by the brightness behind. Hamnet had no words, choking on his emotion, on a throat that had screamed itself to incoherence. A ladder appeared over the rim of the pit and slid down towards him. He dragged himself up it into the daylight, struggling to keep his balance without the use of his tied hands. There was still time. 'Janac?' he managed, as he crawled over the edge, gazing at the figure before him. The man nodded, prodded him to his feet with a rifle butt and waved him forwards. As he staggered upright, he managed another glance at his watch: it was just before eleven.

With the rifle in his back he stumbled towards the closest barrack block. The heat was searing, and he was weak

120

from lack of food and water — giddy, struggling to hurry but his cramped legs and twisted ankle weren't cooperating. Sweat and dirt permeated his clothing, were ingrained in every pore and fold of skin, matted his hair. He fell, and there was a soldier at his elbow, shoving, pushing him up. The world closed in on him, and he focused only on the next yard of dirt, the next step. Then the hand under his arm let him go. He sagged to his knees, head hanging, trying to gather his strength. Janac, he knew that he needed Janac. There wasn't much time.

'Give him some water,' said a familiar voice.

Hamnet raised his head in recognition. There was an overwhelming sense of relief — and with it, of strength regained. He was here. There was still time to see her. It was too late to get her out before the news broke, but he was sure he would at least see her.

A water bottle was shoved in his face. The precious liquid felt heavy and warm in his stomach. He mistimed a swallow, choked and spat. The water bottle was gone. He shook his head and wiped his mouth on his shoulder. He was facing a semicircle of men, most standing, some seated at a heavy mahogany table. Nearest of those seated, at one end of the table and turned towards him, was Janac, legs crossed laconically, thin fingers resting on a kneecap, cigarette smoke drifting into the still air. He appeared to be wearing the same fatigues as on the *Shawould*. Certainly the same heavy revolver lay on the table beside him.

Janac turned to an elderly Chinese figure sitting opposite and raised his eyebrows curiously. 'What's this, General?'

'We think he is crazy trekking tourist, but he want you,' said the general, hands folded neatly in front of him, his green tunic spotless.

Janac stubbed out a cigarette and turned the grey eyes

on Hamnet. 'So, who are you and what do you want?'

Hamnet struggled to compose a sentence, to find words.

'How long's he been in the pit, General Lee?' asked Janac, turning again to address the man opposite.

Lee shrugged carelessly.

'Day-and-a-half,' croaked Hamnet.

'Ah, it does talk,' said Janac, turning back. 'So, who the hell are you?'

Hamnet squirmed onto his knees, tried to get to his feet. Just as he put his weight on them, they were kicked out from under him. He sprawled painfully in the dirt with a stifled moan.

'Stay on your ass. That's how the boys like you,' said Janac. 'And answer the damn question before I get pissed as well.'

Hamnet took a deep breath, composed himself, and looked Janac defiantly in the eye — or as defiantly as he could, flat out in the dirt at his feet. Then he said, 'I'm Phillip Hamnet, and I've come to exchange myself for my wife.'

Something flickered across Janac's face. Then he smiled with a slightly puzzled look. 'Hamnet? Your wife's dead. You broke your silence three days ago.'

Hamnet heard the words with complete comprehension yet a total lack of understanding. He knew everything, yet knew only that the most precious thing in his life was gone. And she had died believing he had failed her. Strength came from a source deep inside him, a well still rich with water after a thousand years of drought. Hamnet rocked his feet under him and launched himself at Janac. But they had kept him sitting for a good reason. He was only just on his feet when the first restraining arm grabbed him. He shrugged it off with a roll of his shoulder, with no more trouble than a well-found ship taking a wave. He was a metre closer when the second and third got to him. But they weren't committed

122

either. They didn't believe this filthy, slightly built, exhausted and bound man could be a problem. They were badly wrong. They had an arm each when Hamnet pulled down hard and spun himself forward into a somersault. They held on long enough to allow him to land on his feet in a squat, but their grip was broken by the final part of the turn. He was free and another metre closer.

Hamnet extended his legs in a single explosive motion and the power of his thigh muscles flung him across the remaining space. But Janac had stood. His forearm and shoulder snapped up, took Hamnet's momentum and redirected it with consummate ease. The throw put Hamnet on his back and momentarily knocked the wind out of him. It was enough. An instant later five men were holding him down. He struggled with all his strength, but there were too many. As the superhuman energy flowed away he was left shaking, sobbing, every muscle rock hard against those who held him. 'I told him, that bastard, I told him to wait!' he screamed. 'We had a deal, that fucker Dubre! Christ, I'll kill him! I swear I'll kill him!'

Janac glanced at Lee quizzically. But the old man was more interested in Janac's fighting skills than the howling wreck buried under his men.

'You still have good move, my friend.'

'I had the best teacher,' Janac replied with a smile.

Lee nodded his serious acknowledgement of the compliment.

Hamnet had exhausted his anger. It was all he could do to suck back air, his body taking over in a recovery reflex.

Janac pulled out another cigarette and said, 'We had a deal, Hamnet. You broke it. Must admit I was a little surprised at how quickly, even for you. But take the consequences like a man, for Christ's sake.'

Hamnet laboured for words between the desperate

breaths, the wracking sobs. 'I gave him the information. But he wasn't to release it for three days, and then only if Anna or I didn't come back. He promised. But he must have told them immediately. As soon as I'd left.'

Janac lit the cigarette, sucking his teeth. 'That is unfortunate.' He blew a smoke ring and glanced at Lee, smiling again. 'You mind if we keep him for a while?'

The general shook his head.

'Take him back to the pit,' said Janac, indicating one of the men with a wave of his hand. 'Give him some food and water. And cut him loose so he can eat.'

Hamnet went tamely. There was nothing left to fight for. The very last of his strength went into cushioning his fall. The trapdoor flipped shut and once again it was quiet.

Chapter 15

By the time they came again, Hamnet had slipped into a stupor. The leaf-wrapped rice balls and water bottle that had been thrown down to him lay untouched. His system was running on vapour, barely ticking over, his breathing slow and shallow, his mind avoiding any confrontation with reality by drifting into oblivion. The shouts from above failed to rouse him. He sat slumped against the wall, unable to deal with the new and vastly different world into which he had been propelled.

The first shot that slammed into the dirt floor half a metre from his right kneecap brought only a flicker of curiosity to his face. He looked up at the rim of the pit, where yelling figures were indicating a ladder. He glanced at it briefly and turned away. But his mind was beginning to stir, if unwillingly. The second and third shots followed quickly and struck a lot closer. Dirt puffed from the impact and drifted over his thighs. Hamnet felt his hand lift almost automatically to brush the dirt away. He sighed a sigh of the deathly weary and pushed himself to his feet. They were leaden as he dragged them one after the other up the rungs of the ladder with immeasurable slowness.

At the top he was greeted by the soft light and cool air of morning. He realised that a night had passed. The only darkness he could remember was despair. The climb finished him; he hadn't the strength to walk. He dropped to all fours, and after some ineffectual prodding, two soldiers took an arm each and carried him. Once again he was deposited in a heap before Janac, who was seated at the same table, picking at a breakfast of mangoes and pineapple. General

Lee again sat opposite, his plate empty. To Janac's right was Tosh — unknown to Hamnet — whittling at a piece of wood, steam drifting from a coffee cup in front of him. The three guards who had delivered Hamnet stood beside the table while one of them addressed Janac. Hamnet heard the account of his refusal to eat and his indifference to the gunshots without understanding the foreign sounds, without listening, without caring.

But Janac's words cut right through him. 'Your children didn't die with their mother.'

Hamnet's mind pushed his body into a reaction it couldn't cope with. The lack of food and water fell on him like a pile-driver as he tried to raise himself. He fainted from weakness. When he came to, there was a water bottle at his cracked lips. The tepid liquid slipped down easily and his body accepted it gratefully. The storm of depression had shifted. He was no longer in the dark silence of the eye, but adrift in the emotional gale that whirled around it. He ate the food placed in front of him — slowly at first, then with a growing anxiety that it would be taken away before he had finished. But when he did finish, they brought him more. Energised by both the food and the knowledge of his new responsibility, strength and life coursed back through him.

Janac finished his breakfast, watching Hamnet in silence. General Lee observed them both implacably, with a faint air of disapproval. Hamnet was visibly slowing, his shrunken stomach already bloated, when Janac spoke again. 'So you're the Lifeboat Man.'

Hamnet looked up and croaked painfully in a voice untested since the day before: 'Where are my children? I want to see them.'

Janac nodded. 'All in good time. We're going to talk first.' Hamnet held his gaze for a fraction of a second before resuming his meal. 'Three could live and four had to die. That's right, isn't it?' continued Janac.

Hamnet kept his head down and his mouth full.

'So what happened out there? How did you choose the three?'

Hamnet looked up, chewing hard, half-heartedly opened his mouth to speak, then closed it again.

'This isn't the Waldorf,' snarled Janac. 'You can speak with your mouth full.'

Hamnet swallowed, then said, 'Why do you want to know?'

'Let's just say that I'm interested in the moral dilemma. And if you're interested in your children, you'll stop fucking me around.' The tone was still harsh.

Hamnet looked at Janac carefully, searching the lean face and the still, cold eyes. This was something he didn't want to talk about. Particularly to this man. But what choice did he have? 'We drew straws. The first one chosen took the supplies and gear.'

'So you were in the draw?'

'I ran it. Got left with the last survivor's straw.'

'And how did you feel when that happened?'

There was a long silence between them this time, punctuated only by the chip, chip of Tosh's whittling and the distant sounds of the parade ground. And Janac let it roll. Hamnet stopped eating and his hands fell away from the remaining rice. He stared, unseeing, at the dirt in front of him. Then he said, 'I prayed for four days that we wouldn't be found.'

Janac nodded, pushed his plate away and wiped his hands on his khaki trousers. 'What happened to the four?'

'Three of them were very weak. They lost consciousness and died in the next six hours or so. The fourth was the Filipino mate. He'd been in good shape right through the storm. He wouldn't swim away, but he went downhill pretty

127

quickly all that day, without fluid.' Hamnet could still see the man's eyes — two unfathomable brown pools. 'He died that night.'

Janac listened to this with a face as expressionless as the general's. Then he said, 'Died? Of thirst?'

Hamnet looked at him, feeling giddy, nauseous — whether from the sudden nourishment or the conversation he was unsure. 'Yes, of course.' He swallowed. 'How else?'

'There were stories about a flare gun, a shooting.'

'Just stories. The papers.' Hamnet shook his head slowly.

'I've seen a lot of men in extreme situations, and I can't believe this Filipino mate just sat there and died,' Janac replied, crossing his legs.

Hamnet shook his head again. 'I guess that's what the journalists thought too. But we had a deal. He was a man of honour.' He wished he felt stronger, that he sounded stronger, more truthful. But he didn't flinch from contact with the grey eyes as he spoke. Only three men living would ever know — and know that they knew — what had happened out there. And however improbable the truth, however unlikely the story, that was the way it would remain.

Janac watched Hamnet closely, held his gaze steadily for a full five seconds. Then half laughed, half sighed, waited a moment and said, 'And the other two?'

'They weren't good. I gave them the majority of the water. It rained on the fifth day. I don't think any of us would have made it through that night if it hadn't.'

Janac tapped a thin finger slowly on the tabletop. 'And then you were rescued, your actions entirely vindicated by events, and instead of hailing a hero the media strung you up for it.'

'Something like that.' Now Hamnet could look away.

'You should've sat on your hands, done nothing, then you might've been dead but not guilty. You can't be blamed for doing nothing — whatever the consequences. That's what they all believe, isn't it? All the little people?' A sneer. 'If they didn't, they'd set themselves impossible moral standards, because they do nothing all the time — every time they walk past a charity box or see another drought on the TV news. And by this marvellous moral code of inaction, they continue to acquiesce silently with the worst evils in the world — and I continue to prosper.'

The sneer widened into a smirk. 'But you, you're different. Rational action —three could live, four had to die. You couldn't have stayed quiet after I had to kill the crew on that second boat — even for your wife. The price was too high.' He frowned. 'She understood that, you know.' He paused. 'Anna — she understood what you would do.'

Hamnet was barely listening. He had never been interested in any analysis of his actions, or his supposed actions, although there had been plenty of it. He knew what was right and wrong, and that was that. But when he heard Anna's name, he thought: That wasn't what I wanted her to think; I wanted her to know I had come for her. And in that he had failed. The thought sickened him to his very core. But for the children's sake he couldn't let despair take over. He concentrated on the feel of the warm sun on his back, the hot aroma of the jungle, the clatter and bustle of the camp. He needed something real to hold onto in this new world.

Janac was watching for Hamnet's reaction as he continued. 'Nevertheless, the death of that crew was unfortunate for both of us. I need the money from these operations' — he waved a hand at the man opposite — 'so that I can buy some of General Lee's very fine heroin. You've screwed that up. But I think you can still help me. Which is why I kept your children alive.' Janac paused as Hamnet looked up. 'You can go home — with one of your kids.'

Hamnet shook his head even as his pulse picked up.

'There's a catch.'

'It's a reward for your courage in coming up here.'

'One child?'

Janac smiled again. 'To get the second will require a little more effort. But we'll talk about that in a moment. Come and see them first.'

Janac stood and watched as Hamnet dragged himself up on to legs and an ankle that would still barely carry him. Then he indicated for the others to follow, led them to an open Jeep and climbed into the front. General Lee sat next to him. Hamnet was helped into the back, with Tosh beside him. The three guards took a second vehicle. Hamnet hung on grimly as they drove quickly through the camp. He saw none of it, thought of nothing but his wife, his children. And the payment he might have to make.

They were soon at the other side of the base, where a collection of shacks clung untidily to the perimeter like a boil on a chin. The Jeeps pulled up outside the first of the huts. Janac stepped out and watched as Tosh yanked Hamnet to his feet and onto the ground. Then he waved Hamnet to a filthy cloth draped across the doorway of the hut. Hamnet stumbled forward and slowly pushed the rag aside. Light tumbled into the room and immediately a baby started to cry. It was a pitiful sound — not the healthy, full-throated cry of a baby that expected to be fed on demand, but a despairing whimper. As his eyes adjusted to the pattern of light and shadow cast across the room, Hamnet saw that it was empty save for a bamboo cot, in which the baby lay, and a mattress against the far wall. On the mattress sat a teenage girl dressed in a dirty T-shirt and shorts, an opium pipe beside her. She looked up listlessly, eyes dull and glazed, then lowered her stare back to the grubby floor.

Hamnet was beside the cot in a moment. His son — so tiny — was lying naked on damp, soiled grass, caked with his own excreta. Flies buzzed and crawled about his face, which was puckered and reddened with tiredness and hunger. Hamnet brushed the insects away, picked his baby up and held him, tears forming in his own eyes.

'So you'll be taking that one then?' said Janac. 'The other's next door if you want to choose.'

Hamnet looked round. He could hear the other baby taking up his brother's cause with a plaintive wail of sympathy. The smell of the room began to overpower him. The heat and the hum of flies swam around him. He knew he had to get out, away from this, away from the child he would leave behind. Away from the thought that he could choose, that there was a twin. He staggered to the door, out into the clear, clean sunlight, and limped off as quickly as he could. Janac fell in beside him, keeping pace with an easy stride. Hamnet had no words for the horror and pain. He could only think that he had to keep walking.

Then Janac said, 'That's far enough.'

The sharpness of his tone brought Hamnet up short. He stopped but didn't turn. His tears mixing and muddying the grime on his face.

'It's simple enough,' said Janac. 'You will be taken back across the border and dropped off on a main road. You tell the authorities that the other kid died in childbirth. That I gave you this one out of some misguided sense of sympathy for their betrayal and the death of your wife. You play on their reaction and get yourself a job with one of the big shipping lines in Hong Kong or Singapore. It doesn't matter which. Then you start feeding me information. I want to know about high-value, easily moveable loads — containerised computer chips are ideal. I want to know loading plans and routes, and I want updates on positions in particular areas. All the good shipping lines now have vessels transmitting position information to head office continuously, so you can hook into that and feed it to me. Without the GPS scam I need to be able to attack the right boats in the right places. And you're going to help, Hamnet. You must find me four ships. The faster you provide the targets, the quicker you get your brat back. Fail to reach four targets and you will never see the kid again. Double cross me and it'll die.'

Hamnet turned to him, holding tightly the fragile, precious figure of his son. Not wanting to negotiate, because that would make what was happening real. 'You can't do this,' he murmured, almost to himself.

'I can and I am. You can deal with it or let it die,' retorted Janac.

'But how do I know I can trust you? That you'll give him back?'

'You know nothing. My reassurances mean nothing. And there's nothing either of us can do about that.' The thin lips compressed.

Hamnet shook his head. 'Even if you do, four ships will take too much time. You can't leave him in that stinking hut under the care of some dope-addled child for that long.'

'The sooner you provide the targets, the sooner you get the kid back. As an incentive I'll improve the conditions each time you deliver me a boat satisfactorily. Someone to look after it, then a decent cot and a water supply to keep it clean. A third ship to get it out of the shack and into air conditioning. And finally, after the fourth ship has been raided successfully, it'll be delivered safely to you.' Janac shrugged. 'I can't do more. You've got till the end of June, the start of the typhoon season. Beyond that we can't operate, and I don't think the kid can be expected to survive in there much longer than that either. But I'll ensure it gets through the two-and-a-half months.' He reached into his shirt pocket for the ever-present Lucky Strike and Zippo.

He lit a cigarette quickly and waved over Tosh, who handed Hamnet a large brown envelope. 'That contains everything you need to know. Tosh here will take you across the border and then drop you off. You should probably read and destroy that before you get picked up. That's all. I trust I'll be hearing from you. Take him away, Tosh.' Janac strode back to his Jeep, where General Lee was still sitting quietly in the passenger seat.

Hamnet was bundled into the back of the other vehicle, which took off in a belch of diesel. He struggled to turn, awkward with the baby in his arms, but just caught a last glimpse of the hut where his other son lay crying as they dropped into the valley he had walked up an age before.

Janac and General Lee watched his departure in silence, Janac drawing slowly on his cigarette. Finally Lee said, 'I think this very bad idea. Too many boats out of Hong Kong and Singapore with drug shipment. You cross Hong Kong Triad like this and even I cannot help you any more.'

Janac dragged the cigarette down to the butt with one final pull, then flicked it into the dirt. 'No choices left, General. How the hell else am I going to get the money to pay you?'

Lee shrugged. 'Must be better way.'

Janac grunted. 'Fuck the Triads. I've had enough of those bastards killing my people in Australia.' He turned the key, slammed the Jeep into gear and took off. As the engine noise receded, the dust slowly settled. And the only sound was the faint crying of a lonely child.

Chapter 16

It was the tears of his other son that kept Hamnet preoccupied as the Jeep bumped and banged its way towards the border. They were tears of hunger and pain. And cuddle, hold and protect as he might, Hamnet couldn't stop the dry, piercing howls. The vehicle travelled on, and occasionally off, a sequence of dirt roads and forest tracks, surrounded by trees with barely a glimpse of sky, let alone an open view. Hamnet saw none of this, only the anguished features of his son. Once, Tosh turned and lashed a sentence at him to make the crying stop. Hamnet returned a stare of such intense hatred that even Tosh thought twice about pursuing the matter. He returned in silence to whittling his piece of wood on the occasional smooth sections of road.

The Jeep came to a halt on a patch of open ground, and Tosh turned again. He met Hamnet's glower with a smile. 'Aye, this is where you get off, soldier. Walk straight ahead through the trees and you'll come to a metalled road. You're already in Thailand. Turn right and keep walking and there's a village. From there you're on your own.'

Hamnet nodded slowly and climbed carefully out of the Jeep, the baby cradled in his right arm. There was a soft thud as his backpack landed in the dirt behind him. He turned and picked it up, rolled it awkwardly onto his left shoulder and started to walk away.

'Hey!'

The shout made him turn back, just in time to catch the piece of wood Tosh threw over to him. He looked down; it was a crude carving of a baby.

'Till you get the real one,' said Tosh with a smirk.

The driver revved the engine, slammed it into gear and spun the wheel. Hamnet watched them go, vowing silently that one day he would wipe that smirk away.

With the Jeep's departure, the silence of the jungle descended on Hamnet like a first snowfall, a soft blanket of suffocating peace. He had stuck his head into the open mouth of the tiger, and the tiger had torn out his heart instead. He was free, but trapped. He sat down, crushed to the ground by the weight of experience. By the mass of what lay before him.

A choke and a whine from the baby broke his stupefaction. He laid the tiny child gently on a soft bed of mulch and rummaged in his pack. Nothing appeared to have been touched — he had money, the passport, food and water. He pulled out the water bottle and tore a strip of material from a T-shirt, then set about cleaning the baby, dabbing at him gingerly as though he were a fragile china ornament. The wide blue eyes followed his every move in ominous silence. Hamnet then wrapped him in the remains of the T-shirt, opened a tin of mixed fruit and dribbled the juice off the back of a spoon into his mouth. The eyes brightened, the baby's appetite was quickly satisfied, and sleep followed even faster. It wasn't much, but it was a start.

Hamnet arranged the pack to form a rough bed and lay the baby back down. He used the last of the water to wash some of the dirt off his own face, and changed into the final spare shirt and shorts in the pack. Then he sat down, pulled the envelope from the trouser pocket he had stuffed it into and read the contents. There were coordinates for the geographical area the ships were to travel through, a list of high-value commodities he was to target, and an email address to which he was to send information. Finally, there were a couple of floppy discs that, according to the documentation, held an encryption program for any messages.

He knew he couldn't remember the list of latitudes and longitudes, so he kept that and the discs. The rest he tore into shreds, which he stuffed into an opening under a tree root.

The next thing was to start walking. He repacked the bag, slung it on his back, gingerly picked up the sleeping bundle and threaded his way through the trees until he came to the metalled road. Then, as instructed, he turned right. The village wasn't far, and he didn't attract any attention as he entered. He found a small roadside restaurant and ordered some food. He learned from the waiter that a bus to Chiang Mai was due to leave from right outside the door in a couple of hours. He finished his meal quickly and walked back out into the heat. It was early afternoon, and nothing moved on the dusty road. No mad dogs, just a single Englishman. He walked slowly up and down both sides of the street, and established that there was nowhere he could buy baby clothes, food or milk. He returned to the restaurant to wait out the hot, heavy hour or so that remained.

Against the oppressive silence of the village, the voices of a young American couple at the next table were bright and cheerful. The woman, dark hair falling around bare, tanned shoulders, smiled prettily at Hamnet and the baby. But neither her smile nor her fresh and lavish good looks penetrated the numbness that surrounded Hamnet. Which was unfortunate, because he could have been better prepared for what happened next. The woman finished her drink, stood up and moved the few short steps towards father and son, while her boyfriend looked on with that faint air of disapproval that young men can have for their partners' broodiness.

She frowned, her nose wrinkling when she saw the ripped T-shirt the baby was lying on. 'What's his name?' she asked, a trace of doubt in her voice, gently extending a slim finger towards a patch of bare tummy.

Hamnet had just noticed her presence when the question crashed in. A name? He'd argued with Anna about that. The matter was unresolved — they had been waiting on the children to see what felt right. The woman was looking at him strangely. Not surprising, really— how could he not know the name? He said the first thing that came into his head. 'Ben. I mean Benjamin — I guess it'll be Ben when he gets a bit older.'

Her doubt was more open now, fired by his hesitation. 'How old is he? He's tiny. Doesn't look old enough . . .' She hesitated. 'Doesn't look very old.'

'A month,' said Hamnet, then fell silent.

The woman bit her lip anxiously, unsure of her right to enquire further, but clearly disbelieving, worried about the baby. Hamnet's shoulders were hunched over his drink, his body tight, his demeanour cold. In the end his bearing turned her away.

'Well, nice to meet you,' she said. And after one last tickle, to which the young Benjamin responded with a blank stare, she returned, reluctantly, to her seat.

Hamnet was left pondering the name. If they'd had a girl, 'Anna' would have been the only choice. But he knew Anna had favoured 'Ben', and that was as close to her memory as he could get. He stared at the dozing baby, suddenly conscious of the load he was already placing on those tiny, unformed shoulders. Ben was all he had now. How much pressure did that put on them both? It was another thought in a long list that had to be carefully placed to one side. Let's just get home safely, he told himself. The false passport would get him back into Singapore. But what about Ben? Overland was his best chance — the train to start with, then a long-distance bus. Usually, the only check at the border was the driver presenting a pile of passports to the immigration officer. Rarely did the officer trouble to match passports to faces, or even bodies. Hamnet knew it would take a few dollars to get the driver to ignore Ben, but if that could be done, immigration need never know.

But getting home was only the beginning. He would have to report his return, deal with the authorities, find a job. And then there was Dubre — he had to settle with that bastard before anything else. He felt his heart thump at the thought, saw his knuckles whiten as he dug his nails into his palms. So much anger, so much fear and hate — but right now he had to clear his mind and concentrate on the journey.

The bus was a welcome distraction when it finally crawled up the street and stopped outside the restaurant. The heat shimmered off the square metre or so of orange roof that wasn't covered with baggage. Hamnet, the American couple and two or three locals filed slowly on board, buying their tickets from the driver. Hamnet deliberately took a seat as far away from the couple as possible and settled down, Ben on his lap, to suffer the journey in silence. Which was more than Ben had in mind. Exhaustion had ensured he slept in the heat and quiet of the village, but on the jarring, roaring bus, fractious tiredness kept him awake. Hamnet could feel the tension rise around him as the crying began to make the other passengers edgy. He did his best, but his baby was tired and hot and wanted something Hamnet couldn't even divine, much less provide. As the journey dragged on, the resentment around him grew ever more palpable.

Then he felt a change in the human field, and found himself looking up into the concerned face of the American woman. 'Let me,' she said simply, holding out her arms. Hamnet shuffled along the seat to the window and she sat down beside him. He handed Ben to her and watched anxiously, and to his eyes she did nothing different — more cuddling, more soft talk. But the effect was a transformation. Ben grew silent and finally fell asleep. Hamnet rubbed his tired eyes with his knuckles. He felt so damn useless. And the woman watched him, trying to figure him out, unsure what to do next.

'I'm Jasmine,' she said finally.

Hamnet looked up, and for the first time took note of her face — saw the concern, the innocent friendliness. And then he lied to her. 'Toliver. Michael Toliver. Thanks for your help, Jasmine, I guess I've got a lot to learn.'

'You look exhausted,' she said.

'Yeah,' he replied. 'I just want to get us both home.'

'He'll be a lot easier when you're not both tired.' She smiled uncertainly before continuing. 'Where's home?'

'Singapore.'

She nodded, turning back to the baby. 'Long way.'

'Yeah,' said Phil. It was.

Jasmine stayed beside him for the rest of the journey to Chiang Mai. He just sat and stared at the sleeping baby, desperately aware for the first time of his lack of childcare knowledge. Of the gulf between his responsibilities and his ability to fulfil them. It was terrifying. More frightening than anything he had faced either at sea or on land. This tiny being was his to care for and protect. And he couldn't even stop him crying.

The bus crawled into Chiang Mai in the late afternoon and rolled to a halt in a dusty concrete bus station. Jasmine led the way off, Ben still in her arms. Hamnet followed her, along with the rest of the grateful passengers. She returned the baby to him silently once he'd hoisted his pack on his back, her face serious.

'Thank you,' said Hamnet.

Jasmine smiled tightly. 'Take care of him.'

Hamnet nodded, half turned to walk away, hesitated, then carried on. He felt guilty, but how could he ever explain? He walked to the taxi rank without looking back, Jasmine watching his every step.

The cab took him straight to the Suriwongse Hotel, where it took him only moments to discover Dubre had gone. There was little doubt he had returned to Singapore. And that was where Hamnet must follow.

He took a room for the night, and paid a maid to buy everything he needed for Ben, relieved at least that Dubre had made him keep the money. The maid helped him feed Ben and showed him how to change disposable nappies and prepare baby formula. It was a short lesson in the basics of childcare — not enough for the longer term, but at least once both of them were clean and fed, they slept for a while.

Ben woke Hamnet at six a.m., just minutes before the alarm call was due. It was the last decent sleep either of them would have for forty-eight hours. The journey was a long, painful nightmare: a two-day overland trip to and through Bangkok, then down the length of the Malay Peninsula. It would have been difficult enough with a ten-day old baby if Hamnet had known what he was doing. But he struggled with the feeding. He struggled with the nappies. He struggled to make Ben feel either comfortable or secure. And so the baby cried, for hour after hour, with extraordinary energy, until Hamnet was exhausted — physically, mentally and emotionally.

He managed to pay off the first bus driver, and that got the pair of them through the slack border controls into Malaysia. But Singapore was a different matter, with a different driver, who, after eight hours of constant crying, had had more than enough of Michael and Ben Toliver. And so, two days after leaving Chiang Mai, Hamnet stepped out of the serene cool of the air-conditioned bus into the noise and heat of Johor Bahru, less than a kilometre short of the Malaysian customs and the causeway to the island state of Singapore. He stood, baby in his arms, rucksack at his feet, watching the bus disappear round the bend ahead, with only a belch of diesel fumes for goodbye.

Ben howled, and now Hamnet understood how parents could strike their children. And he had no idea what to do next. Try and bluff his way through? Local buses travelled the causeway regularly. But he'd have to get off and go through both the checkpoints on foot. What would they say about the baby? There was no way he could prove Ben was his; only once back in Singapore would he have any chance of reclaiming his identity. He could call on friends who knew Anna had been pregnant, friends who would help explain his case. Friends like Dubre. He sank onto the backpack at the thought. Helpless at the betrayal, the loss, that had brought him to this. An exhausted, lonely man, so close to but never so far from home.

Chapter 17

Hamnet didn't notice the car pull up beside him. Barely heard, never mind recognised, his name above Ben's yowling. In fact Anthony Bullen almost wound up the window and drove on, Hamnet's response was so mute. But his wife, Margaret, was more sure of herself. She was convinced that this dishevelled man with the baby was the same man, who, with his lovely wife, had rented their apartment from them for the past couple of years. She knew it was Phillip Hamnet, whatever the papers said about his disappearance. She tapped her husband's hand away from the electric window control, the smile lines around her eyes crinkled with concern. And the higher, more urgent pitch of her voice penetrated Ben's noisy expressions of discomfort. Hamnet heard his name and turned.

The faces peered anxiously at him through the open window of the Rover. He struggled with their sudden closeness, their unplaceable familiarity. There was the dry smell of leather, a waft of air-conditioned coolness, kind eyes. He struggled for words, a name.

Margaret was the first to speak. 'Phillip! My God, what's happened? Where's Anna? Where have you been?'

Anthony interrupted. 'Hey, give the man a chance to speak.'

But Hamnet could only stare in silence. Until slowly, gently, a tear rolled down his dusty cheek. Margaret was out of the car in a moment, one arm round his shoulder, the other taking the baby off him. Hamnet's head was bent now; he bit his lip, sucked back a juddering, shaky breath. 'I can't get home. The baby's not on the passport. I don't know what to do any more. Anna's . . . Anna's . . .'

Margaret hadn't been a nurse and the wife of a GP for forty years for nothing. She knew about priorities, and it was very clear to her what the priority was. Anthony swept a nervous hand through his thick silver-grey hair but protested in vain. 'For God's sake, we can't smuggle the baby across the damn border. God knows what they'll do if they catch us.'

'Don't be ridiculous. We've been across that border a thousand times and they never check us. Quite apart from the fact that the poor dear is incapable of even explaining to us what's happened, never mind to some bossy Malaysian official. Heaven knows what a fuss there'll be if we try to do things properly. Now do as I say and help him into the car and find his passport. I'll look after the baby.'

For his part, Anthony Bullen hadn't been married to his wife for forty years without learning that there were times when you simply did as you were told. He helped Hamnet into the back seat, threw the backpack into the boot and rummaged through the side pockets for the passport. He found it, noticed it bore the wrong name alongside the right picture, and sighed. He slammed the boot shut and returned to the driver's seat before discreetly showing the passport to his wife. Margaret was carefully arranging the baby in a mound of loose clothing at her feet. She looked up and sighed too. 'He's obviously in some kind of trouble,' she murmured.

'Mmm,' said Anthony. 'You read . . .?'

'Yes, dear, of course. All the more reason for getting him home and sorting him out. Drive on.'

Anthony smiled, despite himself. He glanced over his shoulder at Hamnet, who had recovered sufficient composure to take in what was happening and now looked him in the eye and said, 'Thank you.'

Anthony nodded and smiled again, avuncularly. 'Just

let us do the talking,' he said. Then he slipped the car into gear and drove on.

The Malaysian border official had just come on duty. He recognised the spotless old Rover as it slowed on its approach. He'd seen it go past on its weekly shopping trip dozens, if not hundreds, of times, and normally he would have waved it straight through. But this week was different. The financial crisis that had gripped his country and the rest of South-east Asia had led to limits being set on the quantity of certain basic foodstuffs, which could be obtained more cheaply in Malaysia than in Singapore, crossing the border. He had orders to check the Singapore shoppers, and held out his hand.

'Damnation!' swore Anthony under his breath, his ruddy freckled face reddening further. 'He wants us to stop.'

'Stay calm, dear,' said his wife as she wound down her window. 'I'm sure it's nothing. We have to give him Phillip's — I mean Michael's — passport anyway.'

Anthony slowed the car and pulled up beside the official, who bent his head down to the nearside window.

'Sorry to delay you, madam, sir. But we have to check people returning to Singapore. The food allowances, you understand,' he said in accented English.

'Of course,' replied Margaret as though expecting to be searched. 'Our friend here is a British visitor, leaving Malaysia.' She proffered the passport of Michael Toliver and turned to her husband. 'The boot, dear.'

But Anthony was already climbing out of his seat, anxious to divert the officer's attention from the interior of the car, particularly from the baby, who, for the moment at least, swaddled invisibly in the bundle of clothes, was silent. He didn't trust the little blighter to stay that way a moment longer.

Hamnet shared Anthony's concern — from his experience it was clear Ben cried all the time. There was no reason why he should behave any differently now. In a slow-motion, underwater way, Hamnet realised he'd be dragging these kind people into his trouble if Ben was discovered.

Margaret was more confident. She hadn't brought up five children, and helped with six grandchildren, without acquiring a certain skill when it came to keeping them quiet. But it didn't come with any guarantees.

The officer followed Anthony round to the boot. Hamnet's eyes tracked them in the rear-view mirror. The engine filled the human silence inside the car, its revs rising and falling as though it shared their nervousness. The Rover shook slightly as the officer pulled open bags in a cursory search. Ben stirred, sniffled. Margaret shut the window. Hamnet closed his eyes and prayed. There was a final lurch as the boot slammed. A couple of seconds later, Anthony climbed back into his seat and handed Margaret the passport. The official was already walking back to the cool of his office.

'One down, one to go,' muttered Anthony as he pulled away and drove onto the causeway. A kilometre ahead was the Singapore immigration and customs checkpoint. Margaret reached down to her feet and gently lifted a piece of clothing. Ben was still sleeping.

Anthony clicked the air conditioning onto full chill. 'If we cool it right down in here, condensation will form on the outside of the windows and it'll be harder to see in.' He looked in the rear-view mirror. 'Phillip, when we get close, try and make yourself inconspicuous without actually hiding. If you get an entry visa, they'll know Michael Toliver has entered Singapore, and if that happens, they'll want to know why he didn't leave. And they'll come to us for an answer.'

It was Margaret who replied. 'We'll just tell them we never saw him again; that he was a friend of one of the

145

children over from England who stayed for a few days and left. Goodness knows they've sent enough people through our house without seeing or hearing of any of them before or since.'

Anthony nodded slowly. His eyes flicked from the road to his wife and up to the mirror again. 'Hmmm, all right. But look, if they don't stop us, we'll just drive through. It'll be simpler in the long run.' He turned to Hamnet briefly. 'That all right with you?'

Hamnet nodded slowly, as if in a dream. 'Yes,' was all he could manage.

The causeway stretched before them to the island state as they drove slowly across it. Grey cloud loomed, and a few drops of rain spattered the windows, adding themselves helpfully to the gathering mist of condensation. Anthony clicked the wipers onto intermittent to clear the windscreen. Ahead, a car had been pulled in. The leather of the back seat creaked as Hamnet slid into a half-lying position. Once again, Anthony glanced in the rear-view mirror, then at his wife.

'Hold up the passports, please. Two will do.'

He eased the car back to fifteen kilometres an hour as they approached the checkpoint. The only immigration officer visible had his head in the window of the stationary car. The Rover slowly rolled up behind it. The officer looked up at the sound of the engine, saw the Singapore plates and recognised the car. Dr Bullen had treated his child for colic only a few weeks before. He glanced at the two figures in the front seats and the proffered passports — and waved them through. Anthony indicated, checked in his mirror, pulled out and passed the parked car before carefully accelerating away.

Margaret was gazing back through the condensation. 'Wasn't that . . .'

'Yes, I think so,' Anthony replied. He gave his wife an anxious smile. 'I don't think I've got the stomach to ever be a smuggler, darling.'

The Bullens didn't live far from the causeway, and the midmorning weekday traffic was light. It was a little under twenty minutes down the expressway to their Bukit Timah home. As they pulled through the gates the bump started Hamnet awake. Ahead of them lay an extensive single-storey home with red tiles and brick walls, neatly settled into a lushly landscaped tropical garden. Margaret sighed with relief and twisted in her seat.

'The first thing is for you to sleep. You'll stay here for a few days so I can look after the baby for you. Anthony will show you Susie's room — it has its own bathroom. Would you like to eat?'

Hamnet shook his head.

'Is there anything else we can do?'

Hamnet stared ahead as his exhausted mind considered the question. 'No,' he said finally, his eyes flicking to Margaret, 'there's nothing else you can do. You've been very kind. But I'd appreciate it if you didn't tell anybody I was here.'

Margaret didn't even hesitate. 'Of course, there's plenty of time for us to talk about that after you've got some rest.'

Phillip nodded his thanks. Anthony pulled the car straight into the garage so they could unload away from prying eyes. Hamnet followed him to a bedroom that had most recently been their youngest daughter's. Susie had been away at university in London for two years, but had never bothered, on her short return visits, to clear the evidence of her teenage presence — cuddly toys and posters of *Take That*. Hamnet barely noticed, collapsing into the big, soft double bed and falling asleep before the air conditioning had even finished warming up to start cooling down. Anthony watched him for a few minutes, gently took his pulse and checked the regularity of his breathing. Satisfied, he left quietly, closing the door behind him.

Hamnet slept for just over twenty-hours. When he woke, the sun was streaming in through chinks in the curtains. The sheets were clean, the bed comfortable, the air cool. He lay for almost an hour, half awake, listening to the birds outside, putting everything in its place. Finally he rose and found a towel, next to the clothes he had been wearing, now cleaned and pressed in a neat pile on an ottoman. His backpack stood untouched at the foot of the bed.

The shower pinned him against the tiled wall, and he stood under the jet for a long while before drying and dressing. He opened the bedroom door and padded softly down a corridor on bare feet. The corridor led into a big square room, open on two sides to the garden, with three ceiling fans gently stirring the air. Margaret sat at a beautifully laid table in the centre of the wooden floor. White linen, toast, orange juice, fresh coffee and silver cutlery were spread before her. She looked up from the *Singapore Telegraph*, peering over the top of the horn-rimmed reading glasses she allowed to slip down her nose.

'How's Ben?' asked Phillip.

Margaret looked a little puzzled.

'My son, I'd like to see him.'

'Oh of course, the baby. I'm so sorry.' She hesitated, took her glasses off and allowed them to drop on their silver chain so they rested against her crisp white blouse. 'Ben, what a lovely name. Ben's just fine. Anthony had a good look at him — he's a little malnourished. But nothing a few injections, vitamins and some decent rest and nutrition can't cure. He's asleep now. Better not to disturb him. He sleeps very lightly and I've just put him down after feeding.' She paused, eyes gently on his. 'And yourself, how do you feel?'

'Much better for the sleep, though still a little muzzy and dazed — and very hungry,' he added, eyeing the table.

Margaret beamed, her face setting happily into its familiar smile. 'Of course, the arman — the maid — is in today. Would you like a cooked breakfast?'

Hamnet nodded and smiled as he sat. 'Very much.'

He ate solidly for almost an hour — two full cooked breakfasts, endless plates of toast and marmalade, countless cups of coffee and glasses of orange juice. As he ate, he slowly told Margaret the story, from start to finish — leaving out only the incident with the fisherman, Dubre's part in the early release of the information about the *Shawould*, and all reference to Ben's twin. She listened carefully, asked the occasional question, and said all the right things when he came to Anna's death. Margaret had been a child in Singapore during the Second World War and had spent much of it under the Japanese in Changi. After that, she had gone to the Korean War as a nurse, where she had met Anthony, then a serving British army doctor. Tragedy and deprivation were two things she had in perspective. For his part, Hamnet was businesslike in the telling. He knew he had to be — there was too much to do to allow the luxury of emotion.

When he had finished, the two of them sat for a long moment in silence. Hamnet washed down the last of the toast with a final splash of lukewarm coffee, then asked, 'So do you have any idea how much longer he could have stayed in that hut before the experience would have had some permanent effect?'

Margaret sat back. 'My goodness, that's a question. Well, every moment he was there he was exposed to goodness knows what dreadful diseases without having any of the normal inoculations. But assuming he didn't catch anything truly life-threatening, the pace of the malnutrition wasn't so bad as to kill him. Over several months, though, it would have seriously stunted his growth.'

'What about his mind? Would it have had any effect on his mental development?'

'Hmm, certainly with no external stimulus his language development would have suffered. But it would have taken years to affect him badly. There have been some extraordinary studies of children who have been severely neglected — locked away in rooms or chained to beds for years before being discovered by the authorities or neighbours. Even such unfortunates retain the ability to learn a language to some extent — although they require a great deal of personal attention and tuition.' She sighed. 'Really, the greatest danger over a period of months or weeks is disease.'

'You sound like an expert.'

'Oh, I was a mother, and a nurse before that. Now I read all the books — it keeps the mind alert. I've always been interested in new ideas and theories. But it's nice to do a little practical work now and again as well.' She leaned forward and patted his arm gently.

Hamnet smiled wanly, running over her words in his mind: disease, months, weeks. He had no time to lose.

They got up from the table and went to look in on Ben, and then Margaret gave him his second lesson in preparing formula and feeding. Finally, inevitably, she asked the hardest question. 'So what will you do now?'

Hamnet looked up from the hungry bundle in his arms. 'The insurance company and accident investigators, and probably the Indonesian police, will all want to talk to me. I have to explain what happened. Then, assuming everything goes smoothly, I have to find another job, a shore job, so I can look after Ben.'

'How long will it take to sort everything out?'

Hamnet shrugged. 'It could take months, years even. In the meantime I could have my master's certificate suspended, but that shouldn't stop me getting an office job.'

Margaret watched father and son benignly for a moment, then said, 'Until you sort things out you're very welcome to stay here rather than go back to the flat. Once you get yourself settled, I'm sure you'll have no problem finding someone to help with Ben during the day. In the meantime, I'd love to help, and that will be much easier if you stay here.'

Hamnet shook his head. 'I don't know that I could do that to you . . .'

'You must. The house is so big and empty now the children are grown up. I'd be grateful for the company.'

Hamnet looked down at the concentrating face of his baby son, well aware that he couldn't afford to turn down the offer. He looked back up, smiling. 'I can't thank you enough.'

'Not at all, my dear.'

There was a short silence before Hamnet asked, 'Why are you doing all this?'

'Oh.' Margaret waved her hand deprecatingly. 'How could we not help?'

Hamnet spent the day with Margaret and Ben, revelling in domestic calm and orderliness, but always aware that the coming night might change that world for ever. At six in the evening he fed Ben and put him to bed in the room next to Margaret and Anthony's, Margaret having decided Hamnet wasn't yet rested enough to be woken in the night and content to attend to Ben herself. The maid had agreed to come in full-time during the day to help with the house.

When Anthony came home, Hamnet told his story again, with the same omissions. The three of them had dinner together, and both the Bullens agreed that Hamnet was free to stay with them for as long as it took to sort things out and find a job. Hamnet declined coffee and excused himself, saying he was tired but that coffee might keep him awake. Margaret nodded understandingly, and Anthony found him some sleeping tablets.

Back in his bedroom, Hamnet put the bottle of white pills on the bedside table with a glass of water, then sat silently in a chair, in the dark, and waited. Slowly the hum of conversation from the end of the corridor grew more sporadic, then died completely. There were the sounds of doors shutting, taps running, the toilet flushing. It was still only ten o'clock. Hamnet waited another half an hour before gently opening the bedroom door and letting himself out. The house was dark and quiet. The screen doors to the dining room had been pulled shut. He quietly opened one end, leaving it ajar for his return, then strode down the drive, turned left and kept walking. It was time to settle things with Dubre.

Chapter 18

It was a short enough walk through an area that was a traditional favourite of the expatriate community. Dubre's house wasn't quite as impressive as the Bullens', but that was a failure of taste and timing rather than wealth. It was a brand-new, five-bedroom pile that owed a lot to the kind of expensive architecture that dots Florida and California — columns, shutters and stucco walls in bright, fairytale-castle pastels. Hamnet eyed it with a new malevolence as he stalked up the path and rang the doorbell. Violent crime wasn't a problem of any significance in Singapore, and while the owners of such houses in America wouldn't have dreamed of opening their doors to an unknown visitor at that hour, Dubre had no such reservations.

That was a mistake.

The instant it was off the latch, Hamnet snapped the door open with a standing kick. The handle was torn from Dubre's hand as the leading edge of the door smashed into the inside of his elbow. He spun half a revolution under the impact, and had just acknowledged the blinding stab of pain up his arm with a scream when Hamnet's shoulder hit him in the chest. Totally unprepared for this assault, Dubre went down hard, flat on his back. The blow knocked the wind out of him, and as he snatched for breath, Hamnet's hands closed around his throat. Not a word had been spoken. Dubre certainly wanted to speak, but he wasn't in a position to get anything through his windpipe. And if he'd had a choice it would have been air in rather than words out. Hamnet hadn't said anything because he didn't need to. He watched first recognition, then surprise, swiftly followed by understanding and fear, travel across Dubre's contorted features. Dubre realised why he was there, why this was happening.

Hamnet tightened his grip. He knew exactly what the inability to draw breath did to the majority of people. It induced panic. Many died because of that panic, unable to see the route to their next lungful of air. Dubre was such a man. If he had kept his head, with his greater weight and strength he could have pushed his legs against the floor and rolled Hamnet off him. But he didn't; instead, his shoes thrashed ineffectively at his expensive tiles while his hands clawed desperately for a grip on Hamnet's bare forearms. It wasn't enough, and as Dubre's face reddened and his eyes bulged, Hamnet was able to strengthen his hold. The thrashing slowed, weakened and stopped. The chubby red features were mottled with blue, the wild eyes deadened and stilled.

Then something snapped inside Hamnet, and he let go. For Dubre it was probably the very last instant he could have done so to any effect. While Hamnet couldn't finish what he had started, equally he wasn't about to resuscitate the man he blamed for his wife's death. But there was just enough life left in Dubre's body to sustain a reflex to breathe. He sucked back the lungful of air he had needed since his back had hit the floor, and it flooded into his bloodstream and through his body. Another and another — great heaving lungfuls pumped through the fatty tissue and the overstressed organs. He lay like a beached whale, panting, staring blankly at his rococo ceiling. His stunned mind struggled to come to terms with a man who had returned from the dead only to visit the same fate on his own self.

Hamnet sat back against the wall and watched sullenly as the life flowed back into the man he had come so close to killing. When Dubre had recovered sufficiently, he rolled onto his side and slowly pushed himself to his feet. Still wordlessly, he staggered down the hall and through the first door on the left. In less than a minute he returned, and now he was holding a revolver — an old Browning that looked as if it had been left behind by the British army at the end of the Second World War. Hamnet eyed him cynically before finally saying, 'Why don't you? You killed Anna. Finish the job, you bastard. Or haven't you got the guts to do it personally?'

Dubre cleared his throat with an evil wheeze and a coughing fit before finally saying, 'I have no wish to harm you, Phillip.' He waggled the revolver. 'This is just in case you change your mind.' As he spoke, he slumped into a sitting position on the third stair from the bottom. Then he, too, leaned heavily against the wall. He looked at Hamnet for several seconds with a pained and bewildered expression, before finally asking, 'How in God's name did you get back here?'

Hamnet got up and turned to the open door.

Dubre watched him, the revolver barrel lodged on his knee and pointing at Hamnet's stomach. 'Where are you going?' he said, suspiciously.

'To bed,' said Hamnet.

'Phillip, please, stop. There will be lots of people who want to talk to you. You can't just disappear.'

Hamnet turned to face him, shoulders sagging, a thousand years of living etched on his face. 'You know where to find me, Dubre.' And with that, he stepped outside and slammed the door behind him.

Hamnet was woken by a knock the following morning. He stirred slowly and saw Margaret Bullen's head appear round the bedroom door.

'I wondered if you'd like breakfast, or if we should clear it away.'

155

Hamnet frowned drowsily, glancing around for his watch. 'What time is it?'

'Just after eleven.'

His frown deepened. 'You shouldn't have let me sleep that late. I'll be there in a minute.'

'Jolly good. I'll put some fresh coffee on.' And the door clicked shut.

Hamnet showered and dressed quickly, arriving at the table at the same time as the coffee. He exchanged greetings with Margaret and she updated him on Ben's morning, which had been dominated by food and sleep. Her report was detailed and careful, and full of further positive indications that Ben hadn't suffered materially for his ordeal. As Hamnet launched into breakfast, he explained that he ought to go to the flat to pick up some papers and clothes and to start dealing with Anna's things. Would Margaret be all right with Ben, and did she have a spare key? Hamnet knew the answers to both questions before he asked them, and half an hour later Margaret pulled the Rover up outside the building, just off Holland Road. Hamnet looked lugubriously out of the window as the car stopped. He had been dreading this moment.

'Would you mind if I went up alone?' he asked.

'Of course not. Should I wait?'

'No, I think I might be a while.'

'Well, call me if you need me, dear. I can come and get you any time.'

Hamnet managed a weak smile. 'Thanks.'

Anna had hated the lift, so Hamnet took it, avoiding her presence on the stairs. It was a temporary respite. He emerged onto the bare concrete landing and stopped outside their front door. He leant forward gently until his forehead rested lightly just below the plastic number plate. He tried to picture the interior of the flat, to prepare himself for the avalanche of memory, the ambush of sadness, that awaited him. But there was no way to make it any easier, no way to put it off any longer. He suddenly wished that he had brought Margaret with him after all.

He unlocked the door. The tears were coming and he wanted to do his grieving inside. He slipped into the apartment as if sliding into some dark crevasse. In the blackness, despair over a lost future was fuelled by flashes of light, of happy memory. His actions became automatic. A life, boxed and filed — just a few things picked out for her parents.

The phone startled him. He watched its barely discernible vibration with deep suspicion before remembering. He picked it up.

'Phillip?' It was Dubre.

'You can come over,' said Hamnet. 'One thing first. Have you spoken to Anna's parents, or my mother?'

'Ah, yes, three or four days ago,' Dubre replied.

'OK.' Hamnet's voice stayed restrained. 'When will you be here?'

'Ten minutes, if that's all right.'

'Give me half an hour.'

It was early morning in Brittany, where Anna's parents —her mother was French, her father English — ran a yacht marina. They were astonished and delighted to hear from their son-in-law, presumed dead, and utterly distraught that he hadn't brought Anna back with him. The phone call to his own mother was only slightly less painful. She and Anna had become close friends after the death of his father in a skiing accident at Thredbo six years previously. It was then that his mother had moved back to England, to Cumbria, to the family home. But somehow the trauma of others, their readiness to lean on him, made him stronger. He promised to call back soon, they would organise travel plans, there would be a memorial service.

157

Hamnet had just cradled the phone the second time when there was a knock at the door. Dubre entered quickly at Hamnet's call, then slowed. It clearly hadn't occurred to him before he arrived that this was the place where he would most fully confront Anna's death and his part in it. The realisation hit him as he walked through the door and grew as he paced into the lounge. He sat heavily in the chair Hamnet indicated.

Hamnet let him roast — he had brought him there for that very reason. On the walls were shots of Anna winning the Route de Rhum, and the pair of them at the presentation of his Légion d'Honneur in Paris, awarded for her rescue. In front of Dubre sat three boxes of her clothes and papers, her computer on top. Beside him were books she had written, magazine covers she had graced. All around were reminders of her missing presence. The flat was filled with her energy, her ambition and her life. Now it was Dubre's turn to struggle with his emotions.

'Christ, I'm so sorry, Phillip. If I'd thought for one second that either one of you would come out of there alive, I'd have held on.' He blew his nose a couple of times on a large white monogrammed handkerchief, wiped his eyes, and asked, 'Can you talk about it?'

Hamnet nodded. 'He killed her just after you sent out the Navtex warning. I think it was probably quick. He doesn't seem to have taken any pleasure in it, perhaps he even quite liked her.'

'Oh my God.' Dubre looked down at his feet. 'Everybody liked her, Phillip, everybody did,' he mumbled.

Hamnet nodded again, mind rigidly focused on what he had to say, not how he felt. 'Before she died, she gave birth to a baby boy, who's called Benjamin. He's being looked after by Dr and Mrs Bullen, who own this place, at their home in Bukit Timah.' Hamnet continued over Dubre's gasp of surprise. 'That's where I'll be staying for a while. Clearly I have a responsibility to the authorities to report the full story of what happened aboard the *Shawould*, and up to my arrival back here. I'm sure they will want to investigate the matter in some detail. I am offering myself to you for that purpose, and I'd be grateful for your assistance in handling it properly.'

Dubre's face cleared. Relieved to be talking business, he became more assured in his tone. 'Of course, I don't see how any blame can be attached to you. Nevertheless, I'm sure you're correct, and several authorities will want some kind of report on the matter. Just say the word and we'll begin.'

'I think tomorrow morning would be as good a time as any,' replied Hamnet. He reached for a pen and paper from the nearby bureau. 'This is the address and phone number at the Bullens. You can reach me there whenever you need to.' He handed the piece of paper to Dubre. 'Obviously, now I have a son to bring up, I can't return to sea, even if I hold onto my master's ticket. I need a shore job, Dubre, perhaps on the operations side. Can you help?'

'Absolutely. Of course, no question.'

'Good.'

The two men fell into silence. Dubre studied the piece of paper he had been given, his feet fidgeting. Hamnet watched him. Would curiosity win out over discomfort? It did. 'So, Phillip, can you tell me what happened up there?'

'It's simple enough. He let me go. We had an understanding, my side of that was broken, Anna paid the price. There was no more to be gained by killing me or my son.'

'My God.' Dubre flinched as though he had been struck. He stood quickly, eyes cast down. He patted the missing hair anxiously. 'I'll leave you, Phillip. I'm sure you have things to do. Saying sorry isn't much help, I know. But I

159

want you to know that I am desperately sorry. I also realise that it isn't a comfort now, but what happened may well have saved the lives of other seamen — other sons, brothers and husbands. I'll do everything I can to help you, Phillip.' He hesitated, glanced up briefly. 'Will there be a funeral?'

Hamnet shook his head. 'A memorial service. There's no . . . body.'

'No, of course. I . . . I'll go.'

Dubre let himself out, as he had many times before in such different circumstances. Hamnet watched him leave, rolling the plastic pen between thumb and fingers. Other husbands, other sons. The pen snapped.

Chapter 19

Hamnet watched a teardrop of condensation trickle down the side of the glass — gathering pace, pausing for a moment when gripped by some confluence of surface tension and friction, then shooting forward again as gravity regained control. He lifted the glass and caught the trail of water with his tongue just as it rolled off the bottom. Then he sipped slowly at the Pimms, ice clinking under his nose as he stepped from the lounge onto the patio. The sun was sighing into the arms of the Bullens' garden, cicada's serenading its approaching departure. Hamnet sat heavily in the nearest of the soft chairs. There were footfalls behind him and he looked up. It was Anthony.

'You're back early,' said Phillip.

'The sick of Singapore have, for some unknown reason, been overtaken with a sudden rush of good health. I'm sure things will be back to normal tomorrow.' His smile lifted the lines and creased the freckles around his hazel eyes. He pulled up a chair beside Hamnet's and set a freshly foaming beer on the table between them. Anthony had changed his tie for his favourite cravat, and with the mane of silver-grey hair down past his collar, he looked more like an ageing jazz musician than a respectable family doctor.

'Why do you work so hard?' asked Hamnet. 'I can't believe you need to.'

'Addicted to it, I suppose,' replied Anthony, then changed the subject. 'So, young Phil, how's it all going with you then?'

'Oh, another day, another meeting.'

Anthony grunted. 'Indeed. Now tell me about all that. I

catch bits of it, but where do we stand at the moment?'

Hamnet smiled with little humour. 'We stand in the middle of a god-awful mess.' He rubbed his cheek with a hand damp from the glass. 'The *Shawould* was a Liberian-registered vessel, owned by a British-based but offshore-registered company, with a British master and American chief mate. We were attacked in Indonesian waters by an American-led and Burmese-based gang of multinational pirates. And strictly speaking, because it didn't happen in international waters, it was armed robbery rather than piracy.' Hamnet shook his head, picked up the Pimms and took another sip.

'Quite a collection of interested parties,' murmured Anthony.

'Yes. And, inevitably, there's not even the most basic coordination between them. I must have answered the same questions with the same answers a hundred times.' He stopped, and stared unseeing towards the sunset.

Anthony watched the other man's thoughts stall, as he knew they must every time he went through this. None of it was helping him forget, never mind forgive. He shouldn't have raised the topic. Anthony struggled for a question that would move Hamnet along. But it was Hamnet himself who broke the impasse. 'Although,' he said finally, 'four weeks into the judicial process, we are making some progress. The Singaporean government is prepared to ignore my re-entering the country on a false passport with Ben, provided I register his presence and apply for his British citizenship — or are we subjects? Anyway, it's meant a whole pile of paperwork and a lot of visits to the British consulate. Still, it had to be done, and at least it's cleared up the concern about being allowed to stay here.'

'That's all to the good. You do want to stay in Singapore?' said Anthony.

162

'Oh, definitely.'

Silence fell on the two men again. The garden glowed red with the last of the sun as the shadows thrown by the house lights behind them strengthened. They both considered the next question, which neither wanted to voice.

It was Anthony who found an alternative. 'Anyone else come to any kind of a decision?' he asked.

Hamnet nodded, then hesitated, almost reluctant to move on. 'The flag state of the *Shawould*, Liberia. No surprise how eager they were to wash their hands of the affair. As far as they are concerned, the ship operated according to all international conventions and standards to which Liberia is a signatory — quote, unquote — and that's that.'

'That's good, isn't it?' asked Anthony.

'Yeah, sure, for me. But you'd rather they showed a bit more interest, really, from a maritime-safety point of view.'

'What about Indonesia?'

Hamnet laughed, short and harsh. 'Oh, they're quite clear that armed robbery and murder have taken place in their territorial waters. Equally clear is that they aren't that fussed about it.'

'I suppose realpolitik would argue that they have other things to deal with. The collapse of the rupiah, the IMF's austerity measures — the people are restless.'

'Not to say rioting in the streets,' added Hamnet. 'I know. They're not concerned with the murder of a few foreign nationals on a foreign-flagged ship within their waters. Particularly since the majority of those nationals were Philippine. And as the Philippine government have as many or more problems with their economy as Indonesia, they're far too busy to complain about the inactivity. A done deal.'

'What about . . .?' Bullen hesitated. 'The US? You said there was an American aboard. Surely they will act.'

'Yes, Richardson. He was the chief mate,' said Hamnet.

163

'There's no doubt that the Americans are not happy. But the role of another American national in the murders — one they've been chasing for years — leaves them in no position to put any pressure on the Indonesians. And Richardson apparently has no surviving family in the States, so there's no one to discomfort any senators. The result is that the whole thing has been swept under a carpet of finely woven Indonesian red tape.'

Anthony sat upright, swept his right hand through his hair, then reached for his beer. 'That's dreadful. I'm a long way from being an eye-for-an-eye merchant, but even so, that these people can get away scot-free is appalling.'

Hamnet nodded while reflecting that there were also advantages. The death of the fisherman was going the same way. Dubre had let it be known that the boat had been found some miles from the original incident, with the tiller tied off. At the same time he had also told Hamnet that the authorities had elected to ignore the family's original account of the incident. It was easier to put the whole thing down to a fishing accident — with the boat on 'autopilot', the fisherman had slipped, been knocked unconscious, fallen overboard and drowned while his boat steamed off without him. It was a convenient enough fiction with which to close the file and forget the whole thing. Slack Indonesian justice cut both ways, and neither helped his mental state. But he could hardly tell that to Anthony.

'So,' said Anthony into the gathering darkness, 'does anyone care?'

'The Brits. Everybody else takes a statement and issues a press release while the Department of Transport decides the bloody thing needs a full inquiry to see if I can keep my master's ticket.'

'But surely they can't find you at fault in an attack like this? It's the merchant navy, not the Royal Navy.'

Hamnet smiled weakly. 'I'll point that out to them. And fortunately there are a lot of powerful people who want the findings to back my story. The insurance company needs to establish that it doesn't have to pay anybody anything. For that they need the endorsement of my story by the DoT. That will then get charges for fraud brought against the owner. They know that he'll never stand trial — the offices of the company that owned the *Shawould* are empty, and have been since the warning went out about the differential GPS. They'll never find him. But that's not the point. Once the charges have been brought, the insurance company is legally off the payment hook.'

'So you've nothing to worry about, then, my friend. The powers-that-be are working for you.'

'But if the DoT finds I'm culpable, the only conclusion is that my story's fiction. I'll be the next one the insurance company will try to use to wriggle out of having to pay.'

'I don't know anything about maritime law, Phil, but I'd have thought that was pretty unlikely.'

Hamnet let it go — Anthony was probably right. He lapsed into another uncomfortable silence, which Anthony quickly broke. 'So that's why we see a lot of Dubre?'

'Yep. He's everywhere, checking, double-checking, covering and back-tracking. On the phone three or four times a day, making sure I haven't missed any appointments. Or keeping me up with the gossip from the port and city.'

'Do you trust him?'

The question came from nowhere. Hamnet looked up sharply. He could see the moustache of foam from Anthony's last mouthful of beer, grey in the gloom. But the rest of his expression was lost in shadow. With the passage of time and regular contact, Hamnet's boiling hatred for Dubre had subsided first to a simmer and then a quiet steaming. He knew that without Dubre's help he wouldn't have had a chance in the judicial labyrinth.

'At the moment our interests are the same. If the DoT endorses my story, it paves the way for nonpayment of the insurance — and Dubre has a substantial financial incentive to that end. The value of the *Shawould* and its cargo must be well into tens of millions of US dollars. So I have no reason to distrust him. Why do you ask?'

The fading moustache nodded a couple of times. 'Hmmm. It's just that, with all the media interest, I sometimes wonder. When you see the material they have — it must have come from inside, surely?'

Hamnet stared into the now black but still noisily chirping garden. 'It wouldn't surprise me, although I hadn't thought about it before. Initially a lot of the pressure for the inquiry was because of the media interest. Dubre wanted the inquiry, so it would have paid him to fuel the media frenzy. But having got what he wanted, he doesn't have a motive for continuing to feed them.'

Anthony laughed. 'So I can blame him for the trampling of Margaret's prize roses?'

'You can blame him for the sins of the earth as far as I'm concerned,' replied Hamnet. But he was all too conscious of his part in what Margaret and Anthony had been through — the full door-stepping experience, cameramen in the bushes, flashbulbs going off through the windows. At least until Anthony had had a quiet word with some contacts in the government. 'But it could have been worse,' he continued. 'In England they're all over your roses and there's precious little you can do about it. It's been a lot easier in Singapore.'

And here we are again, reflected Hamnet — at the question that needed to be asked. Things had to move on — it was time. In fact he was running out of time. He knew he had been hiding from it for far too long. 'The sublet on the flat must be almost up,' he said.

Anthony shifted uncomfortably. 'Ah, yes, I've been meaning to talk to you about that. Kind of putting it off, hoping that something would turn up. I've had a look around for someone else to take it on for a bit longer, but there's no one. Plenty of people for six months or more, but . . .'

'No, it's OK. I'm ready to move back in.'

'It's no problem to leave it empty. Forget the rent . . .'

'I've had some news on the money front,' said Hamnet. 'Anna had a life insurance policy I didn't know about. It will be a while before they pay, as there's no direct proof of her death.' He paused, still hating to say it. 'There's no body. But the bank has agreed to lend against it in the meantime.'

'You don't want to waste that money by living on it. You'll need it for Ben later on — schools, that kind of thing,' replied Anthony.

'I don't have to. Dubre has found me a job, working in the technical department at Konsan Shipping.'

'That's marvellous,' Anthony beamed.

'The marine superintendent is in the head office back in Seoul, but his man here in Singapore is leaving. He does all the local stuff for Konsan's boats — kind of checks them in when they arrive. I've dealt with all that on the other side for years. Now this guy has been promoted up to head office and he'll be out of here in three months. They want me now, on a trial basis. They're a little worried about me losing my master's ticket. Hard to deal with other skippers when you're a failed one.'

'Surely that will be fine.'

'I hope so.' Hamnet swilled the last of the Pimms and ice around his glass. Unwilling to accept the Bullens' offer to overlook the rent, Hamnet had suggested the flat be temporarily relet, and a visiting doctor doing a locum at another practice had taken it for a month. This had saved Hamnet a lot of money and kept his conscience clear. A few things — clothes, papers, some books and Anna's computer — were either in the Bullens' garage or in Susie's bedroom. The respite had been valuable in other ways. Margaret was fantastically good with Ben, and Hamnet himself was learning fast. The helplessness that had gutted him at the border four weeks earlier hardly seemed possible. But every visible sign of progress on Ben's part was a reminder of his twin and the squalid conditions in which he still lay.

A frightful decision would soon have to be made. Thirteen people had died as a result of his failed attempt to save Anna. While he could blame Dubre for precipitating the final act, he couldn't deny that the chance he had taken with thirteen lives in the hope of saving one was difficult to justify. But the loss of his beautiful, intelligent, brave and loving wife was the single thing that completely dominated his life. He missed her more than he could bear, and the pain persuaded him he had done the right thing.

The thirteen dead didn't weigh on his heart anywhere near as heavily as Anna's absence. Indeed, if he could have wound back the clock and handed Dubre an empty envelope, he would have done so — even if that had meant another thirteen dead. That was how he felt. But he also knew that this was wrong. The conflict and the approaching decision regarding his second son were slowly tearing him apart.

Hamnet had been hiding from it, here in the Bullens' house. While there had been no opportunity to betray another ship, no decision had had to be made. Now that respite was nearly over. He must move back into the flat and take the job to support it. And the operations department at Konsan Shipping would surely give him the opportunity to deliver what Janac wanted. The question was whether or not he was prepared to take it.

He stood, slugged back the last of the Pimms and chewed on the remaining ice cube. 'I start on Monday,' he said. 'In the meantime, I promised I'd help with dinner.'

Chapter 20

It was eight o'clock in the morning when, three days later, Hamnet got a lift with Anthony Bullen to the Mass Rapid Transport railway station. The underground train carried him into the city, to Raffles Place, where he mingled with the throng of impatient commuters. He clipped across the beige marble to the spotless escalator, which glided slowly upwards, stepped out into the sunshine and hesitated. The lawned square was already bustling with people in pressed shirts and elegant skirts. The mirror-finished walls loomed in on him. This was not his world — no space, no horizon.

Konsan Shipping's offices were only a hundred metres away, in a squat concrete building in a far corner of the square. But the ground floor and basement were a maze of shops and food halls, and it took him ten minutes to find an elevator that went somewhere other than the car park. When he had finally succeeded, it bore him swiftly to the tenth floor, where he had been told to ask for Toby. The lift doors opened, and he stepped out into the foyer. An empty room, no receptionist — just four labelled doors, a balding grey carpet and a faded picture of a container ship. He picked the door with the legend 'Konsan Shipping Marine Division' and knocked.

He knocked again, and this time he was fairly sure he heard a reply, so he tried the door. It opened onto a scene of typical office bustle, from among which only a couple of heads looked up. There were ten desks sited erratically round a large, open room. Each desk had a thick skin of paper, through which rose a carbuncular computer screen. There were five side doors, and every inch of space along the walls between them was taken up by ranks of filing cabinets.

'Good morning. Can I help you?' The voice, with its lilting Chinese accent, belonged to a fragile, tired-looking woman at a desk almost behind the door he had come through. Her smooth, unlined face was betrayed by her greying hair, pulled back into a tight, severe bun. She blinked at him through wire-rimmed glasses that magnified the dark rings under her eyes.

'My name's Phillip Hamnet. I've an appointment with Toby.'

A look of concern flickered across the woman's face, though whether for him or about him Hamnet couldn't tell. Then she nodded and stood. She barely reached up to his chest. 'Just a moment,' she said.

She walked through the nearest open door, to emerge in short order pursued by a man who almost leapt out of the office behind her. He beamed at Hamnet with a pure white smile, then shook his hand energetically and introduced himself as Toby. He was already moving back towards his office as he completed the formality.

'This'll be your desk for the next three months.' He tapped a grey Formica top in passing, heaped with folders and books. 'Joan,' — he waved at the bespectacled woman, who had sat back down — 'would you clear the decks here for Phil. May I call you Phil? He's going to be understudying me until I go, then he'll take over. Joan's my assistant — she'll be yours. Ask her anything. Been here forever. Knows more than I do.' He re-entered his office ahead of Hamnet, his jet-black hair jerking with the delivery of each bullet of a sentence.

Hamnet had a brief opportunity to nod acknowledgement to Joan before following Toby into his office, where the door clicked shut after him. Behind the ruthlessly tidy desk was a window, through which Hamnet could see the

171

harbour and some of the hundred ships or more that lay at anchor, awaiting charter or loading.

Toby was still speaking. 'Far as possible, Phil, I think you should just follow me around for the first week — see the kind of thing that's going on. Then while I'm in the office there's a ton of documentation on how we do things here at Konsan.' He lifted a pile of books off his desk, rested them across a belly that demanded much of his shirt buttons, carried them over and dumped them in Hamnet's arms. He flashed the white smile again, his soft brown eyes twinkling at the expression on Hamnet's face. Then he was off again, barely pausing between breathless sentences. 'Which should give you plenty to do while I'm in here shuffling paper. You got any questions, ask Joan, and if she can't help I'm sure I can. Then after a couple of weeks I can start offloading some work onto you, and in three months' time I'll be out there with my feet up while you rush around. I got to go meet a boat half an hour ago but I thought Joan could show you round the office this morning and introduce you to people. OK?' The question was purely rhetorical. Toby had the door back open and was ushering Hamnet out before he'd had the opportunity even to nod. With a battered leather briefcase in one hand, he completed the conversation with 'I'm on my mobile' in Joan's general direction and whirled out of the office.

Hamnet watched him go with the same sinking feeling that had etched itself on his face at first sight of the reading he had to do. He dropped the books heavily onto the desk that Joan was clearing.

'Pleased to meet you, Mr Hamnet,' she said.

Hamnet looked through the lenses into friendly eyes and smiled in return. 'You too. But please call me Phil.'

'He's quite frantic, isn't he? I'm sure you'll get used to it — everybody else has. Would you like a cup of coffee?

172

Then I'll get you settled in.'

The next three hours proceeded a little more at Hamnet's pace. Joan introduced him to the people in the Marine Division, then took him through the other three foyer doors in turn and outlined the activities of each department. By lunchtime his head was whirling with names, titles and faces. He sorted through it all over a bowl of noodles in a sterile cafe in one of the basement food halls. Letting his brain make the connections and sort out the hierarchies. Figuring out where he would fit into the scheme of things, the people he would need, and those who, in turn, would need him. He was still preoccupied with it all when he headed back up towards the office.

'Hello.' The voice was close and he looked up automatically, to find that a strikingly attractive woman was apparently talking to him. Surprised, and feeling foolish, he glanced behind to check, but could see no one else that the greeting could have been directed at. He turned back and took in the dark hair, tied in a loose bunch that flopped onto the shoulders of a pale yellow T-shirt, which was tucked into a short, wrap-around batik skirt. The woman's nose wrinkled prettily as she frowned, and it was this expression that chimed with a distant memory. But she was uncertain of herself now. 'Jasmine. On the bus to Chiang Mai?' she said in an American accent.

Hamnet hesitated for a moment, then said, 'Oh God, I'm sorry. Of course. I've just started a new job — my head's spinning. I never really thanked you properly for your help with Ben.'

'Not at all. I thought the other passengers might lynch you if I didn't do something. How is he?'

'He's great. Really great.'

'Good.' She smiled with gentle relief.

The dark complexion, the slant of the eyes — there was

some Asiatic blood in her, thought Hamnet. Set against this, the Arctic blue of those same eyes was startling. People bustled around them, heightening the sense of hesitation between them. Hamnet managed to fill the gap. 'So are you in Singapore for long?'

'I hope so. Trying to find some work, actually. But it's hard — no work permit,' she added conspiratorially.

Hamnet nodded. 'They're very strict here. I guess your boyfriend has the same problem?'

'Lane?' She frowned. 'He's gone home. He ran out of money and wasn't really enjoying it.'

'You weren't together?'

'Kind of — not really. It didn't work out.' Jasmine shrugged with an American frankness. 'But I have a few dollars left and thought maybe I could pick up some casual work. Enough to get to Indonesia — Bali — then perhaps across to Australia. I'm sure I could work there easily.'

Hamnet nodded, struggling for something further to say, still a little off balance.

'Well, nice to see you,' said Jasmine, starting to turn away.

'Look,' Hamnet jumped in, before hesitating again. Then more slowly, 'Come and have dinner tonight. It's the least I can do after your help. I'm staying with some friends at the moment — I'm sure they'd be delighted to have company.'

'That's very kind of you. I'd like that.' Jasmine smiled with discomforting warmth.

'OK. Maybe if you could get to Bukit Timah MRT station? I don't have a car.'

'Of course, that's easy.'

'Good, I'll meet you there. Seven o'clock?'

'I'm looking forward to it.'

Hamnet watched her turn on her heel and walk away, still smiling. She left a trail of turning heads in her wake.

He rubbed a hand against his cheek and sighed.

Joan greeted him back at the office with a resigned smile. 'I'm afraid Toby's been held up at the docks — something about a ship disappearing. He won't be back this afternoon. He suggested that maybe you could do a little reading?'

Hamnet nodded, with a half-grimace, half-smile. 'I'll do my best.'

Two hours later Joan looked up from her monitor to find him staring blankly into space. She saved the letter she was writing and stood up. 'Coffee?' she asked.

'I'd love one.'

When she returned, she pulled up a chair beside him and said, 'It might break things up a little if I spent an hour giving you some idea of what the computer system can do. There's a lot of detail to learn, but perhaps we could just look at the overall facility. Then the literature might make a bit more sense.' She nodded at the piles of books and loose-leaf binders on his desk. Relief might as well have been stamped across Hamnet's forehead in block capitals.

'I'll log in as me for now. I've asked the system administrator to get you a user account and password, but it'll probably take a week — he's not very efficient.'

Her tone left Hamnet in no doubt that inefficiency was only just below devil worship in Joan's personal morality. He watched carefully as the computer connected and her fingers glided lightly across the keyboard. Too quickly all he caught of the password was that it finished with something from the top row, over on the right. Not much help.

For the next hour, Joan guided him through first the Konsan computer system, then the Port of Singapore Authority's PortNet facility. He was staggered by how much the machine knew and what it could control. The details of every ship that came into and out of the port — routes, arrivals, cargo plans — were available. Every container in transit, whether arriving and departing by sea or land, was tagged with a bar code. Every crane that picked a container up logged the movement using that code. Hamnet could track any chosen container all the way to its final position aboard a ship. And the ships in the Konsan Line were fitted with a Satcom C system with integral GPS. This reported position, speed and course automatically, every six hours, via the satellite communications network. More frequent updates could be obtained by sending a message to the Satcom C from his own desk. The information came back almost instantly. It took his breath away, how easy it would be to do Janac's bidding. The decision was truly upon him. Right here was everything he needed to get his son back. Except a password and a little practice on the terminal.

The door crashed open, and all fifteen occupants of the room looked up. 'Shit, sorry,' muttered Toby to the staring personnel as he bustled towards his office. 'Joan,' he called over his shoulder as he kicked the door open in front of him.

'I guess I'd better go,' said Joan.

Phil returned to the computer and the books with renewed interest. It was six thirty when he suddenly realised that not only would he be late meeting Jasmine, but that he hadn't warned Margaret about the extra place required at dinner. Joan was still in with Toby, so he logged out of the system and phoned. Margaret was unfazed by having an extra mouth to feed. Hamnet retraced his steps of that morning, running, and hopped on a train, impatient with every stop, with passengers who wouldn't get on or off quickly. He was hugely relieved when he got to Bukit Timah to find Jasmine still waiting outside the station. She had changed into a simple floral-print dress and was leaning lightly against the timetable at a bus stop.

He hurried up to her but before he could speak she said,

'I didn't know how formal it was. I hope this is OK? It's my going-through-border-controls dress.' She smiled and spread her arms to show it off. The dress returned the compliment by showing off her athletic figure.

'It's . . . perfect,' said Phil. 'I'm sorry I'm late. First day at work— I didn't like to be the first to leave.'

'Only a few minutes.' She stepped in beside him and they made their way to the house down a quiet, tree-lined avenue. Hamnet made a couple of desultory efforts at small talk while struggling with how to break down the lies he had previously told her. Eventually, after a particularly painful silence, and just before they arrived at the Bullens', he pulled up. 'I'm afraid I've got a confession to make,' he said.

Jasmine looked at him anxiously, saying nothing.

He drew a deep breath, then went on quickly. 'What I told you in Thailand wasn't true. My name's Phil Hamnet, I'm a merchant seaman, and my wife, Anna — Ben's mother — was killed by a pirate gang that attacked my ship about seven weeks ago. It's a long story but I was escaping from them when we first met. When I got back here, the Bullens, where we're going now, took me in.'

'Your wife — I'm so sorry.' Jasmine bit her lip, eyes lowered. 'I've got a confession to make as well.' A hand brushed a strand of hair from her face as she looked back up at him. 'I read about you in the papers. Then when I saw you in Raffles Place I was curious. So I already knew that what you told me was, umm . . .'

'A lie. Yes, I'm sorry. I wasn't able to trust anyone at that point. Fresh start?' Hamnet held out his hand and she took it, smiling.

'It's already begun.'

'Good.'

The smell of Chinese cooking was drifting through the

house when they arrived. Ben was on his way to bed, and Jasmine cooed and ah'd in all the right ways. Margaret had cooked a spicy meal of chicken and rice, throughout which she gently probed the visitor. If she thought it at all odd that Hamnet should be bringing back attractive young women for dinner, it didn't show. By the end of the meal, Hamnet knew that Jasmine was twenty-seven and had been born and brought up in northern California, which was where her father still worked in the computer industry. She had completed a postgraduate degree in fine arts the previous summer at the University of California, in San Diego. After waitressing through the fall to save some money, she had left with Lane on a tour of Asia. Her funds were now almost gone, and if she didn't find a job in the next week or so, she would be forced to return home.

'And what will you do there?' asked Hamnet.

Jasmine sipped at her red wine and settled her blue eyes on him, over the rim of the glass. 'I'm not sure. I'd like to do something with my art, but it's not at all clear how to make a living from that.' She smiled ruefully. 'I wanted to stay away until I'd figured it out, so I could go home and get on with my life with some conviction. I guess I need more time.'

After coffee, Hamnet walked her back to the station. He had already prepared for the parting. 'This is the Bullens' number. Give me a call tomorrow evening — maybe I can help you find some work. There are always expat friends looking for domestic help. Would you be prepared to do that kind of thing?'

Jasmine smiled. 'Of course, anything. Thanks.' She leaned forward and kissed him lightly on the cheek, and before he could react she had turned and gone. Hamnet touched his cheek and wondered if the ache in his soul would ever leave him.

He was still in sombre mood when he got back to the house. Margaret was sitting in the living room, reading. There was no sign of Anthony. The doors onto the patio were still open, and the murmur of the ceiling fans mixed with the chirrup and rustle of cicada social life out in the garden.

'Nightcap?' asked Margaret as he sat down. She had an almost psychic ability to understand when he wanted to talk. He guessed that Anthony had been packed off to bed. He heaved himself back out of the chair and poured two glasses of port.

As he settled back into his seat, Margaret took a sip and asked, 'So are you thinking what I think you're thinking?' For an instant Phil was taken aback, before she added, 'Jasmine will make an excellent au pair. I presume that's why you brought her up here? For me to check her out?' She smiled, eyes sparkling over her reading glasses.

Hamnet rolled a mouthful of port over his tongue before answering, 'I suppose,' then couldn't help but smile. 'Partly. She was on a bus I took up in northern Thailand. She was fantastic with Ben. She saved me on that occasion. I thought dinner was the least I could do.' He grimaced. 'You could do. Thank you.' Then paused. 'I don't really know her at all, but she seems nice, and she's so good with Ben.'

Margaret nodded. 'I'd have to agree with you, dear. She's terribly sweet. And these days you can't even rely on the agencies to vet people properly. Look at all that trouble they've had in America. All you've got to go on is your own character judgement. And I'd say she's just perfect.'

'She needs somewhere to live as well. There's a spare room at the apartment — it would be good for everybody.' It was a simple enough decision. He would ask Jasmine about it when she called the following evening.

The other decision he had all to himself. There was no one to help — and no longer any way to avoid it. Could he trade four ships for his son's life? Would cargo be the only price, or would Janac demand more? He had no way of knowing, and the eternal questioning — and Ben — kept him awake most of the night. Or rather, fear of the consequences did. For, in reality, he had already decided.

Chapter 21

Inevitably, the first deep sleep Hamnet fell into was just prior to Margaret's wake up call. He slipped back under, was woken again, more urgently this time, and finally struggled through to breakfast with puffy eyes and wet hair. He poured down some coffee before returning to his room to struggle into shirt and tie. When he climbed into the car, Anthony already had the engine running and in gear.

The advantage of this small panic was that Hamnet had no time to think of anything else. Not so on the MRT. He stood and stared blankly out of the window, stomach twisting and tightening inexorably as if tied to a Spanish Inquisition windlass.

Joan was at her desk when he arrived. She smiled her welcome and offered him coffee as he sat down. He accepted gratefully and reopened the ring binders he'd been reading the previous afternoon, only this time with more purpose. It was fifteen minutes later when Toby stuck his head through the door.

'Hear about that boat?'

Hamnet looked up. 'No. What boat?'

'Bloody thing just disappeared a day out of Manila. Didn't do the daily report on time. No big deal, but then they couldn't get her on the radio or the satcom. One of our ships went through the same area yesterday afternoon and searched for eight hours — nothing. That's where I got tied up yesterday. Sorry about that.'

'Not at all, that's much more important. What do you think happened?'

Toby shook his head. 'An old bulk carrier like that

could've just broken up. I remember one that did that in Australian waters back in the early '90s. Then a sister ship popped a hatch cover in a storm and went down with all hands in the Western Approaches a year or so later. Too much dodgy tonnage out there in some of those fleets.'

Hamnet nodded slowly.

'Nothing more we can do. They're asking the US navy if they'll help search. Any questions, just knock. I've got the *Enterprise* coming in this afternoon — worth you coming down there with me.' And with that Toby closed the door.

Hamnet gazed with increasingly sightless eyes at the documents in front of him, thoughts drifting away to the lost ship. Had Janac just blazed on without him? A bulk carrier? A cargo of grain or rice didn't really sound like Janac's style. Toby was probably right — too much dodgy tonnage out there. As he himself, of all people, should know.

He forced himself back to work, wading slowly through the documentation. It was a couple of hours later when he turned a page and came to 'Shoreside Software Systems'. He carried on, marking the sections he would need, the places where he would find the necessary information. It was coming together. Lunch time came and went. Hamnet worked through it, barely noticing he had done so.

'You're right into this.'

He jumped.

'I've never seen anyone devour this information so seriously,' Toby continued 'Notes as well. Quite impressive. What are you looking at there?'

Hamnet had been so deeply immersed in his work he hadn't noticed Toby's arrival at his shoulder. He was taking notes on how to use the software to bring up a cargo-loading plan. Not the most obvious area for a new marine superintendent to be researching. 'Oh . . .' he started, looking round, hand twitching guiltily across the page before he got a grip on himself. A kid caught reading a comic by the teacher.

But Toby was already heading for the door. 'Come on,' he called over his shoulder. 'We've got a ship to check in.' Hamnet swallowed dryly, wet his lips, shut the file and put his notes into a drawer in his desk. He had to run to make the lift.

He was still berating himself for his casualness as he and Toby climbed into a car. He had to be a lot more careful. He was going to betray the company, do something that would cost it, or the insurer, millions of dollars. Perhaps more. He forced the idea back. He had to do one boat; he had to know. If Janac took it cleanly, with no casualties, no one would be able to blame him for what he was doing. He had made a decision. Now he had to focus on the task he'd set himself, and not get caught. He sat in silence as the car drove down Shenton Way towards the terminal. And if Janac didn't take the boat cleanly . . .?

Toby lit a cigarette as they waited at the Prince Edward Street lights. He wound down the window and exhaled the first lungful of smoke. The warm air rushed in and flooded the cool of the car. 'I never said how sorry I was about your wife, your crew. It was a terrible thing. A ship goes down, like that bulk carrier, and that's bad enough. But piracy and murder . . ' He stopped, took another deep drag.

Hamnet snapped out of his reverie, uncomfortable. 'Thanks,' he muttered.

The lights changed and Toby pulled forward. Hamnet took the opportunity to change the subject. 'So, Toby, that accent of yours. I've been trying to place it.'

Toby rattled back the answer. 'Sort of general Home Counties — I went to school in Surrey. Pretty good English for a Chinese, huh? My father, you know, he was a success-ful businessman, but in those days there were still many doors closed to him. He wanted them open for me, and he sent me over there when I was five. I learnt English at the same time as I learnt Mandarin.'

'Did it work? The doors, did they open?'

'Everything changed anyway — this is a Chinese town now. But it didn't hurt. I married a nice English girl.' He smiled.

Hamnet didn't want to think about nice English girls. 'What was that ship carrying?'

'Huh?' There was a crunch as Toby missed a gear.

'The ship that went down, what was she carrying?'

'Oh, she was under ballast.'

That, thought Hamnet, settles that. Janac would hardly be likely to raid a bulk carrier full of seawater. And if he had, he really did need some good intelligence.

The car slid under the expressway and into the terminal, then round to E Road by the East Lagoon, where they duly found the *Konsan Enterprise*. Hamnet had been through the routine a hundred times before as ship's master. Now he was starting to learn the job from the other side. Not exactly poacher turned gamekeeper — they were all working for the same company — but he well knew there were always one or two things aboard a ship that the master didn't want anyone poking into too deeply back at head office. The afternoon dragged painfully, particularly as everybody wanted to talk about the lost ship. Hamnet didn't — losing ships was the last thing he wanted to discuss. He just wanted to get back and do what he had to do.

It was late afternoon before they returned to the office and he could finally set about completing his research, rather more circumspectly this time. By five thirty he had finished. He knew where to look for the right containers, how to get from there to the ship's route, and how to keep regular tabs on its position during the voyage. All he needed now was to get on the computer. He didn't have a password, and even when he did, it would be better not to use it. He couldn't be sure what kind of checks were made on users. It would be safer to log in as Joan. She'd been here longer, and her broader role meant she was unlikely to attract suspicion, wherever her computer use took her in the system. He stretched and looked over at her 'Coffee?' he said.

She peered at him, surprised. 'Tea actually, but I'll make it.'

'No, no.' Hamnet was already standing. 'I need a break.'

'Well, thank you. Weak with no milk, please.'

He walked to the back of the office, where a door led onto a small windowless kitchen. He made the drinks and returned to Joan's desk. His eyes flickered across the monitor as he put the tea down beside it. A framed photograph of a caged bird caught his eye.

'Is that your pet?' he asked.

Joan sipped at the tea. 'Mmm, Shashi. She's a cockatoo.'

'Shashi?' Something tugged in Hamnet's head. 'A nice name. What does it mean?'

'It's a Chinese town. Where my parents come from.'

'Of course. A nice place?'

'Very beautiful lake. Or it was. I don't know now. No one from my family has been there for forty years. But maybe soon.'

'They were running from the communists?'

'That's right.'

'Many people have been back.'

Joan nodded and sipped at her tea. Her free hand strayed towards the keyboard. Hamnet got the message.

'I'll get back to my reading. Would you mind just logging me on, as I'm up to the software section now and I think it would be easier if I could look at it as well as read about it.'

185

'Of course.'

Hamnet watched her type the password carefully. This time he had an idea what he was looking for. Again the keystrokes were fast, but he thought he got it. He flipped forward a couple of sections in the documentation and cruised slowly through the screens on berthing schedules. People started to leave for home and the numbers in the office began to thin out. By seven thirty he was almost alone. One woman remained, head down over a sheet of figures on the other side of the room. The light was still on in Toby's office, but apart from that the place was empty. It was as safe as it would ever be. Hamnet clicked his way through the software, using his notes to guide him, until he found the cargo manifests. With the manual open at the right place on his desk, he even had the perfect excuse should someone query him.

It took half an hour to find what he wanted — a medium-sized container ship carrying a small fortune in computer-memory chips out of Singapore. They were in a forty-foot container, near the top of the stack, on the outside. He jotted down the name of the ship and its departure details. Then he paged back to see if there was any routing information. A rustle from the other side of the room alerted him. He watched as the woman collected the papers she was reading into a pile before placing them in a filing cabinet. She glanced up, caught his eye as she stood and said, 'You're working late.'

'A lot to learn,' Hamnet replied.

The woman smiled, nodded and left. As the door closed behind her, he went back to the screen. He found the route and checked it against the coordinates Janac had given him. Everything tallied — he could give Janac the departure date, the route, details of the cargo and the ship's name and vital statistics. There was one last thing. He logged out, then tried to get back in as Joan. Sure enough, the password was 'Shashi'. He felt a surge of satisfaction at this small accomplishment. He was ready. When he left, Toby was still working.

Back at the Bullens', Hamnet learned that Jasmine had phoned and would try again at nine thirty. He ate a quick supper, showered, then set up Anna's computer. He was fortunate that the bedroom had a telephone — he had the machine and a connection to the Internet up and running in half an hour. He disconnected and had just begun composing his message to Janac when the phone rang. He let Margaret pick it up in the sitting room, and a moment later there was a knock at the door.

'Jasmine for you,' she said, poking her head into the room.

'Can I take it here?'

'Just pick it up.' Margaret shut the door behind her.

'Jasmine?'

'Hi! I tried earlier . . .'

'Yeah, they told me. Thanks for calling back. So look, I was wondering. As you know, I've started work now and I'm moving back into our flat at the weekend. I'm going to need some help with Ben. Would you be interested? I can't pay you much, but there's a room there if you want it. So it would be full board and maybe three hundred Singapore dollars a week? A month or two and you could save enough to get to Indonesia, and it would give me a chance to find someone more permanent.' He hesitated. 'What do you think?'

She replied immediately. 'I'd love the job and the room. It's just what I need.'

Hamnet hadn't realised quite how badly he'd wanted her to say yes until he'd heard her say it. 'Fantastic. That's great. I get the apartment back at the weekend, so you can

187

move in any time you like after that.'

'As soon as possible. I'm going slowly crazy in this hostel.'

'I'll meet you there at ten, say, on Saturday morning. Or do you need a lift with your stuff?'

'Not at all. I've only got a backpack.'

Hamnet gave her the address, wished her a good week and put the phone down. That was one thing settled.

He turned back to the computer, took a deep breath and started to type before he had too much time for reflection. He kept it simple — the bare details, with one line for each piece of information, as he'd been instructed. He pulled the encryption disc out of his bag and slid it into the floppy disk drive. The software loaded onto the computer and he ran it on the text file he had just created. Finally, he reconnected to the Internet and sent the encrypted file to the email address.

It was done. He looked up to where Robbie Williams was grinning down at him from the poster and rubbed his cheek. He'd forgotten to shave after his shower.

Ben, installed by Margaret in the room next door three weeks previously, didn't wake Hamnet that night. Hamnet didn't sleep at all. The second time he got up for Ben it was just after three o'clock in the morning. He was wide awake on returning to his own room and thought it might help quiet a turbulent mind if he checked the email. He logged back on, not expecting to find anything, but there was a reply. He ran the encrypted file through the decoding software, and then opened the resulting text file in a word-processing programme. The process took four anxious minutes. The message read simply: 'Require position reports at four-hour intervals after departure time.' Hamnet switched the computer off, thinking hard.

It was not a simple request to comply with. The Konsan computer system was bespoke — custom designed and packaged. It ran on a secure local network and couldn't be accessed from outside the office. A single, daily position report would be easy to do: he could check the data before he left the office and email it to Janac as soon as he got home. A position report every four hours was a lot harder. He could hardly risk emailing encrypted files from Konsan's server. By sunrise he realised there was only one way to do it, and the following evening he went home via the Funan IT Mall. He found a tiny, full-specification PC notebook and the cabling to hook it up to a mobile phone the size of a cigarette lighter. He bought the whole lot on his credit card. Now he could send the email from anywhere, at any time.

He spent the rest of that evening loading software onto the new machine and setting up routines to make the whole process as quick as possible. When it was ready, he tested the system by sending a message to Janac. Hamnet told him that it was impossible to provide position information outside office hours, and that during that period he could only report every six hours without attracting attention. By morning, he had confirmation that this was acceptable. The ship — the *Collingson* — steamed out of the Keppel Channel early that afternoon, and by coincidence Hamnet found himself in Toby's office at the time. He watched her go, and steeled his heart to the risk he was taking.

With everything in place, the final acts of his betrayal were easy. He arrived at work just after seven in the morning. There was rarely anybody else around at that time. He logged in as himself, with his new password, and checked the status of the fleet, including the *Collingson*. He would use Joan's password only to research the targets. When he had the data he needed, he took the elevator down to the ground floor, found a restaurant and ordered breakfast. With

189

the laptop set up on the table, he quickly entered the position, speed and course information into a prepared message, encrypted the file and sent it. It took no more than five minutes from the time he sat down. He followed the same routine at lunch time, and in the evening he repeated it again back at the Bullens'. By late Friday the *Collingson*, blithely unaware of its fate, was sailing through the South China Sea, closing on the Philippines. Hamnet reported her position at 1800, went home and tried to forget about it. He had other worries for the weekend.

He got up early on the Saturday morning and packed his few belongings. When he emerged from his bedroom for breakfast, Margaret was already up. They shared an almost silent meal, then loaded his stuff into the Rover and Anthony drove them down to the flat. Between the three of them they carried everything up in the lift, Anthony helping with the bags, Margaret with the baby. It felt like a real goodbye as he took Ben in his arms.

'You'll bring him to see us, I hope?' Margaret asked as they walked slowly back to the car.

'Of course. Often.' He kissed her on the cheek, and she climbed into the front passenger seat. 'I'll never be able to thank you enough or repay you for what you've done,' he said. 'You know that, don't you?'

Margaret smiled. 'Anyone would have done the same. Come and see us next week.'

He nodded, his face serious, and Anthony pulled away.

It wasn't until he was inside the flat with Ben, with the door shut behind them, that he really appreciated the enormity of the change. The Bullens had propped him up through the most difficult time of his life, and now he was on his own. He switched the television on for company, and put on the kettle.

There was a knock at the door just after ten o'clock. He

opened it to find Jasmine, rucksack on her back, sweat staining the front of her T-shirt and trickling down her face. She smiled broadly, muttering, 'Those steps are a killer in this heat.' Hamnet pointed out the lift as he ushered her into the hall.

'You can put your bag in your room, through here.' He led the way into the box room, which just about held a single bed. 'God, I'd forgotten how small it was,' he said.

'It's perfect,' said Jasmine, dumping the backpack on the only bit of empty floor space.

'At least there are some drawers and a fan,' he added.

'It's fine, really. You should see where I've just come from. Eight to a room, no fans.'

He smiled. 'Let me show you the rest of the flat.'

There wasn't a great deal to show. Through to the kitchen and bathroom, then the other bedroom, where Ben lay sleeping in a cot at the foot of the big double bed. Finally, into the flat's only real glory — the enormous living room, with a balcony that ran its length. The television was still playing quietly in a corner as they walked in. It was the picture that caught his attention — a still photograph of a container ship.

'Wow, this is beautiful,' said Jasmine.

'Shhh!' Hamnet was diving for the set. He cranked up the volume.

The newsreader's tone was sombre. 'The *Collingson* is the second ship to disappear in these waters in less than a week. Authorities are treating the matter as suspicious and have again requested help with a search of the area from the US navy. Elsewhere . . .'

The voice droned on. Hamnet heard nothing but the pounding in his head.

Chapter 22

'Phil?'

Jasmine leaned against the doorframe, arms folded, watching as her words went unheeded. She sighed softly and rested her head gently on the jamb. The coloured light from the screen played on his face in the dark room. Hamnet was completely absorbed in the television, as he had been all weekend. She knew that it was going to be difficult: a recent widower, a young child. Distracted, distant, self-absorbed, even a little teary — she'd expected all those things. None of that bothered her; she felt he was a good man and was pleased to be able to help. And, frankly, she needed the money. But having him sit glued to the television was not on the list of anticipated behaviour.

'Phil!' She said it much more sharply this time — too sharply. She winced after the word had come out.

But Hamnet had only just heard. 'One moment,' he said.

Jasmine glanced at the screen. The credits on the late-evening news were just rolling.

Hamnet looked up. 'I'm sorry. I was miles away.'

'I'm going to bed now. I've just checked on Ben — he's fast asleep. I've made up a bottle for him if you need it overnight. It's in the fridge. Remember to warm it in the microwave.'

'Of course. We'll be fine. Thanks for your help, Jasmine.'

She nodded, pushed herself off the doorframe and turned into the hall.

'Jasmine.'

'Uh-uh?'

'I'm sorry. For this weekend.'

'If you ever want to talk . . '

Hamnet nodded and looked away. Said nothing.

Ben got him up three times that night, and all came as a relief. A relief from lying and staring at the ceiling fan, counting the revolutions. At least with the routine he had carefully devised he could leave for work early. He knocked on Jasmine's door at six to tell her he was off.

The office was inhabited only by ghosts when he got there. He stared at his blank computer monitor in silence before taking a deep breath and switching it on. While it went through the start-up routine, he flipped open one of the ring binders to the page on ship schedules and positions — his unused and still valid pretext. When the computer was ready to give him control of the mouse and keyboard he worked quickly down through the menus. And there it was. Or rather, there it wasn't. There were no position reports for the *Collingson* after midnight on Friday. Janac had hit her a few hundred miles off the Philippines, that much was clear.

He clicked his way up to the main menu and from there went to an Internet marine-news page. The disappearance was the title story, and he scanned the lines quickly. The *Collingson* had failed to report or respond on any communications system since Friday evening. The limited Philippine coastguard search was giving way to a more extensive US navy search later that morning. Beyond that, there was little more detail than he had gleaned from the various television and radio news bulletins over the weekend. He stared at the monitor in silence — wanting to know more, not wanting to know.

'Morning,' Joan chimed brightly as the door clicked shut behind her. Then, 'Are you all right?'

Hamnet looked up. 'I feel a little queasy. Something I ate, perhaps. Not much sleep because of the baby, either.'

He rubbed his temples, then his cheeks, so he stared wide-eyed like Munch's *The Scream*.

'You have a baby?' asked Joan.

'Yes. Excuse me.' He bolted for the men's room. Where it took little effort to substantiate his story of food poisoning by throwing up. He flushed the toilet, turned, and sat on the seat. The dark images from the *Shawould* swam through his head — they weren't so easily expelled. Ten minutes later, he washed his face, rinsed out his mouth and cleared his nose. He stared at himself in the mirror. Pale through the tan. Eyes darkly underlined, blank and accusing. He returned to his desk, where Joan looked at him anxiously.

'Are you sure you're all right?' she asked again.

He nodded slowly. 'I think it's just something I ate. I feel better now. I'll be OK.' He wasn't going to go home and leave the supply of information available in the office.

Joan watched him for a moment, then said, 'I'll make you a nice cup of tea, then you can tell me all about the baby.'

An hour later, when Toby hauled him out of the office for a new arrival, there was still no more news. Hamnet consoled himself with the thought that once on board the ship he would hear of any developments as soon as in the office. But the minutes crawled by in the car on the way to the docks. It was almost eleven before they were on the bridge of the *Konsan Endeavour*, sharing a cup of coffee and some chat with the master, a burly, convivial Norwegian. Toby was just starting to champ at the bit over the enforced inactivity when the radio operator emerged onto the bridge, nose glowing from too much sun.

'Just got a FleetNet message,' he reported. 'The Americans have found the missing boat. She's still steaming at ten knots into the Pacific, apparently. No sign of life, but it looks as though the lifeboats are on board. The Americans will put people on her in the next half an hour.'

Hamnet's hand tightened round his cup in a spasm. Hot coffee splashed onto his hand, but he barely noticed.

The master was looking at Toby. 'Sounds like a bad business, that. Will you have to deal with it?'

'No, they'll manage it from head office. Thank God they found her. Steaming into the Pacific at ten knots with no one on the bridge? That's a disaster waiting to happen. Hard to see what the hell's going on. Could be something crazy like food poisoning, but I've never heard of an entire crew going down with it. She was too far offshore for a small-boat attack, though. As you say, a bad business — especially after Hamnet's experience.'

The master turned to Hamnet. 'You were the master of the *Shawould*?'

'That's right.' He could hear the crack in his own voice.

The older man nodded. 'Terrible business.'

'Yes,' said Hamnet. 'Yes, it was.'

'Let's hope these men are luckier,' said Toby. 'We'll know soon enough. Right, Phil. Finish that coffee up and we'll go and check the deck logs. We'll pop back up in half an hour or so and see if there's any more news — if that's all right with you, sir?'

'Be my guests. Mauso will take you to the deck officer.'

'No need. We know the way.'

The next thirty minutes were the longest of Hamnet's life — not least because they lasted nearly an hour. That was how long it took Toby to satisfy himself that everything in the logs had either been attended to on this stop or was in preparation for the next. Somehow Hamnet kept a grip on the desire to shout and scream that they knew enough, that they could return to the bridge.

Finally Toby was done. They climbed back up through the ship, Hamnet's knuckles white on the rails with frustration and worry. When they reached the bridge, only the radio officer was there, checking through a sheaf of papers.

'Anything on the *Collingson*?' asked Toby.

The young man looked up. 'Yeah, amazing. The crew are fine. They were locked below decks, all the comms equipment smashed. That's all they've released so far. It'll probably take a few days before we hear the rest of the story. Main thing is the crew are OK.'

'Excellent. Thanks for that,' said Toby. 'Don't forget your sun block today.'

Hamnet floated off the bridge and down the stairs to the dockside, a helium balloon of happiness bobbling along on a string behind Toby. No casualties. Just a few containers. He had won the first stage — a proper nurse for his son.

Back in the office, Hamnet fought his way through the arrival report for the *Endeavour*. It was all he could do to restrain himself from switching screens to the ships' cargo details to find another target. He had to be patient — there was too much at stake. The office would soon be empty.

The clatter of keyboards and the low buzz of office conversation slowly died away as the afternoon wore on and turned into evening. Eventually, even Toby clicked his door shut behind him. 'Still here?'

Hamnet looked up. 'Yeah, 'fraid so.'

'Don't work at it too hard. It'll only get worse once I've left.'

'That's what worries me. I want to be ready.'

'You'll be fine. I'll see you in the morning.'

As the door shut and the big office finally fell silent, Hamnet's fingers danced furiously across his keyboard. He knew what to look for this time, and it was only quarter of an hour before he picked up on close to a million dollars' worth of microprocessor chips going to Shanghai the following Friday. He checked the loading plan and found the chips were under two containers full of televisions. Another container held mixed computer parts. Those four containers alone were worth nearly two million dollars. He noted the details and logged out, then followed the same routine as before, emailing the coded file from a basement coffee shop. He threw the shredded notes into a bin on his way to the MRT station. It was almost too easy.

Jasmine was stirring a stew when he got home, having already put Ben to bed. 'You're working really hard at this new job,' she said, looking up from the pot as he entered the kitchen. A light breeze blew through the open window into the hot room, ruffling a calendar on the wall.

Hamnet stepped to the fridge and pulled out a bottle of wine. 'No choice. I have to work bloody hard just to have some chance of keeping up.' He turned to her. 'Glass of white?'

'Please.'

He carried on talking as he uncorked and poured. 'I can't afford this to go wrong. A shore job like this is a huge prize for someone like me. I have to keep it. Going back to sea, with Ben, would be a disaster.' He handed her a glass and offered a toast. 'To the end of a bad patch.'

Jasmine smiled, their eyes met. 'I'll certainly drink to that.' Their glasses hummed as they lightly touched. The wine was cold and slipped down easily in the warm air. The first bottle was empty before dinner was served, the second before it was finished. By the time the third had followed suit, the ice that had formed between the two of them over the weekend wasn't so much melting as flooding the flat.

Hamnet's head was still pounding the following lunch time, but other than that, he had reason to smile for the first time in months. He picked up a paper on his way out. There was a double page on the *Collingson* attack and its background, plus some editorial. The *Singapore Telegraph* leader read:

This plunder was carried out with cold professionalism and skill, and may foretell a new and altogether more dangerous era in piracy in the region. Out in open water, the *Collingson* was attacked by a vessel big enough to remove forty-foot containers, but in a manner that meant the bridge was overwhelmed before the duty officer knew anyone was on board. The crew were locked below from that moment on — until their release by US marines yesterday morning — and claim to know nothing more of events. It appears only the cargo manifest told them they had lost S$3.5M worth of freight. The question for the authorities is whether this is an isolated incident, or the first involvement of major crime organisations in a new, modern era of hi-tech piracy. Until now the threat to shipping has been low-level. And the inaction of the authorities and shipping companies, whilst unacceptable on a human level, has at least made commercial sense. But this new development cannot be ignored. Billions of dollars of goods traverse the world in unprotected merchant ships. This country is completely dependent for its prosperity on that overseas trade and the continued safe transport of goods. We cannot tolerate this threat. Action must be taken.

But not, thought Hamnet, before I've got my son back. It had indeed been clinically clean and simple. And it was going to be all too easy to trade another few million dollars' worth of cargo for a second quarter of his son's life.

The following week went according to plan, until Friday. He maintained his early starts and tried to leave the office at a reasonable hour in the evening. When he logged on to the Internet to make his first position report on Friday evening, there was a coded message for him. It read: 'Weather wrong. Need another target.' It was a bitterly frustrating blow. He had lost a whole week. The clock was ticking — the onset of the typhoon season wouldn't wait. And it would be another two days before he could get back into the office to find another boat.

Jasmine and Ben, without knowing it, were able to take his mind off the situation for much of the weekend. There was a trip to Sentosa Island, another to the zoo. Ben gurgled, Jasmine chuckled and Hamnet laughed for the first time since he'd left Anna in their cabin on the *Shawould*. But it still wasn't easy, and inevitably it was Margaret who noticed, when the three of them joined the Bullens for lunch on Sunday. Hamnet was clearing away the dishes with her while Jasmine and Anthony laid out the croquet hoops.

'You seem tense, Phillip.'

'Hmmm?' Hamnet looked up from loading the dishwasher. He hadn't heard the question, lost in his own thoughts about containers and schedules, risk and reward.

'You seem a little edgy,' she said.

He sighed, 'Yes. New job, working too hard. I don't see much of Ben, unless it's during the early hours of the morning. I haven't had a decent night's sleep since I left here.' He dropped another dish into the rack.

Margaret nodded. 'I'm sure it'll settle down once you've been there a while.'

'That's what I keep telling myself.' But he knew that was a lie.

'How's Jasmine?'

'She's fantastic. Holding us together.'

'Does she do some of the night-time call outs?'

Hamnet poured the dishwasher powder as he spoke. 'No. I don't think it's really fair to ask her. It's only a job, not a calling.'

'What's not fair?' Jasmine had appeared at the door.

Hamnet looked up. 'Uh — you doing Ben at night. It's not fair that you should.'

'I don't mind. I can sleep during the day when he does. You can't. Come on, you two, we're ready.' And she was gone.

199

Hamnet looked at Margaret, frowning.

'Well, why not?' she replied.

'But where's he going to sleep? I mean she can hardly . . .' He stopped abruptly at the expression on Margaret's face.

'Phillip, that's a very stuffy thing to say.'

'I don't want things to get confused . . .' he started, before trailing off, turning, looking away. Out to the garden, past it, off to a point somewhere in an alternative present.

Margaret moved closer, put a hand on each of his arms and squeezed gently. 'It will hurt forever, Phillip, but time will make it bearable. Lots of people will help that time come around. Some in different ways from others. Don't get all uptight thinking that any of them are wrong.'

Hamnet looked round at her, compressed his lips and swallowed, still not quite sure what she had said, or even what he had said. He was even less sure he wanted the matter clarified. He opened his mouth to speak, but nothing came out. Margaret smiled sweetly, closed the dishwasher and switched it on before heading for the garden, leaving Hamnet alone, wondering.

Chapter 23

Hamnet had more luck with the next target he selected. The *Konsan Pinta* sailed into the South China Sea the following Thursday, and he plotted its progress without interruption through to the weekend. He was anxious, but nothing like as wired up as the time before. The *Pinta* was headed east into the Pacific on Monday morning when he returned to work, and still going that evening when he went home. He left the office at a reasonable hour, having almost got control of his official and extracurricular workload.

Just as important, he was impatient to return to the flat, which was now a strong enough cipher for home and family to draw him back at the first opportunity. It made the inevitable moments of dislocation all the more jarring — like when he stumbled into the lock-free bathroom at the wrong time — but for the most part, his life of deceit and betrayal had gathered normality like dust and settled into a comfortable, homely routine. He had started to meet Jasmine and Ben for lunch twice a week, which also meant there was a break from Jasmine's rather average cooking. But neither of those days was a Monday, and he reflected that evening that the lack of cooking skill was something else Jasmine had in common with Anna. Dinner was long over when he decided on a second pot of coffee in an effort to remove the peculiar aftertaste left by her peanut-butter sauce.

'Jasmine,' he started as he returned to the lounge, 'do you still do any painting or drawing?'

Jasmine, stretched out on the floor, looked up from the book she was reading. 'I have a sketchbook with me. But I haven't done much recently. Why do you ask?'

'I was hoping you might like to draw Ben. I'll pay you, of course.' He put the coffee down beside her and settled into the sofa.

Jasmine rolled onto her back and sat up in one movement. 'I'm not sure it'd be worth much. I haven't had enough practice recently.'

Hamnet was about to ask why not when he stopped, listening. A thin wail trailed down the corridor. 'I'll get him,' he said. It was going to be another long night.

The phone slapped Hamnet awake. He came to with a rush of pulse that left him staring bewildered at a blurred alarm clock. It reluctantly came into focus: four o'clock in the morning. He rolled out of bed and almost lost his balance as the blood swilled around his body. He grabbed the wardrobe for support, and the shadowy contents of the room slowly stopped spinning. The phone was still ringing. He stumbled out into the corridor and lurched left towards the lounge. The kitchen light was still on. He peered through the door on the way past, fumbling for the switch to turn it off.

Jasmine was perched on a stool by the window, bare legs crossed, stretching out from under an open-collared shirt. She was supporting Ben on her lap. The baby's blue eyes rolled across to his father as he gave a contented gurgle and chewed on the teat of the bottle Jasmine was holding. Jasmine glanced up, flicked the dark hair clear of her face and smiled with a freshness that gave the lie to the early hour.

'I heard him crying. He didn't seem to wake you this time, so I thought . . .'

'Sure,' said Hamnet, backing out through the door, conscious that he was wearing only a pair of boxer shorts and that she didn't appear to have anything on apart from the shirt. 'The phone, I'll get the phone.' He swivelled round the doorframe and leant back against the wall, closed eyes directed upwards. What was it Margaret had said?

The phone was still ringing. He fell forwards off the wall and hurried down the dark hallway towards the lounge, crashing into the edge of the door. He swore, eventually finding the offending object in a shaft of moonlight reflected off the balcony railing.

'Yes?' he answered.

'Phillip, it's Dubre.'

'Dubre, have you any fucking idea what time it is?'

'Oh, apologies. I'm in Sydney. Didn't think about it.'

'Right,' said Hamnet, not believing a word.

'I just got up. So, how are you chap?'

'How am I? It's four in the morning, you've woken my son up, he's crying and I'm really not in the mood for idle chatter.'

'The au pair can deal with that. She's a cracker, Phillip. Wouldn't mind getting her out of bed myself.'

Hamnet could almost hear Dubre rubbing his hands together. He took a deep breath and didn't reply.

'What happened to his sibling, Phillip?' snapped Dubre into the pause.

The question caught Hamnet off balance. 'What?'

'Anna was pregnant with twins. I checked with her doctor. What happened to Benjamin's sibling?'

Hamnet hesitated, caught a breath, steadied himself. 'Yes. He died at birth. At least that's what Janac told me, and I have no reason to disbelieve him.'

'Did you ever see the bodies?'

'No.' Hamnet hesitated. It was something he'd thought about a lot. His answer was honest. 'Things happened very quickly at the end. I didn't think of it until it was too late.

203

Of course she'd been dead for three days by then. Perhaps it was better that I didn't.'

'She?'

'They. The baby would have been dead for longer. Don't be such a bloody pedant.'

'It's just funny that you didn't mention it before, you see.'

'Dealing with Anna . . . is bad enough. I tell myself Ben never had a brother.' There was a long pause. 'Dubre, it is very early in the morning, and I have to be at work in about three hours. There's a better time and place to have this conversation.'

'Of course. I'll come to the point. Konsan's lost another boat.'

The first question had rocked him, but now his guard was up his reaction was automatic. 'Shit. What have you heard?'

'Seems this one wasn't quite so neat.'

Hamnet felt the back of his neck prickle and start to sweat. The room seemed to fall away from him.

Dubre continued. 'The Australian coastguard picked up a Mayday about three hours ago. I just saw the bones reported on breakfast television and gave them a call. Another very professional job, apparently. Details are a little sketchy, but what is clear is that your friend Janac was leading the attack. He's pretty well known down here after that yacht business a few years back. One of the crew recognised him.'

Hamnet was silent.

'Is that a coincidence, Phillip?' asked Dubre eventually.

'Is what a coincidence?' replied Hamnet with as much innocence as he could muster, immediately feeling he'd overdone it.

'Janac attacking two Konsan ships — the company you're working for.'

204

'What the hell are you suggesting, Dubre?'

'Phillip, I know that I betrayed the confidence you placed in me, and that you have every reason not to trust me.' He took a deep breath, which Hamnet could hear clearly down the phone line. 'But, of course, that cuts both ways. If you don't trust me any longer, there's no reason why you should be telling me the truth. And all I know about what happened up there in Burma is what you've told me.'

'I'm not even going to dignify that statement with an answer, Dubre.'

'Maybe not. But be careful, Phillip. There's a rumour going around that three-and-a-half million bucks' worth of semiconductors wasn't all that disappeared off the *Collingson*. Some sources in Hong Kong are letting it be known that the Triads had a very big drug shipment on that boat. It was there when it left Singapore, and it was gone when it docked in Osaka. They don't think it disappeared of its own accord, either. If I've drawn conclusions, right or wrong, others will too.'

'Dubre, that's ridiculous.'

'Watch your back, old chap.'

'I have enough to worry about — bringing my son up on my own, a new job, a rabbit warren of judicial enquiries — without losing sleep over your wild conspiracy theories. I'm going back to bed.'

'Alrighty. Oh, one last thing. Janac killed the master. Nice old boy — Johansen. You probably knew him.'

Hamnet felt the ground move under him. It kicked his knees out and he sat down hard on the chair behind him. He was struggling to breath, never mind speak — his chest tightening around his lungs, squeezing out the air.

'I'm very sorry. I hope you'll pass that on to your office,' Dubre continued, before pausing meaningfully. 'Nothing you want to tell me, Phillip?'

Hamnet's voice was hoarse, dry, tortured. 'The man's an animal. I already know that. Nothing surprises me.' He laid the phone down with a heavy click. And shut his eyes. The nightmare was real.

Five kilometres away, Dubre listened to the line disengage and then gently replaced his handset. He switched a tape recorder off, wrinkling his brow thoughtfully as he did so.

'You know him a lot better than I do,' said the man slouched across Dubre's leather sofa. 'What do you think?'

Dubre looked round at the visitor who had brought him the news and prompted the idea of the phone call. He nodded his head slowly. 'On balance, I'd have to say I feel he's involved. Now we know there was definitely a second baby, I'm sure he would have mentioned it before if it had died with Anna. And if it's alive, there's no reason why Janac couldn't be using it as a lever. Hamnet's the most obvious suspect. But you can't arrest him on the basis of that phone call.'

'I do have enough grounds to instigate a full surveillance.'

'Certainly.' Dubre hesitated. 'He'll be on his guard now.'

The other man picked at some fluff on his charcoal-grey suit. 'Yes,' he drawled, 'but he's not a professional. It's normal for amateurs to overreact. He's more likely to make a mistake now that we've rattled his cage.'

'That's your party — I'm happy to leave that to you. But no one else, particularly at Konsan, should know about this.'

The man on the sofa nodded. 'I'll keep it tight — just use my own squad. There'll be no leaks from the police. I have carte blanche on this one. The powers-that-be have made it clear that we can't afford this kind of thing to get out of hand. If the media start advertising these losses, they could panic people. Security of world trade — you know the bullshit. You're peering over a precipice at a run on the stock market. Losses so far have already had an impact on the price of computer memory. Normally the system could cope, but not at the moment. Things are fragile enough around here without this.' He paused. 'That story about the Triad drugs — that true?'

Dubre nodded, shivered. The air conditioning was set too high and he was only wearing a light robe. 'Yes, that's what I hear.'

The man shook his head ruefully. 'That'd be ironic, wouldn't it? I spoke to the head of one shipping line at a party a couple of weeks ago. He reckons drugs are the third most valuable cargo they carry. Never know about it, of course, but if you look at the stats, that's the way it comes out. The Triads can't afford this threat to shipping any more than Sony or Daihatsu can. Our opposite numbers on the dark side are probably having this same conversation right now.'

Dubre sipped slowly at a cup of coffee. 'Let's just hope for Hamnet's sake, if it is him, that he gives himself away to us first.'

Chapter 24

Janac grunted with satisfaction. The low-revving thump of the generator and the occasional click from Jordi's computer mouse were the only other human-related sounds, easily discernible against the racket of the forest. He leant on the filthy, once whitewashed windowsill and stared out across the broken shade of the veranda at his new fiefdom. The fortified villa was a relic of overambitious nineteenth-century Spanish colonialism. It stood at the top of a cliff, at the head of a narrow, fjordlike inlet, surrounded and overshadowed — and, when they had found it, all but reclaimed — by the towering forest.

Janac stood in one of three rooms they had cleared of jungle and debris. He stared out across a few yards of open, rocky ground to the top of the cliff, where a stream silently hurled itself off the edge. Less than fifty metres beyond loomed the dark, brooding bow of an old bulk carrier. Had he been there, Hamnet would have recognised it as the ship that had disappeared out of Manila. Its black, rusting hull soaked up what little sunlight struggled through the forest canopy. Her cranes stretched up towards the trees, but not through them. They were invisible from the air, hidden in shadow from anything but the closest and most determined investigation from the water. Janac had to admit that Tosh had done well.

Tosh had found the deep-water inlet after careful inspection of the charts and a lot of time reconnoitring in the RIB, using the bulk carrier as a base for the search. The final test had been to squeeze her in here, with a great deal of care and in moderate sea conditions. The meteorological limits on getting in and out were the only downside, while the house had been an unexpected bonus. It was the perfect spot from which to prey on the shipping lanes around the Philippines. Midway between Diapitan and Palanan Bays, in Isabela Province, on the Philippine island of Luzon, the house was completely isolated. To the west were the mountains of the Sierra Madre, covered by the same, almost impassable, virgin forest that surrounded them. In front and to the east was the Pacific. The only way in and out of the handful of other settlements on the coastline was by boat. It was more secure than Janac's place on Ko Samui had been, relying as that had on the ultimately treacherous locals for protection. With a handful of good men Janac knew this inlet could be defended against a battalion.

The Chinese were the likeliest threat. They had already closed down his Australian operation and cleaned his men off the streets. Things were so bad that the only outlet for the heroin they had taken off the *Collingson* had been wholesale to the Americans, at a fraction of its street value. But even if he'd had to chuck the whole lot into the ocean, it would have been worth it just to take it off the Triads. They would want revenge, and Janac didn't underestimate their capacity to track him down. His team had to deal with the outside world, to sell the plunder and resupply.

The biggest risk was the Triads getting word of the base and offering the New People's Army money to take him out. On their own the NPA could make things difficult if they wanted to, but he doubted they had the will. Communist guerrillas — a dying but familiar breed. If he didn't trouble them, Janac was sure they would leave him alone. In the meantime their activities kept the forces of law and order, such as they were here, busy on the other side of the mountains.

In any case, it would take even the Triads time to find

him, and by then he could make this place impregnable to the kind of muscle they could bring to bear. Those expeditions to sell off the pirated goods could provide him with everything he needed to turn it into a fortress. Then let them come. This fight would be on his territory — in the jungle, not on the streets. In the meantime, he already had the means to melt into the forest and reappear as a respectable businessman in Manila.

'Bugger me,' said Tosh.

Janac straightened and turned from the window to see Tosh leaning over Jordi's shoulder, reading the screen. Tosh sniffed, wiped his nose with the back of his tunic sleeve. 'Must admit, I didn't think he'd play any more ball after you had to shoot that old fart on the last one.' He pulled out a beaten leather tobacco pouch from the cavernous trouser pockets of his fatigues and started to roll a cigarette.

Janac leant back against the windowsill and folded his arms. 'Another dead man and yet Hamnet is apparently prepared to carry on.'

'He must have figured it was an accident. He could have heard the other bloke's story. I mean the old fool was behaving pretty stupidly. If he'd just done what he was told, he'd be alive.'

Janac nodded. 'And if I'd killed him deliberately, what would Hamnet have done then? Johansen had ten or twenty years of life left, his kid might have seventy. So does he think he could trade three more Johansens for his kid and come out ahead? Or does he just feel he has to do this for the child, regardless of the cost?' He sucked his teeth. 'What would happen if he lost two more on the next one, especially if they went down in cold blood?' Janac, as was his habit, answered his own question. 'I think he'd carry on. It's a classic dilemma. He's already lost so much and gained nothing. To gain he has to go on, to risk further loss. I'm sure we've got him, but wouldn't it be interesting to kill a couple next time and find out for sure?' Janac caught the expression that flickered across Tosh's face. 'What's the matter? Aren't you interested in this experiment?'

Tosh almost replied, then shut his mouth, preferring instead to fumble through his pockets for a lighter. His wasn't the sycophantic subservience of Bureya, but even so, he didn't question the boss.

Jordi dragged their attention back to the screen. 'Our boy is a little spooked about something, though. He's changed his email address. He's set one up with somebody else's credit card number. Must've done a little research on the Internet.' He turned to Janac and grinned. The grin froze as soon as he saw the expression on Janac's face.

'Check with Kloc. See where Hamnet was when he sent that email. See if he's still using the cafe, doing it in the open. It's possible he's picked up our surveillance.'

'He wouldn't know who it was,' said Tosh, now struggling with the lighter, which was short of fuel and refused to burn long enough to get the roll-up going.

'Exactly. The last thing we need is to spook our own man. Tell Kloc to back off for a couple of days, keep it real loose.'

'And if it's someone else?' asked Tosh.

'Two possibilities: Triads or the pigs. If either of them takes him out, do we know enough now to manage without him?'

The question was directed at Jordi, who answered, 'It's impossible without someone on the inside. The cargo information we need is almost all on WANs.'

'Spare me the nerd bullshit,' said Janac.

'You can't hack the systems from the outside. The detailed data's carried on private lines. We need someone on the inside. If not Hamnet, then a replacement.' Jordi chewed at his fingernail as he finished.

'So this operation comes to an end when we take the fourth boat?' asked Tosh, turning to Janac, struggling to hide the incredulity in his voice.

'Tosh,' said Janac, with exaggerated patience, 'I made him a deal. You know how I feel about that shit. And the weather turns in late June — the typhoon season will be on us in a couple of weeks. It will make operating impossible for six months. We have plenty of time to replace Hamnet.'

Tosh sniffed again, thinking, thumbing at the lighter wheel. It finally came good and he took a short drag before saying, 'Aye, but we need the four boats if we're going to secure this place against all-comers, keep enough of the boys here for six months and tool up properly.'

Janac turned back to the window, arms folded, heels grinding on the tiled floor. There was another possibility he had to take into account. Maybe Hamnet had already had enough. The police weren't the only people he could turn to for help. Maybe this was a set-up. He spoke to the open window: 'We'll change the attack pattern for this one. Move it inshore, give us an escape route in the RIB. Just in case.'

There was a shriek in the forest, followed by a flurry of beating wings.

'What are you thinking?' asked Tosh.

'We're vulnerable while we're on the target — if Hamnet has had enough, or has been picked up and turned.'

Tosh nodded, but he was still catching up as Janac spun round and strode towards the computer.

'Print out that information for me, Jordi.' A couple of clicks and the laser printer whirred. Janac pulled the paper impatiently from the tray and turned to the charts spread out beside it. 'OK, let's see. The *Kyushu Sun*, a medium-sized container ship headed for Panama from Hong Kong tomorrow evening. We'll pick it up here, in the Balintang

Channel, overnight Friday, Saturday. The eighteen hundred should give us a good-enough fix.' He tapped the chart. 'We put the ship on his starboard bow, coming up from the south and timed to collide with him a couple of miles after this island.' Janac peered closer at the chart. 'Balintang Island. There should be cover for the RIB behind it. If he hasn't spotted you by the time he's approaching the island, Jordi, all you have to do is wake him up and drive him in towards us. Scare the hell out of them — last thing they'll be worried about is a deck watch.' He paused. 'And it's within range of the coast for the RIB. If it turns to shit, we can hit the beach and head into the boonies on the eastern side of Cape Engano. Make sure everyone on the RIB has jungle-survival and fighting equipment loaded. It's a long way back from there to a decent road. But it gives us an option if they're waiting for us on board. Tosh, you got that?'

Tosh, standing beside him, nodded. 'Aye.'

Janac backed away from the chart table and sat in one of the sofas that dominated the centre of the room. 'OK, people, let's figure out the timing. Check the weather and make it happen.'

'A perfect night for it,' said Tosh, and spat into the water.

He was blacked up, balaclava covering all but mouth and eyes. Five other men, similarly attired, Edi and Soey among them, sat with him. A team of three on each side of the RIB, one man cradling a Heckler and Koch MP5 submachine-gun, another a heavier H & K 53, and the third a shotgun. There was another man on the bow with an MP5, and Janac — back-up driver beside him at the console — held the boat on station next to a rocky outcrop just southeast of Balintang Island. The twin engines burped and bubbled almost silently under the sound-proofing covers. The water was mirror calm, albeit a mirror that rose and fell

213

with the slow swell rolling in from a storm way out east in the Pacific. Not that anything could be seen reflected in its inky surface. High cloud obscured the starlight from a moon-less sky.

Janac pulled the encrypted VHF off his belt. 'What's happening, Jordi?'

The radio crackled its response. 'He's ten miles ahead of us, right on the money. Closing speed thirty knots, impact time twenty minutes. He should be a mile south and two miles east of your current position by then if he doesn't adjust course.'

'Heard anything from him?'

'No. Guess they're all asleep.'

'OK.' Janac clipped the radio back onto his belt and clunked the engines into gear. The RIB puttered gently round the back of the island until the bow poked out from behind the last of its extremities. They could see the target for the first time — a red port bow light far off in the night. The minutes ticked by as the light steadily brightened, to the accompaniment of the occasional crash from the other side of the island as a big swell exploded on the rocks.

Janac's radio crackled. 'Still nothing. The bastard's fast asleep.'

'OK, call him up,' Janac replied.

Aboard the bulk carrier, Jordi reached for the micro-phone on the standard VHF, set to Channel 16. 'Vessel steaming east in the Balintang Channel, do you read?' He waited fifteen seconds and then tried again.

This time there was a response. 'Vessel calling, this is the *Kyushu Sun*. Please repeat.'

'*Kyushu Sun*, strongly suggest you turn north. We are on a collision course. Over.'

There was a long silence before a tense reply: 'Wait one.'

Jordi could hear the uncertainty in the man's voice. If he

didn't already know how his sea room to the north was severely limited by Balintang Island, he soon would. And that was where Janac was waiting. Jordi picked up the other radio. 'Herding him in. Coming your way.'

Aboard the RIB the engines continued to tick over as all nine men watched the fast closing red light. Soon enough it was on them, less than a quarter of a mile away, steaming past on the other side of Balintang Island. She had been forced in much closer than her skipper wanted, for the chart marked the island as 'Survey Incomplete'. But Jordi wasn't giving him any choice. A few more seconds, then Janac put the throttle hard down. The propellers bit and the boat surged forward, staggering a little until she rose over her bow wave and started to plane. In these conditions she would comfortably do forty-five knots, but she barely had time to get to half that speed as she sprang from under the radar cover of the island and straight into the blind spot aft of the ship.

Janac throttled back and tucked in under the wide flat stern, which rose vertically above them. Two ropes were already spinning up towards the rails from the grapnel guns. Once locked on, the front men hoisted the climbing ladders on the pulleys and started upwards — three pairs of two, Tosh leading. Once all six were on their way, Janac handed the wheel to the other driver and, with the bowman, followed them up. The driver tucked the RIB in tight under the overhanging stern quarter, from where it could be neither seen nor heard. The first man was over the rail, unopposed, in a little under a minute. The whole attack team of eight was aboard in two minutes. No words were spoken — everyone knew what to do. Janac had worked them hard after the fiasco that had cost Bureya his life.

Leaving the bowman at the ladders, Janac joined Tosh's team and moved off to starboard while Edi led the other to port. Their soft-soled training shoes were soundless as they flowed, two steps at a time, up the companionways. At the accommodation level one man peeled off and took up station at the entrance. Above, the bridge doors were open onto the wing decks. The red glow of night-lights spilled out into the dark as they approached. Janac led and Tosh followed, moving fast, deep into the bridge.

The master of the *Kyushu Sun*, Duncan Fairbrother, was still dressed in his pale-blue nightshirt. He was stooped over the radio, yelling into the microphone, his beard aflame in the red light. One of his officers was glued to the radar screen, the other trained binoculars forward. None of them noticed they had company. Janac stepped up and swung his weapon down. Fairbrother felt something — the air move, a shadow shift — and looked round. But it was too late for him to register surprise. The heavy revolver butt crashed into the face of the radio. Janac had the gun pointed at him before Fairbrother had even begun the process of comprehension. The microphone slid from his fingers and fell to the deck with a clunk. The other two officers stood frozen, mouths open, horrified. They had heard the stories.

'I don't think we'll be needing that any more, do you?' Janac's smile was a yellow smear against the blackened face. 'Is there any comms equipment on this ship that isn't on the bridge?'

Fairbrother stood immobile, too surprised, too terrified, to speak. Janac's left hand leapt out and slapped a blow across his face. The physical contact, evidence that this apparition was at least flesh and blood, seemed to shake the man out of his shock. He gurgled.

'Radio, satcom?' prompted Janac.

'Here. Just here.'

Janac stepped back. 'On the floor, on your bellies, all of you.'

Tosh hustled the two officers towards Fairbrother while

Janac covered him. He pulled plastic cuffs from his belt and fastened three pairs of unresisting wrists, then took a small roll of duct tape from his pocket and stuck a strip across each officer's mouth.

Janac nodded. 'OK, I've got these three. Start working aft.'

Tosh waved two more men in from the wing decks, then moved to the back of the bridge and slid silently through the door, gun raised.

Janac felt for the radio on his belt, still watching the prisoners. 'Jordi?'

'Go boss,' the radio crackled back instantly.

'The bridge is secure, the boys are still sweeping the decks. No trouble so far. I'll turn her to the bearing and speed now. Start to come alongside. Don't light up until I do.'

'Roger.'

Janac backed over to the centre of the bridge, watching the three as he went. There he dialled in the prearranged speed and course. He glanced out of the starboard side window. The green bow light of his ship was passing a hundred metres off their beam. He reached for the packet of Lucky Strike in his tunic pocket. This one had gone smoothly enough so far — a clean and simple take. He lit the cigarette one handed and blew out a smoke ring.

'That's more like it,' he said to the silent, trussed skipper. 'Well, either you're an excellent actor, my friend, or there are no nasty little surprises downstairs. Let's hope the latter. Or surely you will suffer.'

Chapter 25

Tosh stepped onto the bridge, sub-machine-gun on its strap against his chest. Edi was a pace behind him.

'We've cleared the accommodation and have all fifteen crew accounted for. They're under guard in the dining room one floor down,' said Tosh, waving back the way he had come. 'It's at the bottom of this staircase. There are no windows.'

Janac was leaning against the wheel. He looked up from watching the prisoners and nodded. 'No resistance?'

'None.'

Janac stubbed out his second cigarette thoughtfully and said, 'So one's not enough.' He straightened. 'Edi, take these three down with the others. Untie them when you get there.' He waved casually at the three officers still motionless and silent on the floor. The burly Indonesian nodded affirmation before hauling them to their feet one by one and frogmarching them off the bridge to join their crew. Janac watched them go, listened to the footsteps clattering down the staircase.

'Are we ready, boss?' asked Tosh.

'Soon as they're inside,' said Janac.

Tosh strode over to the top of the staircase and yelled, 'OK?'

Janac heard the confirmation as clearly as Tosh. He took three steps and snapped a switch on the control panel. Forward of the bridge the cargo deck was bathed in light. Off on their starboard side the bulk carrier's lights came on a few moments later.

'Let's do it,' said Janac. Tosh nodded wordlessly and

disappeared out of the door onto the starboard wing deck.

The operation took two hours. The transfer of targeted containers into the hold of the bulk carrier was now a smooth and well-practised procedure. The swell slowed progress a little, and although steaming straight into it stopped the ships' superstructures rolling into each other, the constant rise and fall still caused a couple of difficult moments. But Jordi's men worked the cranes on the bulk carrier with great precision and there were no accidents. Once it was done, the hatches were refastened. The pirate ship looked just like any other tramp steamer headed down the coast, touting for anything she could find in the way of cargo. Janac gave the instruction and then watched the two ships slowly sheer away from each other as Jordi turned south, towards their home base, the hulls parting with a sucking slosh as the bow waves separated.

Ahead, the horizon was already swimming with orange. Janac left the course set at due east, steaming into the swell and the sunrise. Then he strode out of the bridge and down the steps to the dining room. There he found the crew huddled together, sitting under the guns of two of his men.

'Let's get this lot outside, Edi,' he commanded. He picked up an empty fruit bowl and a handful of paper napkins, turned on his heel and led them down another two flights, out onto the port-side boat deck. From here the departing bulk carrier was hidden from view. Janac walked straight up to the guardrail and peered over the side. The water below churned and bubbled past at ten knots.

Janac scanned the rail and soon spotted the companionway gate, used when the ship was in port. He led the others that way. Chained to the superstructure nearby was a simple telescoping gangway. Janac waved at two of the prisoners, who were watching him closely. 'Untie this and push it out through the guardrail gate,' he ordered.

The two men turned passive, blank faces to each other.

'Do it,' snapped Janac. He slipped the revolver out of its well-worn holster.

The closer of the two, a slim Chinese man called Deng Chang, with tightly cropped, jet-black hair, touched his hand to his mouth nervously. He turned to the other crewman, who had shrunk behind him. A low voice translated the words into Cantonese for him. Janac's expression hardened at the sound.

It was five minutes before the two men had completed their work. The gangway was a metre wide, made of steel, with two supporting beams running its length. The rusty surface, ridged for grip in the wet, had been worn shiny in places by the passage of countless shoes. It extended five metres out over the water. Welded at metre intervals down each side were slim uprights. At the top of each was a ring, through which a chain handrail was normally fed. This had been removed.

Janac inspected the structure and indicated monosyllabic satisfaction. The pair stepped away, trying to blend back into the group, which only closed against them.

'You'll have realised by now that we are in the business of restoring the noble art of piracy to the position of prominence it deserves,' Janac began, the grey eyes flickering over each of the faces in the group as he spoke. 'It's your misfortune that on this occasion I have decided to resurrect another age-old tradition. Two of you will walk the plank.'

There was a frightened moan, which grew as the brief translations spread comprehension like a lethal virus.

'Any officers, any men, feel they should volunteer?' asked Janac.

The group quietened quickly as everyone sought anonymity. But Janac's eyes rested like searchlights on one after the other of the three men who had been on the bridge. All three stared at their feet, feeling the heat of the glare, shrinking from it. No one moved.

'Well, there's a surprise. No volunteers. The age of chivalry is indeed dead,' Janac went on. 'Fortunately, I have a contingency plan.'

'Boss?'

Janac looked round to find his lieutenant approaching with the rest of his men, all of whom, since completing the unloading of the containers, had been stripping the accommodation and office areas of anything valuable. Finding no one at the stern ready to disembark, they had left their booty and come looking.

'Ah, Tosh, just in time for the games.'

'What's happening, boss?' asked Tosh, staring at the gangplank.

'These gentlemen are about to play for the privilege of walking the plank.'

There was absolute silence — among prisoners and captors alike. Tosh looked back to find Janac's eyes on him. He glanced at the prisoners again. 'Can I have a word?' he asked in an undertone.

'What about?'

The Scotsman's greying ponytail twitched as he took another, more anxious, glance about him and hesitated. He had never questioned Janac's judgement before. All the games, all the murder and mayhem — he'd just let it wash over him. They had still got the job done and that was all he had cared about. But this time it could — did — matter. They needed one more target; they didn't need Hamnet to stop feeding them intelligence. He had to say something. He stepped closer. Janac's hand tightened almost imperceptibly around the butt of the revolver, still in his hand.

'Why?' hissed Tosh in Janac's ear.

'Because I want to see if two more dead men is enough

221

to stop him,' retorted Janac.

Tosh looked down. He could feel a long-dormant fury stirring. The temper that had earned him a dishonourable discharge from the Special Boat Service. A temper he had learned to control only in Janac's brutal, disciplining company. It was a lesson he had learned the hard way, so once again he stepped back. The anger burned in his guts but didn't make the jump to his head. He kept control.

Janac watched Tosh back off, then he knelt. He set the fruit bowl he had brought from the dining room on the deck, spat on a finger and wet the edge. Then he opened a napkin over the bowl, sticking it in place like a smooth white skin. He slipped open the chamber on the big revolver, pulled out a shell and lay it neatly in the middle of the napkin. Then he stood up and stepped back, reholstering the Smith and Wesson, and indicated that the prisoners should gather round the bowl.

'Sit,' he said, and they sat. 'Here's the deal,' he continued, pulling the pack of Lucky Strike out of his tunic pocket. He tapped out two cigarettes and lit them with the Zippo. He drew on both, left one in his mouth, and with the other leant over and burned a tiny hole in the napkin. He handed the cigarette to the man on his left, who took it with a shaking hand. 'You each burn a hole in the napkin until the cartridge drops. Whoever makes the last hole walks the plank.' He waved at the waiting gangway, then glanced round the circle. 'I suggest those of you who can translate, do so.'

There were more voluble words this time, accompanied by fearful glances — at the bowl, the gangplank, Janac. A shiver ran through the group. Janac's men saw the energy and spread out into better covering positions.

Janac nodded at the cigarette, still held gingerly in the first man's hand. 'Let's play,' he said, stepping back to lean against the railing next to Tosh. He drew deeply on the other cigarette and watched the shaking hand burn a second hole close to the edge, well away from the suspended cartridge. He glanced at Tosh, the grey eyes watchful in the gaunt face. 'This takes a while to get interesting,' he said.

Tosh grunted noncommittally, head down.

Janac appraised him. 'If I didn't know better, I could mistake that as a marked lack of enthusiasm for the way I'm leading this merry band of pirates.'

Tosh didn't miss the tone. He looked up, forced a weak smile. 'Nah. Never.'

'Good.'

The cigarette peppered sixty per cent of the napkin with holes before it burned out. Janac lit another, and the game went on. The slow, relatively calm start was surrendering to a frenzy, emotion rising and falling around the ring of captives like a slow-motion Mexican wave. As each player safely took his turn, relief settled over him like a blanket. A relief that steadily frayed and disappeared as the cigarette made its way back round to them. Grey faces, shaking hands, wild eyes brimful with fear, foreheads that bled sweat in the cool air. Paper turned to ash and the napkin grew frail. Janac's gunmen drew closer as the safe areas for a burn diminished and disappeared. Hard, cruel faces alight with excitement, mainlining on the manifest terror before them. Still the cartridge remained suspended, centred in a web of spindly, charred paper. But like a rattling roulette ball gradually slowing, closing out the options, limiting the places it could settle, the cartridge had to fall for someone.

It seemed certain that that someone would be the crop-haired Deng Chang, who had helped lower the gangplank. No one could see where another hole could possibly be made in any of the three arms of paper that now held the cartridge. When he accepted the cigarette, Deng coolly took a drag. He breathed the smoke in deeply and tried to remember what his father had taught him about the martial arts so many years before. He closed his eyes, straightened his back and imagined the napkin whole again. When his eyelids flickered up, he could see it. At the base of one of the arms, right beside the cartridge, so close he would almost have to push the cigarette against the shell, was paper enough that it might just take another hole. He sucked hard on the cigarette until it flared fiercely, rolled it on the deck to a tip, then reached out quickly with an arm that was rock steady. The napkin burned for the briefest moment. A tiny hole appeared. The paper held.

An incredulous gasp greeted Deng's unexpected reprieve. Emotion ripped around the players as he bowed his head and passed the cigarette to his left. Jose Mendez, a young Mexican chef on his first voyage, took it. His face was ashen. The acrid taste of vomit burned in his mouth, such had been the nauseating rush of fear when the cartridge had remained suspended. He couldn't believe the cigarette had come full circle back to him. Now, like Deng before him, he tried hard to compose himself. He sat and breathed deeply, closing his eyes. But still his hands shook. He stared at the napkin. There was one place, at the base of another of the arms. It might hold. But the greatest possible precision would be required, and Jose's hand was still shaking as it reached out with the cigarette tip. Silence fell. The next man in line crossed himself and started to pray under his breath. Mendez's hand trembled, he left the burning tip in place a fraction of a second too long. The paper glowed, flamed and cindered. The shell dropped into the bowl with a rattle. A tremor shook the little man's body. The cigarette butt dropped from his fingers, following the cartridge into the bowl. It continued burning, slowly, a thin wreath of smoke rising from a miniature funeral pyre into the midst of the grimly silent circle.

Janac grimaced at Edi. He'd have preferred it to be the Chinese man, but games were games and rules were rules. 'We have our first plank walker. Tie his hands and blindfold him.'

Edi stepped forward, pulled Mendez to his feet, clipped on plastic cuffs and tied the hapless man's own neckerchief across his eyes. Mendez was so frightened he could neither speak nor stand. Edi and Soey had to carry the frail figure to the rail. Only then, when he felt the breeze and heard the rush of water beneath him, did he come to life, kicking and squealing. But blindfold and bound as he was, it was easy for Soey to push him a couple of metres along the gangplank. Mendez tottered, trying to gain balance, the gangplank wobbling slightly under his weight. Right at the edge, he stood rooted to the spot. He was still wearing his chef's apron; the wind flapped it around his knees. The ocean churned, mawlike, below him.

'Walk,' said Janac.

Mendez didn't so much as twitch a muscle. And then he found his voice. 'Please. Have wife and child. Please.'

'Goddamit, walk!' bellowed Janac.

The Mexican sank uncertainly to his knees, in prayer, in supplication. The gangway twisted under his shifting weight. The ship rose slightly on one of the bigger swells and he swayed unsteadily.

Janac turned to his crew and grinned. 'Now I know why those old timers used to carry cutlasses. Something to prod the bastards along the plank with.' He turned back and raised his revolver. The bullet struck the steelwork a few centimetres from Mendez's left knee, sending shards and sparks flying. Mendez jerked away, his knee skidded and suddenly his balance was gone. His thin wail of terror rose to a squeal as he lunged his shoulder down to where he hoped there was solid steel but found only air. He slipped from sight into the shadow of the hull. His fading cry was terminated by an indistinct splash. He was gone. The ship swept onwards. Another sailor lost to the ocean.

All the radios squawked at once. 'RIB here. What the hell was that? You want me to pick it up?'

Janac snatched the VHF off his belt. 'Would I have thrown it overboard if I wanted it?' he snapped. 'I'll tell you when I want you to pick something up.' He clipped the radio back into place. 'Let's set it up and play it again.'

'No.'

Janac looked around for the voice. 'What?'

'I said no. If anybody else is to die, it had better be me.' The voice was resigned, slightly tremulous.

Janac recognised the skipper. He nodded, apparently satisfied. 'Chivalry lives after all. A brave man.' His tone wasn't so mocking this time. There were no voices raised in protest.

Fairbrother proffered his hands to Edi, accepted the plastic cuffs but shook away the blindfold. His red beard, flecked with grey, quivered around his chin. Janac nodded his agreement. Then Fairbrother took four careful, slow steps out onto the gangplank. He emerged from the shadow of the superstructure, and felt the warm sunshine on his face. He stood for a moment and listened. The silence of horrified, exalted anticipation from the men safely on the other side of the rail rang in his ears. So, too, the churn of the ocean, and the faraway thump of the engines he had presided over for so many thousands of miles. A lifetime of earning his living on the sea lay behind him. He was seven months from retirement. He had always known the risks, but had never expected it to end like this.

'Let's do it,' snapped Janac.

Fairbrother turned and faced his tormentor. 'So what are

226

you going to do now?' he asked. 'Come on, come out here and push me. My hands are tied, surely that can't be too hard.'

'Jesus wept, a hero,' snarled Janac. 'For God's sake, time's up.' The big revolver swept up and took a bead in the same motion. The report cracked out across the short space. The bullet took Fairbrother in his left knee. He spun away and crumpled simultaneously. Almost in slow motion, he started to fall. But this one didn't scream. Not a sound. Just the flap and rustle of the nightshirt as he fell. A white spatter and he was gone. Janac's men leant over the rail eagerly. Fairbrother didn't reappear. The splash was quickly smothered by the ship's wake.

Janac shouldered his weapon and muttered, 'I'll bring the cutlass next time.'

Chapter 26

Jasmine carefully tucked the thin sheet around Ben a little tighter. Then she looked up from the buggy in which he was quietly sleeping. Singapore's commercial waterfront churned past as the ferry motored them home. Her blue eyes flicked towards Hamnet and studied the grim, intense expression trained on the container terminal of Tanjong Pagar. If only he'd smile, she thought; he had such a gorgeous smile.

The last few days had been the worst so far. After recovering a level of good humour, Hamnet had become hopelessly preoccupied again. She had suggested an outing to Kusu Island to try to break the mood. It had failed, and not because of the overcast and unusually chilly weather. Hamnet had sat and stared morosely at the handful of families cooking lunch, listening to his radio through a headset. She had been left to entertain Ben alone, the pair of them completely shut out. She knew she should just walk away. Leave this difficult, complex man to look after his own son. Yet, at the same time, she knew she couldn't. Hamnet felt her watching eyes and turned.

'A good day out?' she asked with her bright smile. He nodded and struggled for an equally enthusiastic response, before glancing at his watch and fumbling for the radio in the daypack at his feet. Jasmine frowned, opened her mouth to say something, and then shut it. What was the point? All this had something to do with the late-night phone call, she was sure of that. She was also convinced it wasn't just about Anna. There was something else. A couple of times she had tried to probe, but the silence had been so stiff and painful she had quickly moved the conversation on. She settled back and closed her eyes, struggling to get comfortable on the hard, wooden bench seat. Perhaps one day he would feel able to confide in her.

Hamnet had the headset in place and the radio on just in time to hear fading music replaced by the serious tones of a newsreader. He listened intently to further gloomy predictions of the region's economic prospects. Then he shut his eyes as the words drilled into his head. He swallowed dryly, focused on not letting a further shred of expression show on his face. He had prepared himself for this. He listened to the scant details: another attack on a merchant ship north of the Philippines; two casualties reported; the piracy discovered by chance that morning, after the unmanned ship had almost rammed an oil tanker; the captive crew released by men put on board by the tanker's master to investigate. It was enough. He knew where the *Kyushu Sun* had been the night before, and he didn't need to be told this was the ship that had been attacked. He had been wrong. Horribly — probably fatally, murderously — wrong. He shut the thought out. He knew what he must do now. Everything had been made ready in case this happened. It had been an acknowledged risk. But he needed Jasmine to help.

He peeled the headset off and dropped it in the daypack. He glanced up at her face — so serene, so beautiful. He rubbed his right hand slowly against his cheek. What he had to tell her would shatter that peace. She didn't deserve that. It was no reward for her patience and kindness. Perhaps she wouldn't do it. The Bullens were a last resort, but they were really a little too old for the kind of journey he had in mind. Jasmine was his best chance.

He glanced sideways. They were coming up to Marina Park. Clifford Quay was around the next corner, in the bay. He would have to be quick. Despite being prepared, he had

229

been lucky to hear the news now. He knew he was under surveillance, and was certain Dubre was responsible, given the suspicions he had voiced over the phone. But there were only ten people on the ferry — unsurprising on a day that had constantly threatened rain. They were all families, and Hamnet was sure his police tail had pulled back, fearing identification in such company. But the cops would be waiting for him, if not on Clifford Quay, then at home. And there was every chance they would have instructions to pick him up. At best that would waste time, at worst it would scupper his plan before he had even started on it. He had to get off the boat unseen, before it docked. He tightened his grip on the pack. It held everything he needed. Would it survive a swim?

Hamnet shook Jasmine's arm gently. She opened her eyes and looked straight into his. She knew immediately. 'What's wrong?' she said.

Hamnet casually glanced up and down the boat. Everyone was in the bow taking photographs of the city. He reached for Ben's buggy with one hand, the pack in the other.

'Come with me.'

He led her to the stern, pushing Ben in front. He moved to starboard — the offshore side — behind the toilets, out of sight of the bow. He sat, and turning to Jasmine indicated that she should do the same. No one paid them the slightest attention.

'We don't have a lot of time,' he said. 'I desperately need your help.'

Something flickered across her face — almost relief. 'This is something to do with the radio?' She glanced at the bag. 'What did you hear?'

Hamnet hesitated. 'I can't say yet. It's better that I don't tell you what's happening, or where I'm going. Will you help me? Will you help Ben?'

'What do you need me to do?'

'Take Ben to England. Take him home, to my mother.'

Her blue eyes widened. She bit her lower lip nervously. 'To England?'

Hamnet nodded, leaning forward. 'Jasmine, I'm really sorry but we don't have time for questions, barely for thinking. Will you do it? Please?'

She didn't hesitate, but nodded hard, her dark hair falling across her face. 'Yes, of course.'

'You've got your passport? I have everything else you need.'

'I always have it with me, after you told me I should.'

'Good. I don't want you to go to the airport here and wait for a flight. I want you to take a taxi from the quay, straight across the causeway. Don't go home, don't stop, don't do anything other than drive direct to Malaysia. The police might want to stop you, but even if they're following, you'll be across the border before they can react. Hopefully they'll be too busy looking for me, anyway, to worry too much about you. Once you get to Johor Bahru, get on a bus or train or another taxi — whatever you can find — and get to Kuala Lumpur. Once you get there, fly to Britain on the first available flight. This is Ben's passport and enough cash for the tickets.' He discreetly pulled a manila envelope out of the bag. 'Once you're both there, send me an email message to let me know. Give me a return address so I can reply. Then you can also call the Bullens and tell them where you are. They might be worried.' He held out the envelope. 'Everything you need is in there — addresses and money.'

Jasmine took the envelope. 'You want me to do all this without any explanation of why?' she asked.

'It's a lot better that you don't know until you get to England. I'll send a separate message to my mother, explaining everything. Once you get there, you'll know as much as I do. And hopefully, by then this will all be over.' He hesitated, looked at the envelope in her hands. 'There's enough money in there to get you back home to the States, from England.'

Jasmine dropped her gaze. 'Who said I wanted to go home?' she replied, mouth down-turned.

Hamnet's brow knitted. 'You were going to Australia, weren't you? It might get you there, if you can find a cheap enough flight. If not, my mother will help. I'll make sure she knows.'

'You'll come to England? When this is over?' Jasmine looked up.

'As soon as I can. I'm finished out here. Just this one piece of business to deal with.'

She nodded, tilting her head, searching for his eyes. 'I'll wait, in England. I'll wait for you, and help your mother with Ben. He should have someone familiar around.'

Hamnet looked up, too, but couldn't hold her gaze. He glanced away, at the shoreline. The corner of the headland before Marina Bay was closing fast.

'That plastic carrier bag we brought lunch in — do you still have it?' he asked.

Jasmine looked confused for a moment, then dug into a pouch on Ben's buggy. She pulled out half a baguette and handed over the bag. Hamnet dropped the daypack in it, tied the handles together then stood and grabbed the life ring hanging on the rail nearby. He strapped the pack to it as best he could. It wasn't perfect, but it would have to do.

'I'm getting off at this corner of the park. There's a good chance the police will be waiting for me at the pier. If anyone stops you or asks you a question, tell them I met some friends on the island. That I'm staying for the last boat, that you brought Ben back for his dinner and bed. Then get in a cab and don't stop for anyone until you're in England.'

He glanced forward, round the corner of the toilet block. Passengers and crew alike were still intent on the approach to the bay; no one was looking aft. Nor was there anyone on the Marina Park shoreline. It was the break he needed. He stepped over the rail, the life ring tucked under one arm. Jasmine stood quickly, suddenly understanding, realising that this was it. He was leaving, she was on her own with Ben.

'No!'

'Shhh.' Hamnet had his finger to his mouth, and now their eyes met. He leant against the rail and kissed her. Her lips were soft and warm.

'I will see you again?' she asked.

'Of course. Just make sure you've finished that picture of Ben by then.' His voice started to crack.

'Promise me? We need you.' She turned and picked up Ben.

'Yes.' He could manage only the one word, feeling his knees, his resolve, weaken. He ran his hand gently across Ben's forehead — the touch, her expression, burning itself into his memory. He knew he would never forget that face, that look, as long as he lived. But nor could he forget what had already happened, was happening. Before he could go forward, he had to go back, finish this. He quickly lowered himself off the rail until his feet were trailing in the wash. Then he let go.

Hamnet was kicking himself back up as soon as he hit the water. He lost touch with the life ring for a moment, but surfaced beside it. It was still the right way up. He looked over and caught sight of the ferry as it rounded the corner away from him, into the bay. He ducked behind the ring and started to paddle gently for the shore. No one emerged from the tree line before he was able to haul himself quickly onto the rocks and then up into cover. He jogged deep into the thick of the landscaped park. Then he stood still and listened. The distant hum of traffic, a low rumble of thunder from the long-promised storm. Otherwise it was quiet. He knelt and fumbled in the plastic bag. The backpack was damp round the top, but no water had penetrated inside. All his precious equipment was dry.

Hamnet stripped to his boxer shorts and hung his clothes on branches. Then the storm hit and it poured with rain — a windless, vertical downpour with a fierce sound-and-light show. At least it rinsed the salt out. The sky cleared as the thunderstorm departed, and with a couple of hours' daylight left, the sun still had some power to dry.

Once the rain had stopped, he was able to get on with the next task. He needed to find a ship. It didn't matter what it was carrying, it simply had to travel the same route as his last target — up past the northern tip of the Philippines. That much he knew he could ascertain from the published schedules of the shipping lines, which were accessible on the Internet. With the laptop hooked up to the mobile phone, he made a search query on each of the companies operating out of Singapore. From there it took him ten minutes to find what he was looking for — a Hanking ship that was leaving early Monday and heading for Osaka. He sent Janac the standard message about the target, making up the cargo details. The benign weather in the South China Sea had to hold for just a few more days — one more thing to worry about as he lay sleeplessly in the rough nest he fashioned for himself in the scrub.

At first light, he dressed in his slightly damp clothes and walked to the Marina Bay MRT station. He took the train one stop, to Raffles Place. From there he walked quickly south to the Telok Ayer food centre. The dazzling skyscrapers loomed threateningly over the untidy square of stalls.

He buried himself deep under the red-tiled roof to eat a furtive breakfast and drink a reviving coffee. The ceiling fans beat away the minutes, drawing the occasional whiff of rotting food up from the gutters. As the heat and humidity built around him, so did the bustle of people, and by eleven o'clock it was easy to lose himself in the crowd. He was grateful Singapore was a city that never stopped shopping.

He walked up through the steaming streets, posting the letter to his mother at the first opportunity. Then he bought a sturdy holdall. In a men's clothes shop he found a dark suit, a white shirt and a formal collar. The next stage was harder. At the Funan IT Mall, it took him a couple of hours to find the phone he was looking for — one that could use the new system of low-earth-orbit satellites. It would check first for access on a terrestrial mobile network, and then switch to the satellites if it couldn't find a standard station. He also bought the cables and PC card he needed to connect it to the laptop, along with a couple of hundred dollars' credit on calls. He paid with cash. The shop assistant helped him set up the system and check he had Internet access. It was the middle of the afternoon before he walked back out into the mall, satisfied at last.

The next item was both easier and cheaper to acquire — a hand-held GPS unit. It took him three shops and ten minutes to track down, and a little under two hundred dollars to buy. But now the loan he had secured against Anna's promised life insurance money was almost gone. There was just enough for some food.

Out of the cool of the mall and back on the hot streets, he found a supermarket, where he stocked up on dry biscuits, a few tins of fruit, some Granola bars and bottled water. Concerned at the amount he was now carrying, but unable to do much about it, he took the MRT to Tanjong Pagar. Then he walked down Maxwell Road to Shenton Way, which he followed southwest. By now his calves were cramped and his feet sore, he was caked in sweat and dust, and his nose and lungs were clogged with exhaust fumes. But the elevated section of the expressway that ran across the bottom of Shenton Way was his final destination. He turned left, parallel to the road above, then, with a quick glance around him, stepped into the scrubby shade that ran beside the pavement. He walked fast, moving deeper under the expressway, ducking round the occasional bush that survived in this insalubrious environment.

He knew that the most northerly road in the container port, between Finger Pier and the Tajong Pagar workshop, ran beside a chain-link fence. On the other side of the fence was the wasteland he was now walking through. He was confident it would provide access to the perimeter under good cover, and he wasn't disappointed. Out from under the shade of the expressway there was a thick growth of trees and bushes, which took him right up to the fence. Beyond was the twenty-four-hour bustle of the port. He found a spot on the edge of the cover and sat down to wait.

He had two final jobs to do to complete his preparation. He hooked the laptop to the satellite phone and logged onto the Internet. Then he checked his email. There was nothing from Jasmine, which didn't yet concern or surprise him. She had only had a day — he needn't start feeling concerned until the following night. But there was confirmation of the target from Janac. It seemed the weather forecast was good — the high pressure would hold over the northern Philippines. He logged off, shut down the computer and packed it away — after pulling out the heavy roll of linen that had sat in the bottom of his pack since Dubre's early-morning phone call. Hamnet hadn't looked at this since Moh, Naisborough's man, had given it to him in the Burmese jungle. He assumed he could thank General Lee's men for his continued possession of the weapon, for their apparent failure to search his bag. That he had brought it all the way back to Singapore undetected was more the result of luck than cleverness. He'd completely forgotten about it until he had emptied his backpack at the Bullens'.

He unwrapped the gun for only the second time, on this occasion to examine it properly. It was a nine-millimetre, semiautomatic SIG Sauer. He found the magazine catch between the trigger guard and the grip panels. The magazine clunked out easily enough, and he established that the weapon was loaded. He rolled the gun back up and packed it neatly beside the computer and phones. He was as ready as he'd ever be.

Chapter 27

At midnight Hamnet pulled the suit out of the holdall and changed. He arranged the stiff white collar back to front, but with no mirror to check how it looked he just had to hope it was convincing. After a little careful repacking, he managed to fit the contents of both bags in the holdall. He then hid his discarded clothes and the empty daypack under a scrappy shrub. Littering, he thought, was probably the most serious Singapore law he'd broken — so far.

He crept up to the chain-link fence and started to move along it. On the other side, floodlights blazed down from high towers and loading cranes danced ponderously in the glare. It didn't take him long to find the best spot. On the edge of a pool of light, there was thick foliage on both sides of the fence. A double strand of barbed wire at the top, set in a V, was the only thing that gave him any trouble, but once over that he was able to drop to the ground inside the container terminal, still hidden in the dank, green cover. The next stage was more difficult. He knew the site was covered by security cameras, and that creeping around it was the easy way to get caught. He had to front it out, and the hardest part was going to be stepping out of hiding. He pulled his orange, high-visibility vest out of the holdall — courtesy of Konsan — and slipped it on over the jacket.

He crouched, waiting for one of the double-stack container lorries to make its way down the road. He didn't have to wait long. The crash of gears announced the machine's presence a hundred metres away. It rumbled closer. He didn't hesitate. As it passed, he stood and walked quickly out from his cover, behind the lorry and across the tarmac. There was no howl of sirens, no response from the site security. Nothing altered in the background growl of port activity. He strode down the line of stacked containers, hauling in deep, slow breaths. Now he had to find the right ship.

The Tanjong Pagar terminal was a highly orderly operation. Containers, in stacks five high, were arranged in strictly parallel rows, laid out between the tracks of the four-legged overhead cranes used to lift them. Hamnet headed east first, across the top of these rows, towards Finger Pier. When he reached this, he turned and walked south, ships and water to his left, towering piles of containers to his right. He glanced up occasionally to check the names of the boats. The *Hanking Empire* wasn't among them. Still, no one paid him any attention. He crossed the pier at the bottom and worked his way north, along the East Lagoon. Halfway up he got lucky. There it was, painted in white on the flat black stern — *Hanking Empire*.

Hamnet's eyes roved over the vessel, quickly assessing his options as he approached. A single companionway ran up from the dock, thirty metres from the stern. It reached the deck at the base of four storeys of accommodation. Above these rose the smoke stack, while forward of this was the bridge superstructure. The starboard wing deck hung out over an open companionway, and behind it was a lifeboat on derricks. That would make an awkward hiding place. It wasn't overlooked, but any noise he made would be audible to anyone on the companionway below or on the wing deck. Another lifeboat looked more promising. It was slung from derricks on the third level so that it hung just above the aft railings on the open second deck. It was overlooked by an observation deck on the fourth level, and any noise might be picked up by anyone on the three lower decks. But those decks would see a lot less traffic than the wing deck and forward companionway. He made his decision.

The aft lifeboat would be his target.

Hamnet continued his steady pace towards the ship — he hadn't missed a stride since spotting the name. Loading was still taking place inside the hull, but he couldn't see anyone on deck, and the dock was frequented only by cranes. It was now or never. The machines continued in their labour as the distance peeled away — sixty, fifty, forty metres.

There was a clatter from above. Hamnet's head jerked up to see a slight figure in overalls and orange vest loping down the companionway towards him. Somehow Hamnet kept walking evenly, focusing on his stride length to keep his mind off the danger. The crewman reached the dockside before Hamnet arrived at the companionway. Hamnet did his best to smile. The man took a quick glance, his face hidden in shadow. Then he tapped his head. Hamnet didn't understand at first, then realised he wasn't wearing a hard hat. He broke his stride, and with a rush of inspiration held up and waved the holdall. The man understood but didn't approve. 'You should put it on, Father,' he said in a Mancunian accent, with a faintly scolding tone. But he didn't wait for a reply, let alone to watch Hamnet comply. Instead, he hurried on towards the crane working on the forward half of the ship.

Hamnet exhaled a long sigh of relief as he made his way tremulously up the gangway. The ruse had worked. The priests who ran the merchant-marine hostels were regular visitors to ships in ports all over the world and rarely rated a second glance. They would palm a few hands, smile and promote their mission with a curious mix of God and cheap booze. It was the perfect cover. He hesitated for only a moment as he stepped aboard, then turned sharp left towards the stern. He took the companionway up to the second level before continuing aft. In a few steps the lifeboat was right in front of him. He slowed as he crossed the deck towards it. The plastic cover was hooked down with elastic ties. He looked back over his shoulder, and then upwards. There was no one on either this deck or those above. Why should there be? They had a schedule to keep, a ship to load.

He stopped next to the lifeboat and swivelled slowly round. He couldn't be seen from the cabin of the crane, but the man from Manchester was visible on the quay below. Hamnet slid over to the port side of the ship to get out of sight. Then, in one swift movement, he released a couple of the ties on the cover and pulled it back. He dumped the holdall over the gunwale, climbed up the railing and followed it in. It took longer to reattach the ties from inside, and his hands shook as he fiddled with them, feeling for the hooks. But finally it was done. He was under cover, undetected. He slumped on the wooden deck, nervous tension pouring out of him. There was only one act left to play, and that was about three days away. It was a comforting thought, and allowed him to sleep.

Hamnet never knew what woke him, but he came to with a suddenness that didn't match the soporific rumble of engines beneath him, the humid air that enveloped him, or the gentle motion that rolled him first one way and then the other. They were moving. He glanced at his watch: eight a.m. They had probably been moving for an hour or two. It was already hot under the cover.

Janac would be expecting a position report. He lay still and listened. Minutes passed. Nothing changed, nothing was moving outside. Struggling with stiff muscles, he raised himself onto one elbow and unzipped the holdall. Piece by piece, he pulled out all the electronic equipment, carefully set it up and switched everything on. The GPS went through its opening routine quietly enough, searching quickly for the satellites with which to calculate its position. But the computer's hard disk clicked and rattled as it started up, unnervingly loud in the stifling silence of his hideaway. He was relieved he'd thought to turn off the machine's speakers back in Singapore.

On the one hand he wanted to take things slowly, to pause after each step to check for movement outside. On the other hand he knew his gadgetry had a limited battery life, and that he would be pushing it to make it last all the way to the Philippines. Gingerly he switched on the phone. Meanwhile, the GPS had found itself and reported his latitude and longitude as well as a course and speed. They were doing fifteen knots to the northeast, which meant they were already in open water and clear of the Strait of Singapore. He opened the email application on the laptop and, depressing each key slowly so that it didn't click, typed in his standard message and encoded it. Then he opened the Internet software and made the call on the satellite phone. The computer linked down the phone line and his position report was gone in an instant.

Hamnet smiled briefly with satisfaction. As far as Janac was concerned he was reporting from the Konsan office, just as he always had done. He would have the element of surprise on his side as they entered the endgame. Then the smile evaporated. No incoming emails — still no message from Jasmine.

Quickly he moved on to the marine-news website, downloaded the 'latest updates' file, logged off and powered down the phone and GPS to conserve their batteries. Then he looked at the news stories. The account of the execution of Mendez and Fairbrother verged on the hysterical. He switched off the computer and fell back against the deck with a thud he didn't even notice.

The decision to provide Janac with a third boat had been an agonising one. But the *Pinta*'s first mate's account of Johansen's death had been unequivocal. The gutsy old skipper had died because he had recklessly tried to overpower their guard. Hamnet had had too much to lose to give up after this apparently unnecessary death. But now he was facing the consequences of his decision. He had gambled and lost — two more lives. Janac had coldly and deliberately raised the stakes.

Hamnet had all day to sweat over it, as the heat in his enclosed hiding place steadily increased. He knew that the response he had planned might lose him his second son, perhaps his own life, but there was no question now, it had to be done. Except — where were Jasmine and Ben? Had Dubre had Jasmine arrested, or simply stopped from leaving Singapore? If he'd forced her and Ben to stay within Janac's reach, he was powerless. He couldn't take any chances with Ben's life, with Jasmine. Not after Anna. He simply couldn't bear to lose them. But then how many crewmen was he prepared to see die? How could he just stay hidden in the lifeboat and watch? It was an impossible choice.

He made his two further reports that day in the hope that while he was on line word would come of their safe arrival in England. On each occasion the computer and phone seemed to emit impossibly loud sounds — never mind that such reason as he could muster told him the clickings and beeps were muffled by the heavy lifeboat cover and likely to be drowned by the background noise of engines and ocean. But still there was nothing. Wherever Jasmine was, she hadn't, or couldn't, let him know she and Ben were safe.

The night brought cooler temperatures and an end to the day's reports. But sleep was impossible. Lying in a lifeboat for the first time since he had been pulled out of one half-dead, he was tormented by swirling demons old and new, too many to count.

As warmth and light began to penetrate the plastic cover,

he realised the seemingly endless night was over. With cramped and shaking hands he switched the equipment back on for his early-morning report. He forced himself slowly and silently through the routine of measuring the ship's position, of composing a message, of encoding it, of logging on and sending.

This time the computer flashed up the notice he'd been hanging on: 'You have one mail message waiting.' And there it was, one line: 'Arrived safely. A plea from all three of us for news. Love Jasmine, Ben, Mother.'

Hamnet wilted under the relief — the strength-sapping release that seemed to soak into the wooden deck beneath him. It was a couple of minutes before he could compose a brief lie in reply: 'Happy and safe in Singapore. Business nearly settled. Will be in touch by phone soon.'

Now things were simpler. The transaction was clearer. It would be completed in a day or two. But that day or two crawled by with excruciating slowness, extracting a full pound of flesh in exchange for its passing. The air moved even less than Hamnet himself, terrified as he was that a single noise might lead to his discovery. He came to know every square centimetre of his voluntary prison. The streaks of grey that ran down the outside of the cover, visible against the daylight, lost at night. The broken deck-board that threatened to creak and poke him in the back every time he moved. The spreading stain of sweat where his body pressed against the wood. He counted the screws in each rubbing strake, the knots in the wood of each thwart. He rolled a quarter turn every quarter of an hour to try to avoid sores. Each movement performed so slowly and carefully. When what he really wanted was to leap and stretch and scream.

Once, a noise sent a rogue chill through him — the clatter of a door opening and shutting, passing footsteps. But only on that one occasion did anyone come near the lifeboat. For the rest of the time, little marked the passing of the hours. There was a slight change in the ship's motion as the breeze freshened briefly from the southwest, sending ripples across the not-quite-taut lifeboat cover. There was the return to a smoother passage as this quickly died, the *Hanking Empire* advancing under the umbrella of high pressure that still soothed and protected the South China Sea. The big moments were the two-hourly sips of water and biscuits. The four-hourly Granola bars. The eight-hourly tins of fruit. He urinated into the empty bottles. And defecated into the empty tins.

But time always passes, events always come to hand. No matter how long or slow or painful the wait, the end always arrives. Hamnet told himself this, and while he waited in the lifeboat, he built a future. Just like he had the time before. Then, Anna had made it worth carrying on. Worth taking one more dry, painful breath of hot, salty air across cracked, parched and bleeding lips. He told himself that this was easy by comparison. He had enough food, enough water.

This time he had Ben to carry on for. And Jasmine — was she waiting? Would she really be there when this was finished? He didn't expect her to stay in England. For the most part he had made her life miserable since meeting her. Nor did he think he should expect it. Not so soon after losing Anna. It wasn't right, was it? He didn't really know. How did these things work? But her face, when he'd left her. He could hold onto that. For now, it helped.

Chapter 28

The chink of metal on metal was very close. Just the other side of the hull. Hamnet tensed against the shudder that prickled up his spine. It had started. He lay motionless in a flood of adrenaline. Fighting to control his breathing, to relax muscles hellbent on tensing. Another chink. A rustle. The sounds were coming from behind, on the port side. Then a scuffing noise — beside him, just forward of the lifeboat. He had control of himself now. His heart was thumping, but his mind was focused. Oh, so totally focused.

There were only a couple more noises — thin sounds, steadily moving away, forward. He listened to them go, then waited three minutes, carefully timed on his watch. Nothing but the beat of the engines, the breeze against the superstructure. No sound of any guard left behind. When was it time? Now. He should go now.

Just at that moment, he heard a gunshot — flat and dull, distant. He hesitated. And was lucky to do so. The buzz of radio static was right next to him. His pulse screamed through the two-hundred-a-minute barrier. Then a voice he recognised, on the radio, calling for support on the container deck. Janac was on board. Footfalls, muffled but distinct, faded at a run. A door banged open and shut. He daren't consider how close he had been to blowing it.

Instead, he felt in the holdall for the SIG handgun. The warm plastic grips slipped against the sweat on his palm. He wiped his hand on his sodden shirt to little effect. He grasped the butt harder, until he could feel the pattern bite into his skin. He rolled onto his side and, supporting himself with his gun arm, gently unhooked and lifted the lifeboat cover. The darkness was tempered by a sliver of moon, and he could see the aft deck through the narrow gap he had opened. There was no movement. But there was the sound of another shot — again from a long way forward. He had to get on with it. He flipped the cover back and rolled out of the boat in a single motion, dropping to the deck in shadow. Nothing else moved among the windlasses, the coils of chain. He turned and checked astern, looking for the power-boat. He could see nothing but the cool, moonlit, blue-white wash against the dark ocean.

Cries and shouts now. And a short burst from an auto-matic weapon. Hamnet whipped back round, wiped his mouth with his gun hand. There was a war going on. The rules had changed. He wondered what had happened after the murder of Fairbrother and Mendez. Had the crews been armed, told to defend themselves? Or had they prepared to fight individually? He knew the latter was most likely. Prac-tically and legally, the arming of untrained crew, with or without instructions to repel borders, was a nightmare. He felt an ice cube of guilt slip into his stomach. But he couldn't have warned these men — they would have just pulled out, headed home, taken another route. This was the only way.

The sentry who had been called forward for support had headed into the accommodation superstructure. Hamnet wasn't anxious to follow him. He knew the way he wanted to go — he'd had plenty of time to plan this. He tucked the pistol into his belt and stepped up onto the top of the stern railing. Supporting himself with the rope from which the lifeboat was suspended from the derrick, he straightened slowly until he was peering across the floor of the next deck up. He scanned the empty space — only a couple of metres before a set of three individual doors that led inside. He grabbed the lower railing half a metre above his head, and pulled himself up so he could lift a knee onto the deck.

Silence in front of him, the edge of another deck three metres directly above.

He hopped over the railing and threw himself into the shadow at the side of one of the doors. No response — just another distant burst of automatic fire. The crew were obviously fighting a solid defensive action. He cupped a hand against the dark glass in the top half of the door and peered through. He could just make out an open area of tables and chairs that looked like a dining room. All that mattered was that it was empty. He stepped back across the two metres of deck, then up onto the railings again. This time he could only steady himself by bracing his left hand against the deck above. Slowly and carefully he stretched up, until he could peer over the lip of that deck.

There was movement. He ducked back down. His mind replaying what he had seen. One man, back towards him, standing in an open doorway, some kind of weapon held at his right side. He was a good ten metres away, at the entrance to the accommodation block. Beside him was a ladder that led up onto the top of the superstructure. From there, Hamnet knew he had only to go forward past the smoke stack to reach the bridge. He teetered on the railing, half-crouching, left hand pushing up against the deck to steady himself. He wiped his right hand again on the stinking, sweat-soaked shirt. He ran his tongue across his lips, pulled the gun from his belt. He would give the man a minute. He stared forward into the blackness behind the glass of the doors. He felt horribly exposed, perched out in the open. He daren't glance away from the glass to look at his watch, counting the seconds instead. He had reached fifty when he heard a noise above him. He moved his head out just enough to look up.

The shotgun muzzle was the first thing he saw. It was one of those moments when there was no time to think, only to act, to react. To be a survivor or a casualty. Hamnet snapped his legs straight, jumping, left hand snaking out and up from under the deck. He felt the coarseness of the fatigue tunic under his fingers, locked on at the touch, half-aware of the stunned surprise in the face he yanked down towards him.

A moment before, Soey had been resting casually on the rail, staring out at the silver sea, the accommodation block supposedly cleared and secured. Now both men were falling in slow motion, Hamnet's weight dragging Soey over the rail. Then a sudden resistance as Soey got a grip, both of the situation and with his free left hand. They stopped with a jerk. Soey was bent tight over the railing at his waist with Hamnet hanging off the handful of collar that he had a life-and-death hold on.

Hamnet saw the weapon move very clearly. He hadn't taken his eyes off it. But it had to come up and over the railing, and even the short length of the sawn-off shotgun was a handicap in this hand-to-hand struggle. Hamnet was already powering into a single left-arm pull-up he wouldn't have thought himself capable of, closing into his opponent, making it even harder for Soey to use the gun. The SIG came up in Hamnet's right hand. He buried the muzzle of the nine-millimetre deep in the soft flesh above the Adam's apple. Coursing with adrenaline, he once again forgot all about the safety. But this time it didn't matter. His finger achieved the twelve pounds of trigger pull required for the SIG's double action to push back the hammer and fire. Then the semiautomatic recocked, the single-action, four-and-a-half pound trigger pull so light in comparison the second shot was unintended.

And unnecessary. The first bullet drove up through the centre of Soey's skull. Hamnet's eyelids twitched and quivered as blood and brains spattered his face at each report. Soey died instantly, his left hand opened. They both started to fall again, but this time Hamnet was the only one who cared. He turned and twisted, desperately trying to push off the body and onto the boat. His left heel just clipped the railing and kicked him the right way. He hit the deck hard, with a jarring impact on his right knee. A moment later he heard the body land, with a wet, bloody slap, on the cover of the lifeboat below.

'Shit, shit, shit,' he hissed, desperately wiping his face with his shirtsleeve. Hands, arms, body — all were trembling violently. But his instincts were already clearing the gory mess from his mind, if not his face and shirt. He refocused on the next move, pushing distractions aside.

He stepped back to the railing, barely noticing the shooting pain from his damaged knee, and looked out and up for just an instant. No gunfire, no shouting, no lights. The dead man had been alone. He stuffed the gun back in his waistband and reached for the rail above. Still wet with blood, his hands struggled for a grip, but he managed to haul himself up and over. He scurried across the open deck to a ladder and started to climb. He was just in time. As he rolled onto the top of the accommodation block, the doors crashed open below him.

Tosh and Edi swept their MP5s across the deck. The Sure Fire torches built into the stocks caught the dark gleam of blood on the railing. The pair looked at each other, the whites of their eyes luminous in their blacked-up faces. Their advance onto the open deck was cautious, professional. But they heard nothing, saw nothing. Hamnet had backed another five metres away from the ladder, the SIG now trained on the top rung. He couldn't see the scene below as Edi took a cautious first look over the railing. But he heard the sharp gasp as the big Indonesian caught sight of Soey's body. Tosh, finally satisfied there was no immediate threat, joined him at the rail.

'Christ, half his head's gone. Let's check the deck below.' He was already reaching for the radio to report the find to Janac.

Hamnet listened to the two men's footfalls as they passed through one of the doors beneath him. He rolled to his feet. Adrenaline, fear, hate —all were forcing him forward. So close now.

His right eye was weeping badly — something was stuck under the lid. Through blurred vision, he could just see that the deck stretched forward to the back wall of the bridge. It was divided in two by the smoke stack, up the side of which ran a ladder onto the roof of the bridge. He pressed himself against the base of the stack and crept towards the ladder. The din of the engines bellowed and blubbered through the steel wall of the chimney. He dabbed his eye with a cleanish piece of shirt, blinking hard, tears trickling. Gradually it washed itself clean, and as it dried, clear sight returned. Yet again he wiped the palm of his right hand, and the gun grip. Then, cautiously, he climbed the ladder and wriggled onto the roof of the bridge. To his left, the lifeboat derricks, sticking up and out; to his right, the aerial tower that held the communications links. He was almost there.

With infinite stealth, he paced fifteen metres towards the leading edge of the roof. Five metres short he slid to his belly. He inched forward, gradually increasing his view of the container deck. It was dark below him, in the shadow of the bridge and accommodation superstructure cast by the moon. The fighting seemed to have stopped. He could hear nothing, could see no sign of activity. Had Janac gained control? He watched for a few moments, and then, in answer to his question, out from behind the nearest stack of containers trooped a shadowy line of figures in single file. As they approached the foot of the accommodation block some twenty metres below, someone threw open a door.

White light spilled onto the deck. Hamnet counted twelve men with hands clasped behind their heads. To the rear, one to either side, two armed guards. Janac had control.

Hamnet glanced left and right. On the port side, a heavy green polythene sheet was stretched tight above the wing deck. He writhed silently over to it. It stuck out at right angles from the accommodation superstructure. He crawled aft, past the first lifeboat davit, from where he could see the wing deck was empty. He stretched for a fuller view. Red light fell on the deck; the bridge door was open. The lifeboat was little more than a metre below him. He eased himself over the edge and down onto the lifeboat cover. He crept forward, the material sagging under his weight. The bow sat a third of a metre short of the top railing of the wing deck. He stepped onto the railing, pulled in tight against the bulkhead beside the door and slid down onto the deck. He was just in shadow — a shaft of red from the night-lights fell on the deck at his feet.

He had arrived. This was it. A tremor shook his gun hand. His heart was bashing against his rib cage. His throat was suffocatingly tight. He hesitated. Ben and Jasmine were safe. He didn't have to go through with this. He shut his eyes. Anna's face swam into view. But nothing would bring her back. Not even this.

Three metres away, inside the bridge, MP5 slung diagonally across his chest as always, Tosh patted his trouser pockets and pulled out his leather pouch. He tapped a line of rolling tobacco into a cigarette paper. Janac listened to his report, but didn't take his eyes off the only other person on the bridge — the ship's skipper, trussed and gagged, lying at his feet along the back wall. Janac was still, dangerously still.

'Dead?' he said. 'But I thought we had them all trapped forward?'

'No,' Tosh mumbled past the completed cigarette. The disposable lighter wouldn't fire again. He stabbed repeatedly at the ignition wheel, annoyed that he hadn't replaced it.

'And now?'

Tosh caught Janac's tone this time, looked up, pulled the cigarette from his mouth to speak. 'Almost — the whole crew accounted for, a couple wounded, no dead. But we have an extra on board like you expected. Someone's been covert in the aft lifeboat. It's full of piss and shit, some food, a GPS, computer, satphone. All the toys. Me and Edi had a pretty good look around but we couldn't find him. The lads will sweep the boat again with a full squad as soon as the rest of the crew are secure.'

Janac smiled now, stubble bristling under the face blacking, his body relaxing a fraction. 'So he is here. I thought he must be. Couldn't see how he was reporting the position otherwise. What with the entire Singapore police force looking for him. Good job we brought the kid.'

'We have to find Hamnet first. And he's armed and dangerous — as they say.' Tosh went back to his cigarette. It still wouldn't light.

Janac listened to his lieutenant's futile efforts with the lighter. 'We'll smoke him out the same way as last time if we have to,' he said. 'But I suspect he'll wait for us to start the fun and games, then show. He probably wants to swap himself, rather than the crew, for the child. Like he did with his wife. If only it were that simple.' He snorted a short, vicious laugh. He tapped the heavy revolver three times against the chart table he was leaning against.

It was the first sound Hamnet heard as he inched closer to the door. He had found him. Tap, tap, tap. Just as he'd heard at the beginning, all those weeks before. And now it was the end. All he had to do was step round the corner.

Chapter 29

Tap, tap, tap.

Anger started to boil. The sense of helplessness Hamnet had felt on the *Shawould* was gone. This time he could do something. He raised the gun to his shoulder, left hand supporting, his right index finger laid gently against the trigger. He tried to get a bearing on the noise. But it issued from the doorway with little hint as to whether the source was forward or aft of the opening. He took a long, slow, silent breath. Blinked hard to clear his eyes. Filled his mind with the image of Janac. He was the target. Turn, find the target and squeeze. It was as simple as that.

Hamnet rolled round the doorframe, extending the weapon in a smooth movement. The vertical white bead of the gun-sight tracking across the room. Janac was fifteen metres away, under one of the red night-lights. He was facing Hamnet, leaning against the side of the chart table, the back wall of the bridge to his left. It was less than a second before the white line danced on Janac's face, but it was still too long. Janac had heard the faint rustle of motion and looked up from his prisoner. He didn't have time to swing the unholstered revolver up, across and onto Hamnet, only to raise the muzzle a few degrees. A barely discernible motion. But the Smith and Wesson was now aiming its .45 calibre load at the back of the skipper's head. Hamnet met Janac's eyes with three-and-a-half pounds of pressure on the trigger and hesitated.

Three metres away and at ten o'clock, to Hamnet's left, Tosh had his back to the new arrival. The Scot had been too preoccupied with the recalcitrant lighter to notice anything amiss. Until he saw Janac's gaze shift, his gun move. Lighter and cigarette slipped from his fingers. He tensed to turn and fire. But he had way too much to do from such a slow start.

'I'll kill him!' Hamnet half-shouted. 'Don't move!'

Like Hamnet, Tosh also hesitated. His right hand was halfway across his chest, only centimetres from the trigger of the MP5. The chest sling made the weapon as easy to ready and shoot from there as any other. But he had to turn and locate Hamnet, and the safety was on.

'Hands away from the gun!' Hamnet's voice was still wild.

No one moved. Tosh looked across to Janac. But the grey eyes were consuming Hamnet, a vision smeared and splashed with Soey's blood, glowing in the red light like some ancient demon.

Nor was the demon about to take his eyes off Janac. But it was to Tosh that he spoke again, cooler now. 'Don't do it. I've got time to drop Janac and you before you can get any-where near that trigger. Just ease your hands out where I can see them, away from the gun.'

Tosh still didn't move as he assessed the situation clini-cally. His initial, instinctive reaction had been the right one, he thought. If he had gone for the shot, Janac wouldn't have made it. Years of loyalty to his boss had checked his hand. Hamnet would have pulled the trigger, of that he was con-vinced. He had seen Soey. But now, for the first time, there crept into his head another question. He started to look at the situation differently, easing his hands away from his body, just far enough for Hamnet to be able to see them. At the same time he began slowly, smoothly, to turn.

Janac still held Hamnet with an implacable stare. If he was angry that Hamnet had evaded his men and got the jump on him, he didn't show it. He knew that anger was no help to him now. And like Tosh, he also had no doubt that

Hamnet would fire if provoked.

'But equally, Phillip, I think you'd have to agree that I will kill the skipper as you kill me.' A trace of a smile appeared on the thin lips, a touch of colour in the blacked-up face. 'Always assuming you can hit me with a killing shot from fifty feet with that thing. Then it's Tosh's turn — and you die. And then your kid dies. He's on our boat, Phillip. We've been expecting you. He's yours now — this is the fourth ship. So just lower the weapon.'

'Stop the turn!' snapped Hamnet. He would have picked up the sudden movement if Tosh had gone for the MP5. But it was an unpleasant surprise to realise the Scotsman was now almost facing him on the edge of his visual field. Nevertheless, he didn't move his eyes from Janac. 'Tosh, is it? Hold it there — hands a little further away from the gun, please.'

'Aye, OK. Relax.' Tosh had frozen, staring at Hamnet, breaking down the angle, looking at the timing. It was tight. If Hamnet had been a professional, Tosh knew his chances would have been zero. As it was, Hamnet might still be good enough. Tosh didn't share Janac's confidence that he would walk out of there. Nor was he ready to murder a baby. But he figured Hamnet wasn't to know that.

No one spoke or moved in the heavy silence that had settled following those last words. Hamnet's knee beat out its damage in pain. But the SIG's barrel remained locked on Janac. Tosh's right hand was now a foot from the trigger of the Heckler and Koch. Janac's Smith and Wesson still drilled at the skipper's spine.

Hamnet swallowed hard. He traced his upper lip with the tip of his tongue. The skipper would die. Janac had the reflexes, unless he could get him with a head shot that closed down his nervous system instantly. Hamnet didn't doubt there were people who could do that. But he knew he wasn't one of them. He moved the sight down onto the bigger target of Janac's chest and held it there without a quaver. He was pleased at how steady his hands were.

Janac watched the tiny movement of the barrel before repeating, 'We've been expecting you. You can have your kid back. Don't blow it now.'

A noise came from the skipper, muffled through the gag. His feet beat briefly on the deck before Janac stamped on a twisted ankle. 'Silence,' he hissed.

Why, Hamnet asked himself? Why did it have to be difficult again? The skipper was the price. Could he pay it? And would it be the last? Could he stop it there?

'It's him for me, isn't it?' said Janac. 'I can see it going through your mind. But that's not where it ends. You die too, Phillip. And your kid. Tosh will see to that. He's the only one who walks away if you shoot.'

Hamnet adjusted his grip fractionally on the weapon. He felt Tosh tense, but his eyes never left Janac. 'Don't do it, Tosh. Don't even think about it.'

Tosh froze once again and repeated, 'Aye, OK. Relax.'

Hamnet nodded before speaking again, matching Janac's quiet tone. 'Yeah, you and me relax, Tosh. That's good. Because I don't think it's going to happen like Janac thinks it is. I think there's a price to pay. That's what you've been teaching me, isn't it Janac? That there's a price to pay?'

'You've paid already, Phillip. You've paid.'

'So send Tosh to fetch my son. I want to see him before we do a deal.'

The grey eyes narrowed, the crow's feet at their corners tightening. And in them Hamnet saw that Janac now knew for certain — that Tosh was the only thing preventing him from squeezing the trigger. He would pay the price of the skipper's life.

'No. Not till you lower the weapon,' Janac spat. 'Lower

the weapon or shoot. What's it gonna be, Lifeboat Man?' he whispered, lips twisted in a sneer.

'I'll pay the price. You should know that.' Hamnet paused for an instant at the muffled sound of a choking wince from the skipper, again cut short as Janac put pressure on the ankle. 'But what about Tosh here? Think about those Triad drugs, Tosh. With Janac gone you can negotiate, cut them in. They'll trust you, but they'll never trust him. Think how much easier it'll be with him gone. Triad informers for cargo-routing in Hong Kong and Singapore — with this operation you've got it made. And I'll take him out for you. Just keep your hands away from the gun. Then you take what you can find, leave my son and go.'

That was it. He'd played his card, the only one he had. But he thought he could see the first sign of uncertainty. Janac's sneer was gone. But the gun hand was rock steady.

Janac was quick to speak into the silence. 'Divide and rule. Nice idea, Phillip. But Tosh and I go back a long way and this little venture has a great future. Triads or not. We're not negotiating with those assholes. Or you. It's make-your-mind-up time. Kill him on the count of five, Tosh. One.'

Hamnet could feel the sweat spring between his finger and the trigger. He didn't want to die. He wanted to bring up his children. He wanted to see Ben again. He wanted to see Jasmine. He'd promised her.

'Two.' Janac's voice betrayed not the slightest shred of emotion. The deep rumble of the engines was all that disturbed the warm, heavy air between counts.

'Three. Put the gun down, Lifeboat Man.'

Hamnet's finger tightened the pressure on the trigger by another half a pound.

'I can't get him, Janac,' said Tosh. 'He'll take you out.'

Hamnet's eyes still hadn't left Janac's face once. And they didn't now. 'All I want is the child, Tosh. Take your hands away from the weapon. Let us finish this.'

'And the skipper, Phillip, the skipper?' said Janac.

Hamnet could hear it now, in Janac's voice. Uncertainty. 'Like you said, Janac, there's always a price,' he growled. 'I think this is as low as it gets. There are no better deals going today.'

There was a stifled sob from the floor.

'Four,' Janac bit back in response.

Hamnet daren't breath. He needed the tiniest trace of uncertainty in Tosh's mind. He thought it was there — that moment's hesitation was all he needed to take out both of them. And, finally, his eyes flickered away from Janac towards Tosh, to see his face properly, to be sure.

It was exactly the mistake Janac had been waiting for. All too often, the hands follow the eyes. Janac knew only too well that Hamnet's glance at Tosh should take his aim off his own chest. He also knew that with Hamnet prepared to let the skipper die and Tosh's intervention questionable, this was the best chance he would get — and he took it.

The revolver came off the back of the skipper's neck and tracked towards Hamnet. Its motion was a blur. But such blurs are what the peripheral vision of wild animals is for, and Hamnet had the sharpened instincts of the hunted. He knew he didn't have time to think, never mind look back at where the SIG was pointed. He didn't even try. He just squeezed the extra half-pound on the trigger. He was moving the weapon before he had even controlled the kick. His eyes were still on Tosh, who was spinning the MP5 down and across his chest, his thumb already flicking the safety. Hamnet fired a second time on instinct. This shot and another bellowed simultaneously. The combined report in such a confined space shook the air.

Hamnet felt the impact swat him, but at first nothing else. It flung him backwards, spinning and crumpling at the same time. He slammed into the doorframe and slid awkwardly down. His mind, which had been so focused, was suddenly scrabbling for a priority. Then the pain tore through him as he hit the floor, and he was slipping and sliding towards blackout. But he saw Tosh — lying on a bloody right thigh, his gun trapped underneath him. Then he realised he couldn't feel his right arm. The comforting weight of the SIG grip was gone. He lowered his eyes — the gun was lying some half a metre in front of him. He looked down further. And felt the nauseating landslide in his mind. He could see bone through the hole torn in the flesh that had been his forearm. Somehow he tore his fascinated gaze away. Tosh was struggling to clear the MP5 from under him. Their eyes met. Hamnet lunged for the SIG with his good left hand. He fell on his stomach, snatching up the gun and swinging it round as he did so. Pain shot through his shattered arm. Consciousness tripped and tottered.

'No!' screamed Tosh, agony etched across his face. The barrel of his weapon was still stuck in the bloody folds of his leg. But he almost had a bead through what remained of his thigh.

'It doesn't have to be like this,' croaked Hamnet, eyes half closed. 'I only want my son back.'

Tosh didn't say a word. Just looked away. Hamnet followed his gaze. Up against the back wall of the bridge Janac lay in a broken heap. The hole in his chest was neat; a bloody stain spread across his tunic. Hamnet's hand hadn't wavered at all.

The skipper hadn't moved either. Hamnet couldn't see if he was dead or unconscious. He couldn't see a wound. Perhaps he had just fainted. Then the grey eyes flickered in Janac's ashen skin. They moved so slowly now. From Tosh to Hamnet. The revolver still lay in his open hand. He struggled for the strength to fire it one last time. But the weight, the pull on the .45 calibre — both were heavy. Hamnet looked back to Tosh.

'It doesn't have to be like this, Tosh. Take your men, your boat, and go. All I want is my son.'

Janac's thin lips trembled as he tried to speak. A trace of blood trickled down his chin through the blackened stubble. All three men continued to bleed in the silence.

Chapter 30

Radio static crackled through the charged atmosphere before a disembodied voice sparked another few volts into the stand-off. 'Janac, it's Edi. Over.'

Tosh's gaze swivelled back to Hamnet. Only the hazel eyes moved in the black face.

'I would suggest you stall them if you want to work this out,' said Hamnet.

Tosh moved his left hand slowly towards the VHF on his hip, while his right shifted the gun barrel under his damaged right thigh, up towards Hamnet.

'Steady,' threatened Hamnet, blinking his sight clear.

Tosh grimaced. 'We've no done any deals yet, soldier.' But the muzzle stopped moving. He found the radio and pushed down the transmit button. 'Just wait a couple, Edi. Small problem with the captain. It's under control — the show'll be back on the road soon.' His voice buzzed through the bridge, a feedback loop starting from Janac's radio.

'Roger, Tosh,' replied the speakers in stereo.

Tosh reattached the VHF to his belt, the pain of the movement tugging at his carefully composed expression. He looked back at Janac. The eyes were closed. The body limp. Just the faintest rise and fall of the chest indicated the boss was still alive.

'Janac was expecting you. Had you tailed, knew you'd gone to ground and figured you'd turn up out here. That's why he brought the kid. He had this great little scene lined up. He wanted you to make the decision between the kid and three of the crew walking the plank. Bollocks to that. You should collect — there's a Triad contract out on him.'

He gave out a hoarse, pain-laced laugh.

'Tell them to send it to a charity for merchant-marine widows,' said Hamnet. The nauseating head-spin had gone with the first rush of pain. Now there was only a dull throb, his arm didn't feel broken, the bleeding had slowed a lot, and he wasn't going to pass out. Not now — not this close.

Tosh grunted. 'So if we don't kill each other, how's it going to work?'

'Simple. Give up the gun. You'll stay here until all your men are off the boat and I have my son back. There are no semiconductors on this ship as far as I know. I made that up. But you can take any payroll cash from the safe.' The skipper shifted and moaned but the two injured men ignored him. Hamnet continued: 'You tell your men on your radio to collect the money and get off. Bring my son here. Then I'll let you go.'

The ponytail shook slowly. 'We need more than that. We need another big take from this boat.'

'You can have whatever you can find on the cargo manifest. If you want to stick around. I sent a Mayday message before I left the lifeboat.' There hadn't been time or opportunity to start up the equipment to do that, but even if Tosh suspected he was bluffing, Hamnet knew he couldn't be sure.

Tosh considered. The money wasn't worth the risk. He could claim he'd put Janac out of circulation, get the Chinese off his back, and he wouldn't need to fortify the villa. Then maybe he could strike a deal for the future, with the Triads supplying the cargo and routing information for a cut of the proceeds, just as Hamnet had suggested. And his leg needed attention. Soon.

'How do I know you'll let me go once you have your kid?' he asked.

'Because you have a boat full of armed men who might

just come back for you,' retorted Hamnet. 'I keep saying it, all I want is my baby.'

Tosh hesitated, then smiled faintly. 'Aye, I guess it'll do,' he said.

Hamnet nodded. 'Push the gun away. Can you get over and free the skipper?'

'Aye.' Tosh carefully rolled backwards off the gun and over again until his weight was on his good left leg. Then he dragged himself painfully across the linoleum to where the now motionless skipper lay. Hamnet followed him with the SIG. A Bowie knife came out from a shoulder sheath and Tosh cut the plastic cuffs. Then he heaved himself up against the back wall, beside Janac, as the skipper stirred and ripped off the gag.

'God almighty, I thought I was dead,' said the skipper in a thick voice. He propped himself groggily on his elbows, revealing a tanned, lined face and neatly clipped grey beard.

'What's your name?' asked Hamnet.

'Mandal, Fredde Mandal.'

'OK, Fredde.' Hamnet nodded towards Tosh and Janac. 'Take the revolver away, and find something to bind up his leg and my arm.'

Mandal looked bemused. He glanced at Janac and grimaced. He shifted, then reddened, wiping a hand across his face. The smell that spread as Mandal stood told the story — bowel and bladder had opened at the first shot. Face down, he'd had no idea Janac had moved the gun off him to shoot Hamnet. The stench mingled with the smell of cordite. Hamnet just said, 'Get on with it.'

Mandal picked the Smith and Wesson out of Janac's limp hand and slid it towards Hamnet. Tosh's knife followed. He then walked uncomfortably over to a cabinet, marked with a red cross, on the starboard bulkhead.

'Do him first,' said Hamnet, indicating Tosh as he pulled

the Smith and Wesson towards him. He eased himself up and back so that he was sitting against the doorframe, and propped the SIG between his clenched knees. He watched Tosh push away the morphine shot. Mandal shrugged, then tied a tourniquet round the thigh and dressed the wound. It was rough and ready, but it staunched the bleeding.

'Good,' said Hamnet. 'Now come over here and strap this up. Tosh, get on the radio and tell them the new plan. Pick up the cash, get your men off the boat, then fetch my boy and bring him here.'

Tosh nodded, unclipped the radio from his belt and started talking.

Hamnet listened carefully to the instructions. He smiled when he heard Tosh tell Jordi to get as far away as he could, to maintain a full radar watch and get ready for a search, as the coastguard were on their way.

Mandal worked in silence on Hamnet's arm for a couple of minutes before he whispered, 'You're letting them take the payroll? There's a hundred thousand dollars in that safe.'

'They're only interested in the money now,' Hamnet murmured back. 'We give them what they want and they'll leave us alone. There's still a crew of heavily armed men on your boat. Once I give them Tosh back, I don't want them to have any reason to do anything except leave. You have a radio anywhere else on board?' He flinched on the last word as Mandal lifted his wounded arm towards his left shoulder in a sling.

'Sorry. No we don't.'

'I have a satellite phone in the lifeboat. Or I did have, but they could destroy it or take it with them on the way out. We can't guarantee getting any help. We give them what they want. I trade Tosh for my son.'

'Your son? I don't understand.'

'It's a long story.'

265

The skipper nodded. 'Would you have let me die?' he asked.

Hamnet looked down. 'That's a long story, too.' He hesitated. It wasn't something he wanted to think about anymore. He had done what he knew to be necessary. 'Janac had to be sure I would. Let's leave it at that. When you're done, take a look at the course, check the radar. No one's paid it much attention for a while.'

'What about him?' Mandal nodded towards Janac.

'I'd take a shower and change those trousers before worrying about him.'

Mandal helped the pirate crew into the safe, then they returned to the bulk carrier to fetch the baby. Tosh and Hamnet waited in silence as Mandal resumed command of his ship and then examined the still unconscious Janac.

The doors at the stern of the bridge banged open. A tall, blond, well-built man in his early thirties stood in the doorway. His white uniform shirt was sweat-soaked and filthy. 'Capsson, first officer,' he said in a heavy Scandinavian accent. 'Your child's here. With one of them.'

Hamnet nodded. 'OK, let's go. Help him.' He waved at Tosh, who was now visibly struggling, face pale under the black paint, lathered with sweat, eyes wide.

'I'll stay here,' interrupted Mandal, looking up from Janac. 'He's in a bad way, but we should do what we can.'

'You watch the bastard. He's dangerous until he's dead,' said Hamnet.

'I've filled him full of morphine. If he does come round, he won't even know where he is.'

Capsson took Tosh's right arm round his shoulder and almost carried him down to the brightly lit boat deck. Hamnet followed, his wounded arm in its sling, the gun now solidly in his left hand. Half a dozen of the ship's crew were waiting for them, armed with knives, a hammer, a single shotgun.

They stood around Edi at the top of a rope ladder over the stern rail. The RIB buzzed fifty metres off.

The baby was tiny, cradled in Edi's huge left arm. It was crying loudly, dryly — no tears on the red face. Hanging from Edi's right shoulder, the strap twisted tight round his forearm, was a sub-machine-gun. It was levelled at the man with the shotgun. Tosh limped over to him and slumped against the stern rail.

'Listen up. This is how it's going to happen,' said Hamnet, with the SIG pointed at Edi. 'Tosh goes down the ladder. Then you hand the boy over and go. Jump if you're worried. The RIB can pick you up.'

Tosh turned, glanced at Edi. 'That's good,' he said.

Edi nodded silently, turned the gun onto Hamnet.

Tosh hauled himself over the rail, and laboriously, using his arms and good leg, lowered himself down the ladder. The group waited in silence, listening to the baby wailing, for the two minutes it took Tosh to get safely into the RIB. A shout told them he had made it. Edi eased himself, one leg at a time, over the rail. The weapon never left Hamnet. Edi stood on his toes on the outside edge of the deck, leaning forward so as not to fall. He held out the baby by the back of its yellow jump suit. Capsson had taken half a step towards the rail to take it when Edi let go and pushed backwards at the same moment.

Everyone dived forwards, but it was Capsson who just caught the howling bundle. Hamnet was only a second behind, the gun finally slipping from his hand and rattling onto the deck. He took the baby in his good arm. It had finally happened. The second son, the one he had turned his back on, was safe. The joy that welled up through him was so powerful he shook. A single tear trickled through the blood that still smeared his face.

He held the baby so tight for so long that Capsson laid a

hand on his shoulder, worried he would suffocate it. Hamnet pulled back a fraction and looked the baby over. The yellow jump suit was dirty, the face still red, but the crying had stopped and the blue eyes were huge, curious.

'We're going to be OK, the three of us. We're going to be OK now. I'll never leave you again,' said Hamnet in a choked voice. He looked up at the surrounding faces, all beaming. 'We have any milk, anything we can feed him with?' he asked.

'Sure, in the kitchen,' said a big man in a chef's apron. 'Follow me.'

Hamnet trailed after the chef, into the accommodation block, up three flights of stairs and into the dining room he had crouched outside so fearfully such a short time before. The kitchen was at the back. Hamnet carefully laid his son down on an empty stainless-steel surface. Behind him the chef busied himself with warming some milk.

Hamnet ran his hand through the tousled dark hair. Anna's hair, he thought with a jerk as he carefully unzipped the jump suit and started to unfasten the nappy. 'Oh my God.'

He could feel what little control he had left slipping away. His throat tightened, he bit his lip, his jaw clenched. But his eyes blurred and filled with tears. His son was a girl. He dropped his face into his good hand and cried like he had never cried before. The grieving had finally begun.

Hamnet had no idea how long he had been there. But he could tell that the firm hand squeezing his shoulder wanted something important. He looked up, breathing hard through his mouth, sniffing, wiping his face with his left arm. It was Capsson.

'The pirate leader, he's conscious. I think he wants you.'

Hamnet glanced at the chef.

'I'll look after the baby,' said the big man. 'You go.'

Hamnet strode after the Swede up to the bridge, still

wiping away his tears. When he got there, Mandal — in clean trousers, Hamnet noticed despite himself — was bent over Janac. The bridge was bright under the white lights that had been switched on. Janac looked small and insignificant in the dark pool of his own blood.

Mandal looked up. 'I've stabilised the bleeding and we have an IV bag coming up from the med room. He could make it if we got him to a hospital. But I think the bullet nicked his spine — he can't feel or move anything below his chest. We don't have much morphine left though, and the last lot's starting to wear off.'

'Check the aft lifeboat, see if my satellite phone is still there. Maybe we can get some help,' said Hamnet as he crouched down beside Janac. Mandal stood up and moved away, waving to Capsson to go and look.

At the sound of Hamnet's voice, Janac's eyes flicked open. But his breathing was barely perceptible. He looked at Hamnet for a long moment. Then his lips moved, faintly, barely making a sound. Hamnet bent closer, his ear to the thin lips. Now he could hear.

'Did you kill him?'

Hamnet pulled away, puzzled. 'Who?' he said, and leant back down for the answer.

'The Filipino. In the lifeboat,' rattled the whisper.

Hamnet smiled.

'I have to know,' Janac murmured eventually.

Hamnet rocked back onto his heels. He rubbed his cheek, looked at the blood-stained hand that came away. So much killing. Only three living people knew what had happened. None of them had ever told a soul. There was no need to change that now. Hamnet leant closer again, whispered right in Janac's ear.

'After what you put my wife and kids through? Fuck you.'

For a moment their eyes locked. Hamnet knew what the grey pools were telling him. He stood up, looked round the bridge and saw the MP5 still lying where Tosh had left it. He walked over and picked it up, feet sticky on the bloody floor. Then he turned and walked back to Janac. Mandal watched him, not quite understanding or believing. Until Hamnet leant down and placed the muzzle on Janac's forehead. The grey eyes closed. Hamnet barely heard the shout behind him. He turned his head and for the last time pulled a trigger. The report crashed round the bridge, the reverberation seeping away under the doors. The expended cartridge rattled on the linoleum. Hamnet didn't look back. Just pulled the gun off and threw it on the floor.

'What the hell do you think you've done? Who do you think you are?' Mandal's voice was tremulous with righteous indignation, shock and more than a trace of fear.

Hamnet looked up at him, sighed a thousand-year sigh. 'We don't have the morphine to get him to a hospital. And even if we did it would have cost a fortune to treat him. And for what? To execute him? Jail him for life? I'd rather the money went on something useful. He's better off dead, and he knew it. Why shirk the responsibility for the bastard?'

He didn't wait for an answer. He pushed past Mandal and strode across the bridge, down the steps and away, back to his Anna.